AWOKEN

ALEX SOUTH

Proofread by FiveJsDesign

Cover art by Amanda Mills

ISBN 978-0-692-27959-5

Printed in the United States of America

First Edition

For Dave Sutherland

Acknowledgements

When I first began this journey I had no idea it would engulf my life the way it has. To all of the family and friends who put up with my obsession, thank you.

From the books inception, my good friend Julien Folstrom has been there to listen to my ideas. He worked with me to shape the overarching plot of this book, and has been a general source of encouragement. Special thanks goes go out to him for being part of the driving force that helped me get started.

My parents have been supportive since the beginning, reading my rough drafts as I churned them out, albeit with grimaces at times. They have been there to watch the story grow and mature as it has gone through the rigors of editing. I cannot thank them enough.

As this adventure neared its close, Rachael Wenzel joined in to run a fine tooth comb through the dialogue. This was one of the toughest edits I went through but I believe it has created a story you will better enjoy, and for that I cannot thank her enough. She gave me the boost I needed to sprint to the end of this project.

Finally, no book would be complete without a cover, and what a cover Amanda Mills has created. Her skills took the vague concepts out of my head and set them in painted art form. The cover art is by far my favorite part of this book. Thanks for the hard work, Amanda.

Without further ado, I cease my yammering and allow you get to the story. Enjoy.

But now at last the sacred influence
Of light appears, and from the walls of Heaven
Shoots far into the bosom of dim Night
A glimmering dawn. Here Nature first begins
Her farthest verge, and Chaos to retire,
As from her outmost works, a broken foe,
With tumult less and with less hostile din,
— Paradise Lost, II, 1034-40

PROLOGUE

Sentient life form detected.
Activating memory banks.
Retrieving most recent log.
File accessed.
Initiating playback …

Footsteps crunched up the steep slope, upsetting the sharp gravel. Ohm marched on, leaving behind soft depressions in the ancient soil. The ridge was barren with only the wind as its companion. At his intrusion, the wind whipped over the ridge with a vengeful jealousy. The fury of the current caught Ohm's coat and threw it open to reveal a worn body of alloys and plates, seemingly ravaged by time and wearied by life. Deception lurks in appearances, for his stride was sure and quick, filled with purpose and a will that could outlast the alloys and energy veins that gave him form. Cresting the hill, Ohm refastened the buckles that had come undone on his coat. He reached over his shoulder and lifted a tarnished metallic pack off his back. Ohm knelt and rested the pack on the coarse grit.

Then he stood to face the mountain, an endless peak that sprawled out into all of existence. As high as Ohm was on the ridge, the mountain stood, still taller. The pinnacle of the monolith was shrouded by the sky: a sea of churning clouds, dark and heavy. He lifted his face up toward the roiling gray ceiling. Streams of energy coursed through the clouds, heavy white crackles that moved slowly, leaving behind a burning trail of color. The peak pulsed numerous times, sending out a new wave of color with each flash. Ohm allowed the plates on his face to emit light in a rare display of emotion, mimicking the ever-changing beauty of the sky. Each new flare of color was full of unique character, fleeting and haunting. The story in the sky amended itself as it found more ways to express its glorious nature. Ohm, the observer, stood still as stone in somber reflection, paying respect to the glory that the sky displayed for all who would look.

Many waves of light passed overhead before Ohm finally moved again. Involuntarily, his hand reached up to grasp a chain hanging from his neck. Ohm's hand closed around a beautiful white crystal—a soul ember that had once held the spark of life, now lifeless and dim. So much had come before to bring him to that desolate ridge. So many experiences culminated in the obsessive desire for the future to reconcile the past. As Ohm stood, his faceplates returned to their usual expressionless grey. Only his single remaining visual receptor stayed aglow. The ocular plate was angled sharply and it burned with a cold blue fire. Ohm watched the mountain with keen focus. His bandaged right arm rested on the pack while his left hand clutched the soul ember. Ohm maintained his vigil, an enigmatic plea for the universe to remain still. The future need never unfold. The past could be preserved forever in the lone figure standing before the mountain under the ever-changing sky. But it was not to be.

The ground rumbled briefly; and a light began to grow rapidly in the center of the sky, brighter than all the previous pulses of the mountain. A lone object streaked out in a brilliant white arc. It flew far over the land toward the edge, toward the Void. Ohm turned around, watching the object until it disappeared from sight. He knelt down next to his pack.

"Will you track the cell for me, Fred?" Ohm asked softly.

"Affirmative. Relaying the projected coordinates now," Fred replied.

"It landed very close to the edge," Ohm said, sighing at the distance.

"Calculations place it close to but not past the edge," Fred confirmed.

"Funny. It would have been in keeping with Creator's character to let us watch our hope hurtle into oblivion," Ohm griped with mock humor.

"I do not hope," Fred replied bluntly in his monotone voice

"Of course not; that's why I keep you around," Ohm retorted.

"I have identified the reason to be your lack of friends," Fred's robotic voice quipped.

Ohm chuckled slightly. "Quiet, you! I'm supposed to be the clever one. Now let's move. Whatever that thing is, it couldn't have landed any further from us," he said, less than excited at the distance they had to travel.

Ohm shouldered his pack and slipped the soul-ember neck-lace back behind his coat. Turning from the mountain, he walked off the ridge, leaving it to the solitude it was accustomed to. The wind was appeased; and it calmed as Ohm's figure moved away from the ridge, walking towards a distant idea waiting to be realized.

EPISODE 01

THE EDGE

Nothing.

Nothing.

More nothing.

Then there was Oa. He was awake in an instant, emerging into consciousness. He had awoken—he was *one* of the Awoken, the identity originating from an unseen corner of his mind. What had he been doing up until this moment? Where was he? Oa's mind raced, trying to keep up with the sudden influx of questions and sensations. The most important uncertainty he needed to settle was whether or not he had a body. Almost as if in response, two triple-fingered appendages appeared in front of his face, rotors whirring as the digits extended in the dim light. Oa sighed in relief, listening to the sound of his own voice as it projected from the vibrating cones implanted behind his faceplates.

Hands are a good start, Oa thought to himself. *Maybe now I can explore. It's what I've always wanted to do.* He realized the relative humor of his thought and began to wonder how long he had been awake. Then he wondered how long he had been asleep. He felt an instinctive need to measure the moments flying by his awareness. The urge to create a method of time measurement pulled at Oa briefly, but it soon bored him so his mind brushed past it. He was more interested in his surroundings and in the individual moments he kept encountering.

The entire universe is either a cylindrical pod with a cracked window looking out at nothing, or I'm just stuck in some strange capsule, he thought to himself.

Oa peered through the window. He realized the dim light was coming from outside the window. It had been a deep red, but now it was a burnt orange. The light allowed Oa to see a panel to his left with three buttons; the button on the left was pressed flat into the panel while the others were still protruding from the metallic plate, tempting him to push them. After a moment of indecision, he pressed the center button, enjoying the new experience of using his hands to accomplish a simple task.

White lights flickered to life in the pod, and something hissed as a seal was broken. The hatch in front of Oa fell forward to reveal a hard rocky ground that extended outwards away from the pod. The barren rock continued for a short distance before it ended in nothing. Oa was bemused and a little disappointed as he stepped forward, trusting his legs to work for the first time. The motors in his legs whirred quietly, smoothly propelling him out of the pod. He took three more cautious steps to make sure he understood the concept of walking. Feeling ready, Oa began to stroll toward the edge. He enjoyed the excitement of his first excursion. He walked in a straight line; and before the trek grew dull, he found himself on the edge of the rock which dropped off below into nothing. Oa stood on the fringe of the sheer cliff, staring out into empty air. Then he noticed it: an oily black so deep he felt he could reach out and touch it.

A great desire grew in Oa. The emptiness was so close it appeared to be only an arms length away. He slowly reached out toward the *nothing*. The spot he was about to touch pulled back, and the rest of the vacuum seemed to push forward. Oa moved his hand side to side; but existence clung to him, never allowing his hand to enter the inky black wall. The impenetrable vacancy swelled out around his arm, attempting to either engulf it or escape its touch. Unsettled, Oa pulled his hand back and the depression flattened, receding slightly. He noticed that to either side of him, the emptiness was touching the rock, softly eating into it. Only around Oa did the darkness refuse to push forward and grab hold of the rock.

Oa stood for a moment pondering what he was witnessing. He decided to let the darkness be and explore elsewhere. He glanced down over the bit of cliff where he stood to see the abyss hovering below waiting for him to leave. Oa obliged; he turned around and stood with emptiness at his back, the world before him. The young Awoken was amazed, wonder and excitement returning to him. He gazed upon an endless expanse of rock, faceted yet smooth. The stone was organically random in shape and size, but each slab fit perfectly together. It was as if the floor of the world had been cracked and was about to shatter.

Oa's gaze extended outward, looking toward the horizon. There were canyons and jutting spires, and the ground sloped inevitably upwards toward the center of the horizon where a single point stood out to meet with the sky. The sky gripped his attention like nothing else had thus far. Oa had wondered about the strange light before, but now he understood. Brooding dark clouds churned above as rippling strands of energy crackled and slithered through the clouds, burning incredible hues of color and casting an ever-changing light on the ground. Oa basked in it, enjoying how his surroundings constantly changed, becoming beautiful in a new way every moment in the changing light. Veins of glossy material in the rocks reflected the light, allowing for the ground itself to glow. The veins of light in the sky crackled and built to a crescendo. Oa loved it. Overjoyed to be witnessing such beauty, he watched as the leading strands of light crashed into the darkness behind him, disappearing into it forever.

The brilliance faded, leaving the landscape in dim light. The remaining strands of energy wound through the sky, slowly burning out. The glow was not gone though from Oa's face. His visual receptors radiated pure wonderment as he looked toward the peak on the horizon, the origin of all sky light. It gleamed brighter than any other spot. From it, the lights crawled outwards to the ends of the world. Oa knew he wanted to follow the glittering trails above; he had a strong urge to be at their source, to be in the midst of the far-off storm.

Oa returned his gaze to where he had started. A fair distance away, his pod lay at the base of a gradual hill. Looking closer, he realized that other Awoken were scuttling around it. Intrigued, Oa decided to be impatient and attempt running instead of walking to get back to his pod. His feet were swift, and he enjoyed the thrill of speed as he raced back toward his pod. When the Awoken noticed him coming they backed off his pod a few steps. They stared at Oa as he sped up to them, halting just in front of his pod. There were three Awoken: one short, one tall, and one that would be a normal height if he wasn't slumping over. They all looked worn and were clothed in threadbare rags. Underneath the tattered fabric, Oa could see that they were missing pieces. Strange oily black veins streaked from their hands up their arms, spreading across their bodies. He heard them whispering amongst themselves as they stole occasional glances at him.

Amazing! So they talk, Oa thought to himself. *Maybe I can, too.* He decided to listen to them for a few moments before joining in. He noticed that as they spoke certain panels on their faces glowed pulsating rhythmically with each syllable, the intensity and color of the glow seemed to accent the tone and emotion of their voice.

It's like the sky, Oa thought to himself. He enjoyed the parallel as he listened closely to decipher their whisperings. At first, it was all babbling and gibberish. Then gradually the sound cleared and sharpened into words—like the ones in Oa's mind, the language he thought with.

"How did this open?"

"I dunno. We've been trying to break open the stupid thing for a while now. There's no way he opened it himself. No cell opens from the inside. I must have loosened it!"

"The only thing you've been loosening is my patience!"

"Wha …?" One of the strangers gasped as they did a double take at Oa. "He has no soul ember!"

All three heads stared in astonishment at Oa before the short one refocussed them sharply.

"Shh! We've got nothing left to barter, so let me do the talking. He just woke up. He'll be easy to control."

Oa looked at the Awoken before him, then down at himself. Despite differences in appearance and design, they all were made up of some sort of plates, energy veins, alloys, gears, and motors. Then he saw the difference that alienated him from the group: there was an empty cavity in his chest. Oa looked at the other Awoken and realized that they each had a bright white shard in their chest.

I'm strange, Oa thought. *No, I'm unique*, he affirmed himself.

"You remember your name?" asked the short one, stepping toward Oa. The face and limbs of the short one were angular in design, slim with sharp features.

"I-I," Oa stuttered slowly as he emitted words for the first time. "I am—Oa." *Not the best of starts, but it will have to do,* he thought to himself.

"Did you come from this birth cell?" The voice was light but raspy around the edges. A new part of Oa's mind involuntarily activated, identifying the Awoken as feminine.

"I did," Oa replied evenly, listening to his own voice out of curiosity. His was deeper and smoother than the high, scratchy voice of the Awoken in front of him.

"Where am I?" he asked.

"You are on the edge of the glorious Great Planes, or what's left of them anyways. Just a bunch of rock and dust really," the female Awoken said with disinterest.

"I ask because just woke up. I was over there looking at that black mass. I can't seem to touch it though," Oa explained as he pointed behind himself.

She laughed, and her faceplates flashed slightly. Then she replied, "We try that sometimes, too, when the shaking starts; but you won't sleep that way. If you want to dream, you gotta have something to trade with the distributors."

Oa was puzzled by her statement. He wanted to ask more, but the trio had grown impatient. They shifted about in agitation.

The taller one spoke up gruffly. "We have been trying to steal your gear from this cell; but it's locked to anyone but you, I suspect. So how about you show us what's inside?"

Oa noted that the Awoken stood on a shaky leg that looked ready to buckle at any moment. The trio did not seem very threatening despite their tone.

"Why would you want things meant for me?" he questioned, too innocent to understand theft.

"We will decide who it's meant for. Now open it!" the tall Awoken barked.

The harsh words grated on Oa and for the first time he felt irritation at the unfriendliness of these strangers. He pushed the unpleasant feeling away, hoping their tense moods would lighten if he remained friendly.

"I didn't mean to make you angry. We can all see what's inside," he replied diplomatically.

Oa walked back up to the birth cell. Inside, he saw no visible mechanisms other than the three buttons. Only one remained unpressed. He reached in and pushed it.

The three Awoken huddled in closely to watch as a panel in the back of the cell slid down to reveal a stack of cloth. Atop the clothes rested a silver metallic sphere with intriguing markings carved over it's surface.

Oa waited for his mind to reveal the identity of the objects in the same strange way it had attributed meaning to the Awoken's words and gender to their voices. Nothing happened. *I guess some things I must figure out myself,* he thought in confusion.

"What are these?" Oa asked the three Awoken surrounding him.

The feminine-voiced Awoken responded, "Just clothes. Use them to cover up that chest of yours. I don't want your deformity to scare the distributors off. You shouldn't even be alive without an ember." She pointed to the silver sphere greedily. Her hand trembled slightly from some unknown ailment. "That looks valuable. We'll be keeping that."

Oa instinctively grabbed the orb and took a few hasty steps back away from the trio. He perceived innate ownership over the silver sphere. Instantly, he felt as if he had discovered a piece of himself that he had been previously unaware of. Oa noticed a sudden rush as his mind became more conscious, transcending his current understanding. He sensed more now. It as if his visual receptors had been off or not fully activated and were only now seeing properly. He was able to peer into his surroundings. Oa's altered sight permeated everything, turning the environment around him to a string of symbols. He looked at the figures in front of him. Oa could see another image, a faint aura of white light, emanating from them like a projection. Their auras were tainted, blemished by a murky darkness. The moment was brief and fleeting. All at once, the vision was gone. The young Awoken shook his head, wondering what had just happened. He turned toward the three Awoken who were attempting to stand threateningly around him. Oa now had a sense of how truly tired and worn they were.

"Don't take this from me. It feels like mine. When I am holding this I feel …" Oa paused, searching for words, "more complete." He decided it was time to stand his ground on the matter. "I can't quite process all of this yet, but I believe I can help you."

"Yeah, everyone everywhere has felt the same way too. Now hand it over," the female Awoken said jadedly as she reached for the sphere. The orb began to hover and glow with a white-hot light, searing the greedy Awoken's hand. She recoiled sharply, her comrades face plates flashed in surprise.

"Fine," the Awoken hissed. "Keep it, but you're coming with us." She smoothly regained control of the situation. "We will see if you're of any use to us. Put those clothes on and come along."

Oa was surprised that the Awoken didn't want his clothes since theirs were ragged and patched. The Awoken seemed to put little value in their appearance. *Perhaps clothes don't make a good trade with these distributors,* he thought in realization.

Using the appearance of the other Awoken as a guide, Oa figured out what to do with the first article of clothing he grabbed. The piece was composed of two long cloth sleeves merging together at the top. The sleeves slid over his legs and the whole thing buckled around his waist. *Pants,* the word popped into his mind, followed by a sudden realization of how to use the remainder of the pile. Oa accepted the information his mind had revealed, and he continued to dress. He draped a heavy cloak over his shoulders, it hung loosely. He buttoned the tunic up over his chest, conveniently covering his empty ember socket.

Next, Oa knelt down and slid a pair of sturdy boots over his metal feet. *These seem unnecessary,* he thought as be buckled them. Oa considered removing the shoes. Then he heard a faint grinding noise coming from the gears and motors in the Awoken's bare feet as the trio walked off. The metal skin of their feet had worn away in parts, exposing the joints. The rusty Awoken didn't seem to care as they plodded on drearily. Oa looked at the hill they were heading up. It was full of jagged rocks and fine sand just waiting to scrape through his alloy skin. He decided the boots were a decent precaution. The last article of clothing was a simple bag with a strap. Oa placed the metallic sphere in the open satchel and then looped it over his shoulders. The strap was snug and held the bag tightly to his side.

Oa hurried to follow the trio. They were already halfway up the hill behind his pod. As he walked up past his birth cell he noticed a marking on the top. It was nearly obscured by burn marks and scoring that had come from the high impact of the pod's landing. He looked closer and brushed away some dust, revealing a symbol. He paused and focused, waiting patiently. With a slight jolt, a new path opened in his mind; and he was able to read the symbol. It was a number *One.*

"Hurry up back there, Empty!" the female Awoken called back. Oa quickly stood back up. He started jogging up the hill to catch the trio. He didn't care for the nickname; but he kept quiet, listening hard to hear their conversation as he raced to catch up.

"I think he's cursed," the tall one said.

"You're too superstitious," the female Awoken replied.

"Remember Buri when she came out of her last immersion? She said she met one of the ancients. She woke up all wild and scared, babbling about the Destroyer; now we meet this guy walking around with no soul ember. It's creepy timing," the tall one insisted.

"Yeah, that's one of the reasons we immerse: to hear those exciting legends. To get a rush. Sheesh, Birk! Don't be so scared. It's only stuff from the past. It can't hurt you, and neither can Empty," the female Awoken snapped in annoyance.

"But his birth cell did say *One* on it. I have heard things about number One in my immersions. They say he was an unstoppable killer," the hunched Awoken added.

"There is no way Empty is the first Awoken. The First One would have died a long time ago. You saw how burned Empty's pod was, the rest of his number just got scraped off," the female said, explaining away her companions' worries.

"What if Buri is right, and the legends of the Destroyer are true? What if the Destroyer has come back?" the tall Awoken called Birk asked, glancing back at Oa.

"So you think we need to be scared of Empty because of a number and some fragments of an old story Buri heard in her immersion?" the female asked mockingly. "The Destroyer is already back, stupid; he's our generous supplier. So worry about pleasing Eol, or he'll end us all. Don't put too much trust in the immersions. I'm not sure how much of the stuff we hear is really accurate history. All I know is that it's a crazy, fun ride." She shook her head in annoyance at her paranoid companion. Oa had no idea what the haggard Awoken were talking about, but he found the conversation intriguing. He stored their words away in his mind to revisit later.

Oa rejoined the group as they reached the top of the hill. The rough gravel of the hill stretched down into a modestly sized valley below. Several insignificant mounds of rock huddled together at the base of the hill.

"How do you like our home?" the female Awoken asked smugly.

Oa looked around for a moment, then replied, "I don't see anything. Do you just stand around in the dirt?"

The female Awoken laughed and pointed at the mounds of rock. Oa looked closer and realized that the mounds where actually dwellings. The rough soil of the valley was scattered over scraps of ancient machinery to make it appear like a pile of debris. He could tell from the scoring and dents that the metallic scraps had once been a part of some structure built long ago.

"Hard to spot, isn't it?" the female Awoken said proudly.

Oa nodded, though he was curious why she would be proud of the village's obscurity.

"Loads of good that camouflage will do for us if our own start turning," Birk said resentfully.

"Shut up, Birk. I am monitoring all our immersions. I have it under control," the female shot back.

"Great. I'll go tell Buri. She's going to be thrilled," Birk replied with grim humor.

"I'll get her more immersions. That's why we have him," the female said, flinging her hand toward Oa as she started down the hill. The other two trailed behind her while Oa looked over the valley one more time. All he saw beyond the shallow depression in the terrain was just the same broad expanse of rock. He followed the trio down into the decaying village. They ducked through a narrow opening in one of the rusty scraps of machinery. Inside, a feeble Awoken laid next to a flickering loop of energy contained in a clear cylindrical device. It gave very little light, but Oa was glad for the warm glow.

"Go ahead, try and help this one," the female Awoken sneered at him. "She dreams most of her cycles away, and she'll probably snap the next time she wakes up. Or she won't wake up at all." Her face plates betrayed emotion as they throbbed deeply. "She doesn't need your help she needs more immersions."

Oa ignored her mocking tone, deciding to remain amiable. He knelt down beside Buri. She turned weakly toward him. Her face plates flashed chaotically. Oa saw that most of her body was infected with the veins of darkness that the others had. He knew he could do something, but he had no idea how to achieve it. If only he could see as he had when he first touched the orb. Go, *super-sight!* Oa thought to himself in amusement. Suddenly he felt his mind being dragged into higher awareness.

"Your will shall be," a voice from within coursed through him. Immediately, the strange orb floated out from the bag at his side to hover above his hand. He could see the Awoken's aura and the murky blackness infecting her. The strings of symbols that permeated the Awoken's being had been jumbled. The story in the symbols did not make sense but Oa saw that he could fix it. He could rearrange the symbols and bring sense to the chaos. The sphere began to glow, now floating between both his hands. It glowed brighter; and a stream of light began to emit from the sphere, flowing down in many shimmering tendrils to touch the Awoken's broken body. The infection receded, and her broken plates grew back. Motors and gears that had not turned in a long time began to spin anew. The other three Awoken stepped back in awe, all visible signs of hostility gone, replaced by shock. Oa could sense them whispering. His heightened senses overheard their words.

"Still think he is the Destroyer?" the female mocked.

"Shut up. Can we trade him even though he has no ember?" Birk asked begrudgingly.

"I don't think so," the hunched one replied.

"Trust me. This will make him even more valuable to the distributors," the female Awoken said with assurance.

"Not too soon though. Let him fix us first," Birk reminded her.

The shortest of the three Awoken stepped up and put a hand on Oa's shoulder. He remained in a trance, still at work. She spoke in a deceptively welcoming tone.

"That's the first time not stealing has worked in our favor. I'm called Swift, my tall friend is Birk, this quiet fellow is called Kane, and the one you're saving now is Buri. You might want to work on remembering those names because you're one of us now," she said sweetly.

Oa felt as if he was outside his mind, looking in. He watched his indignation boil over at Swift's hidden intentions. Then he heard himself speak to the Awoken.

"You all seem to care for each other to some degree, but that care doesn't include me. You only need me to perpetuate your sorry state. I don't like what I see, though. Your actions, whatever they are, have broken the symbols," he accused.

Swift drew back, "What symbols? You don't know anything about us! You just woke up."

Suddenly, explosions rocked the hut. Screams of "Marauders!" and "Run!" filtered through the chaos around the village, echoing to the group inside. Oa felt himself turn to look at the entrance just in time to see it blasted open by some unseen force. Three healthy and armed Awoken burst in. *Marauders*, Oa assumed. Birk grabbed the first Marauder by the shoulders only to crumple as a blinding white energy, accompanied with a sharp crack and hiss, seared a hole through his torso. Birk's dead body fell to the floor revealing a smoldering weapon in the Marauder's hand. Then the weapon was pointed at Oa. Yet he could not deviate from his task to respond to the danger. He had no control. The power flowing from the orb had nearly rid Buri of the last of the infection, when suddenly an unseen force surged from the infection sending Oa reeling back. His focus was broken and he returned to himself. The sphere darkened instantly and fell into his hand. Oa remembered he was in danger and he rolled backwards. A piercing white beam ripped through the space where his head had been a split second earlier.

The leader of the Marauders turned and knocked Oa's attacker back, shouting, "No! Don't kill him! He's levitating a lump of light, and that's got to be the most interesting thing I have seen in a billion cycles. If you damage him, I'm gonna have lieutenant Bota feed you to Eol."

The Marauder named Bota chimed in. "Sorry Captain, but Murd's head is too thick to eat. Eol would spit him back out."

The Captain turned to Bota. "Ha! Good point. Anyway, grab this stranger." He pointed at Oa. "We'll deal with the rest."

Oa scrambled back to Buri, knowing time was short. He stared down at the dying Awoken, the infection having returned even stronger than before. She was beginning to shake uncontrollably. Oa tried to see the symbols again; but before his inner sight could return, he was grabbed by the Marauder lieutenant. Bota dragged him out of the now ransacked hut while Swift's bitter voice followed them out.

"Let this be your first lesson, Oa: accept that your good intentions are just going to rot like the rest of us. You won't ever fix anything here."

Oa wanted to struggle, but he froze in shock as the other two Marauders raised weapons toward Swift and Kane. He turned from the sight as execution shots where fired. Glancing back, he caught a glimpse of the Marauders pulling the lifeless soul embers from the corpses. Oa gripped the silver sphere tightly in his hand, trembling in terror at the brutality of the world he abruptly found himself in. He had never encountered death before and it frightened him immensely. The young Awoken deactivated his visual receptors. Retreating from his senses, he let his mind grasp at the vision he had been so close to realizing. Buri was gone; but Oa could still see her burned in his memory, as she would have been. He felt cheated. His efforts had been thwarted.

But how? Oa thought, remembering the mysterious force within Buri's infection. He longed to understand what he had witnessed. And he promised himself he would find the answers.

EPISODE 02

EXCHANGE

Oa was dragged through the harsh shale for a short distance before he was roughly pulled to his feet and shoved forward. He allowed his sight to return quickly. The irises in his visual receptors widened to let light in as his foot caught the edge of a metal deck. He barely had time to put his hands out in front of himself as he tripped and fell onto the floor of one of the Marauder's Mark IV Reapers.

Oa quickly glanced around the interior of the dropship. He appeared to be in a spacious hold located directly in front of the vessel's engine. Luminous strips embed into the walls cast a faltering glare. In the flickering light, he could make out the slowly spinning turbines of a powerful jet through a grate in the back. He felt heat emanating from that area of the deck. Oa reasoned that the airflow through the open passage helped keep the engines cool. The space where he stood served as a platform that the Marauders could carry passengers and cargo on. Two other Marauders were already on board: one of them laid wounded on the floor of the ship while the other knelt, working with strange tools to fix the damage. Oa peered up to see a pilots seat nestled in a small alcove above him, surrounded by buttons and dials. A windshield bulged out of the top of the ship allowing the pilot to see where they were going.

Lieutenant Bota stepped in after Oa and leaned up against the wall. He reached up and casually grabbed a handhold. Oa noted several other makeshift handholds welded to the inside of the dropship. *I hope this vehicle isn't wild enough to need those*, he thought as he shuffled to the back of the hold. Oa sat against the warm grate watching the other Marauders warily.

"See, Jad, you can't go calling a cycle unlucky before it's over," Bota said, motioning to the wounded Awoken. "Those Howlers may have got hold of Coop, but they led us right to a camp. We just made our quota."

"You were fortunate it wasn't another Howler den, the way you all went rushing in there," Jad replied somberly as he hunched down beneath the long green coat he wore. Patched and faded, the coat concealed various surgical implements strapped to the old medic.

"It was a close call. One of them was turning, but this one here was doing something strange to stop it. He seems to be a healer like you," Bota said glancing back at Oa. The Lieutenant was an imposing figure, clad in an array of combat gear. Plates of cloth armor belted tightly over his torso. Slings and bandoliers hung across his shoulders. A belt around his waist supported his weapon and whatever other implements of war he carried in the numerous utility pouches of his pants. Goggles covered the Marauder's visual receptors and a rag concealed the rest of his face below. Three antennae protruded straight up from a groove cut into the left side of his dome skull.

"Come up here and give Jad a hand," Bota commanded. Oa quietly picked himself up and moved cautiously over to Jad. "If you ride with us, you have to be useful. If you're no help to Jad, I'll deal with you myself." Bota stared menacingly as Oa passed by. The young Awoken nodded and sat down next to Jad. Bota yelled up to the pilot, "Kiri, let's burn out of here! Best not keep Eol waiting. Also, keep in formation for once."

"You know I can't do both at the same time, sir," Kiri called back. Bota shook his head, muttering something to himself in amusement.

The engine came to life, rumbling with a deep hum that filled the air. Oa placed his hands down against the floor, trying to gain stability as the Reaper began to rise up into the air. He looked down at the wounded Marauder. There was a grizzly gash in the Marauder's side where the mangled metal sparked and leaked clear fluid. Jad was focused intently as he worked to mend the wound. The pair of immaculate white gloves he wore sparked with a bright green energy that darted between the glove's fingers sporadically. At frequent intervals the energy arced directly out of the digits, into shiny dust clouds hovering around the wound. The shimmering specs streamed out of slim tubes on the gloves. The tubes traced back to cylinders strapped to Jad's chest, and they ran down his arms to each digit of his gloves. The green energy seemed to be controlling the clouds of shimmering dust, guiding them in the process of repairing the broken Marauder. As Oa stared down, his keen eyes could see the alloys being mended while wires and tubes were reattached by the microscopic tools.

"What are those things?" Oa asked. He turned to Jad. The medic had only one faceplate amid the angular metal ridges of his blocky head. His rectangular visual receptors glowed with a kind emerald light that matched his surgical implements.

Jad kept working as he replied in a sociable voice, "These are known as microburs. You can think of them as very, very tiny machines that replace the lost materials with new ones that are fed to them. The process is delicate, and the repairs can be messy, but I am one of the better healers still around so this fellow's scar will hardly be noticeable; even if he won't be able to feel this spot anymore." Jad turned to look at Oa for a second before continuing. "You don't strike me as a medic. How about you show me why Bota believes you are one?"

Oa reached into the satchel at his side and pulled out the metallic sphere. "I used this, but I wasn't able to finish my first attempt. I don't know if I can do it again." He tried not to re-member the event his vague explanation referred to.

"You might as well try. It's a better idea than getting thrown off the ship by Bota over there," Jad said, nodding toward the leery Lieutenant quietly watching from the side.

Oa looked down at the wounded Awoken who appeared to be sedated somehow. "Can he see me?"

"No, his consciousness has been temporarily suspended us-ing that stasis ring. It'll slow the flow of the primary and secon-dary bloods in his body," Jad explained as he pointed to a tight metal coil fastened around the wounded Awoken's soul ember, "It won't last for long, so we need to be done before he wakes up and bleeds out. I am going to work on replacing these alloys along his side. I need you to reconnect the veins there." Jad pointed to a spot deep in the wound.

Oa shut of his visual receptors, not quite sure how to reclaim the sight he had achieved in Swift's hut. Then he remembered the words he had heard from within. "Your will shall be."

I hope I work well under pressure, Oa thought as he attempted to imagine how to fix the wound. He pictured where the veins would flow, what they would connect to, and how the alloys would stitch over the wound. To Oa's surprise, the image came naturally. He wondered if his mental creation was original, or if he was merely discovering something he already knew within. All at once his inner sight flashed open. Confusion surrounded him as the symbols battered his mind. There was no internal force aiding him this time. He had to struggle to maintain the gaze. The experience was too chaotic for Oa to discern the strings of information that tumbled past him. He could barely remember what he was supposed to do. The sphere began to glow and hover between his hands. A stream of light extended, winding around the orb randomly. The power was wild and unruly. Oa focused harder trying to direct his will, but his mind refused to stay in one place and time. He reached out his left hand, using his physical form to guide the stream toward the wound.

Jad looked up from his work and watched as Oa held the light in one hand, straining to guide it with the other. In the midst of the blinding glow, veins began to reform. Jad looked over Oa's shoulder to see Bota watching. A slight white glow of surprise leaked out from the faceplates hidden underneath the cloth mask the Lieutenant wore.

Jad turned back to Oa's work and watched as the light faded, leaving no sign of any damage. Jad quickly guided the microburs in patching up the remaining alloys before turning to Oa. Exhausted, the young Awoken was sitting back and staring in bewilderment at the silver sphere in his hands.

"That's no form of medicine I have ever seen," Jad said, baffled and impressed at the same time.

"I don't know how it works either," Oa said with a slightly frustrated tone. "And it's not consistent. I meant to repair all the damage, but I only fixed the veins."

"That could be a sort of fusion device like these microburs, but there's nothing feeding it materials to use. That's quite possibly the strangest thing I have ever seen," Jad said perplexed. He turned to Bota. "This fellow will do just fine. His talent with healing far surpasses mine." Bota nodded silently and stared out at the landscape below.

Oa helped Jad lift the unconscious Awoken into a sitting position against the side of the hold, then went to sit down near the front so he could see where they were going. Jad knelt down and began removing the stasis ring from around the wounded Awoken's ember.

Jad completed his task and sat next to Oa, striking up further conversation. "He will come out of stasis soon enough. You have done good work. What's your name?"

"My name is Oa," he said evenly, wary of the strange friendliness of his captors. Before Jad could continue the idle conversation, Oa confronted him bluntly. "They killed all of those Awoken. Why would they do that?"

Bota turned sharply ready to retort, but Jad held up his hand calmly. "Don't take too much offense, Bota. We would have responded the same way once," he said, defusing the situation. The Lieutenant returned to staring quietly out the ship.

"We don't kill—we survive. You're going to be a part of it too if you want to stay alive," Jad explained. "You're strong and skilled like us. Unfortunately, the reality of our lives is that we need to fight to stay alive. It's not all bad though; we are wonderful musicians when we have the time for it."

Oa sat and listened, silently staring out at the landscape below. The seemingly endless terrain of rock sped underneath him. He was still troubled by Buri's death. He did not miss Swift or her gang but the idea of life being taken disturbed him. The Marauders fight seemed rather one sided. Then he thought of the mysterious force that had pushed back when he was healing Buri, it hadn't happened when he healed the Marauder. Perhaps it had just been a fluke. His attention was diverted when he noticed the smoldering wreckage of what used to be a small town off in the distance. Reentering the conversation he pointed and said with disgust, "Like that? Is that what it takes to keep you alive?"

Jad answered, "Yes, we value uninfected life. And while there are few pleasures left in this world, we fight to keep them: camaraderie, a good ship beneath our feet, and the rush of the air as we soar.

"Look there, Oa," Jad pointed off to the horizon. The peak had begun to glow brighter. It pulsed in a flash of white light. The wave of new energy slowly spread, creeping toward them.

"A new cycle begins. As long as we see that, we know we have done right."

Oa gazed in wonder as the distant blaze moved toward them, brightening the dim landscape with a pale jade light. The peak's glow dimmed, but the new ripple of life remained, a far-off hope. The tide of the new cycle would eventually reach their spot. He looked up at the sky. A few remaining wicks of orange and yellow light burned wearily through the dark clouds. *Soon the light of my first cycle will forever rest in darkness*, Oa thought to himself.

Oa sat quietly as the Reaper flew on, heading toward an unknown destination. He watched the sky as the light in the distance came toward them. To pass the time, Oa tossed the silver orb back and forth between his hands. He inspected it, trying to decipher the symbols and markings all over it. At one point he even let Jad hold it. Oa explained what he felt whenever he activated the power of the sphere. Jad tried to replicate it but was unable to. They both returned to gazing below at the cracked landscape as it sparkled and glowed. The cycle of the sky reached its brightest point for the travelers. Feeling uplifted by the light, Oa turned to Jad and asked, "With all this freedom, why do you choose to take the lives of others?"

"We don't choose!" Bota snapped, irritated by Oa's words.

Jad held his hand up in a calming gesture. The Lieutenant shook his head in frustration but did not speak any further. Jad answered Oa, his voice growing grim, "A long time ago before I awoke, there used to be governments and order. That's all gone. Now there is one law that we must answer to, and that law's name is Eol. Recently his grip has tightened. He actually sets foot on our land now. It's not just his soldiers we have to worry about anymore."

"You will understand soon enough," Bota added, rejoining the conversation. "Eol has an appetite for soul embers. If he is not fed, he eats away at the edge lands in search for them. I won't let Eol devour my home, or my crew! So I feed Sleeper and Howler embers to him, to keep the peace."

"Then you serve rather than fight, to keep your lives," Oa reasoned as he began to understand.

Bota stared evenly at him. "Either way, Awoken are going to die. We have the strength to decide who it is. Did you see those Sleepers back there? They wallow in Eol's grip already. Once you fixed them, they would have ripped your ember from you and sold it to Eol's distributors. They do anything to barter for just one more Void immersion. There is no reasoning with their addiction. They are worthless beings destined to become Howlers. It's them or us; that's the way Eol keeps it."

"Oa, you must be young—" Jad mused, "too young to have made hard choices yet, but you will one of these cycles. You will discover a great desire to keep yourself and the ones you love safe. Allow us to be your friends, and you can care for us the same way you tried to care for those miserable Sleepers. This time your good intentions won't be misplaced."

Oa wanted to protest, but he could not. Words wouldn't come to him to explain to these Marauders any other way they should live. He still did not know enough. Oa disliked the situation but remained silent.

Jad could sense the young Awoken's inner conflict. He put a hand on Oa's shoulder for a moment before speaking. "We used to be more like you Oa, but times change. We didn't always need to kill to survive. Eol has made that our reality now."

Oa nodded and decided to change the subject. He had many questions, and Jad seemed smart enough to answer a few of them. "The Awoken you killed back there talked of the Destroyer. Were they referring to Eol?"

Jad laughed and shook his head. "Those fools go soft in the head from their addiction, and their crazy dreams ruin the ancient tales. I'm the oldest living Awoken in these parts. Everyone else is too young to know, but I'll tell you the real story. From my early cycles I remember a fellow called the Traveler. He came through my town a few times before the place was torn down by Sleepers. He was a storyteller and a very old Awoken with a single piercing blue ocular plate. The other half of his face was covered in a strange mask. The Traveler roamed all about the edge lands carrying a talking pack, trading his stories for supplies and rides. My favorite story he told was of the Destroyer—an Awoken, the very first Awoken. He was a hero, not some monster like Eol. A great leader and peacekeeper until—"

"We are rapidly approaching the exchange point!" Kiri yelled down, interrupting Jad's tale.

"Yes, we know you fly fast!" Bota yelled back. "Slow us down so we can arrive in formation with the Captain." He turned to Oa and Jad. "Alright, story time is over. Let's see if our luck holds through this new cycle. You're one of us now Oa, so have your gear ready. Interactions with Eol can end badly."

"We will finish that story some other time," Jad said apologetically to Oa.

The Reaper slowed down and began to descend. Jad looked out over the deck's edge to see where they were heading. He cursed, muttering to himself, "The Void has moved again." He turned and shouted to Bota, "The old exchange zone is gone. The Void is advancing farther." Intrigued, Oa poked his head out of the hold to see that they were flying toward the end of a steep ravine. The walls of the gorge sloped down into a flat field of rock that led to the familiar dark abyss.

"Are you sure?" Bota shouted back to Jad. The old medic nodded, and Bota sighed. "Then we need to track the Void's movement. Ever since Eol started walking, the Void has been following, eating away at our land. It must stop."

Only Oa heard Jad's muttered response. "We would have better luck trying to fold the world."

The Marauder dropships landed on a wide flat area of the canyon just shy of the Void's edge. Oa glanced around and counted six of the rusty Mark IV Reapers in total, all facing the black abyss. Bota got out and began walking toward the Void to meet up with a dozen Marauders who were starting to group together. Halting his stride momentarily, Bota turned and yelled back, "Stay in the ship and keep the engines hot in case we need to run off."

"If we can," muttered Jad. "Eol can chase us himself now."

Kiri gave an affirmative signal with her hand. Once Bota saw it through the cockpit window, he turned and jogged over to the group standing around a case, hands ready on their weapons. Bota took his place to the right of the Captain, whom Oa recognized as the same leader from the village.

For a moment, nothing happened as the armed Awoken stood facing the Void. Oa was about to turn and ask Jad what was going on when two figures emerged from the darkness, stepping out of abyss to stand in reality. An oily dark sheen seemed to trail behind them with every move they made. They wore long black high collared coats, with boots and gloves to match. An eerie breathing apparatus concealed their face. Twin black conduits snaked out from the bottom of the apparatus and connected up to a round viewport in the center of the mask. A metal helmet with a narrow brim sat atop their heads. Oa could see no part of their bodies, only an evil crimson glow that poured out of their viewport. It looked like an eye.

A third entity emerged, clothed in many folds of tattered cloth that wrapped around its body like a shroud. The ends of the numerous rags trailed down around its ankles. The lower half of the figure's face was covered by the wrappings, and on its head lay the smoky remains of a strange wild creature. The bottom jaw had been torn away leaving the top jaw draped over the figures head like a cowl. The carcass's dead, black eyes cast a fierce look. Two vicious slits of a deep glowing red seethed from beneath the shadow of the dead creature. The eyes of Eol.

The ominous Void dwellers walked up to the group of Marauders. The shrouded one stepped forward, standing tall and menacing in front of the Awoken. Oa wished he was close enough to hear. He saw the Captain motion toward a case another Marauder was carrying. Oa jolted as he heard a strange voice all around him. The voice was smooth and calm, yet rather unsettling.

"You have brought me an abundance, and I am very grateful. That is why it pains me to inform you that I require something more." The Captain must have replied because the voice continued. "There is something strange among you, an anomaly."

Bota glanced back in their direction, then stepped in close to the Captain, leaning over to whisper something.

It must be me. I'm the anomaly, Oa realized looking down at his covered chest. The Captain turned and said something to the shrouded figure. Oa waited.

A moment later the voice snarled. "Lying to me will only bring chaos. You force me to restore order!"

Oa jumped slightly as he witnessed the shrouded monster move with unnatural speed. The Marauders jumped back in shock. The crimson eyed figure stood with his arm extended, a solid black staff held straight out before him. The weapon was protruding through the head of the Marauder standing to the left of the Captain. The Marauder's body stood stiff for a moment before dissolving away completely. The case he had been carrying fell to the ground with a clatter that Oa heard faintly.

The Captain stepped forward and gestured frantically toward Oa and the dropship he was in. The voice laughed and taunted the Marauders, "So much for your honor, Captain. Consider our treaty broken, as you have failed to uphold it. If it's any consolation, I was never going to abide by any rules, even those of my own making. Your use to me is at an end, but you have my gratitude for finding him."

The Marauders responded quickly, drawing their weapons. The two Void minions sprang forward into the Marauder midst. Oa had trouble seeing what was occuring in the confusion. Fists flew and shots were fired; rays and sparks of energy arced across the landscape. The two black warriors were overwhelmed. Oa glimpsed Bota firing into one of them. The wraith dispersed into a cloud of smoke as the energy beam ripped through it. The Marauders took a few steps back, their numbers dwindled. Oa could still see the Captain and Bota. They stood back, warily eying the shrouded figure.

Eol had not moved. He stood, still pointing his staff at the Marauders. Out of the Void more soldiers emerged. They began marching toward the Marauders, glowing red viewports glinting in the dying green light. Overhead, the cycle burned a poisonous green as rivers of energy flowed into the Void. Bota snatched the case from the ground, carrying it under one arm as he followed the Marauders in a full retreat. Oa now assumed the case contained soul embers.

As they ran back toward their Reapers, the Marauders turned and fired their weapons back at the soldiers in an attempt to slow the march of the deadly wraiths. The dark warriors reached into their coats and, in unison, pulled out compact streamlined pistols; similar to the ones Oa had seen the Marauders wield. The soldiers pointed their weapons at the Awoken and fired. Instead of noise, the air was filled with a deafening silence as black beams streaked out from the weapons, leaving behind an oily sheen in the air. The Marauders dodged and continued to run. Some of them fell and dissolved as they were ripped apart by the Void weapons. Oa saw Bota dive down behind a protruding rock and fire his weapon, obliterating several of Eol's minions. The Lieutenant jumped to his feet with explosive speed and darted the last few steps to his ship.

"Get us out of here!" Bota yelled up to Kiri, as he bounded on board and tossed the crate to Jad. Jad immediately began strapping the metal box to the deck with gear from a compartment in the floor that Oa had not seen earlier. Kiri piloted her craft up into the air, joining other Marauder vessels in retreat. Eol's soldiers never slowed their assault. After finishing off the stragglers on the ground, they redirected their attacks toward the fleeing Reapers.

Bota and the other Marauders returned fire from decks of their ships, but their weapons hardly made a dent in the ranks below. Oa watched as the nearest Reaper crashed down. It exploded on impact, sending a flash of light and sound rocketing up towards him. He stumbled back and then fell to the floor of the ship. He tried to get up but the ship began to shake from the impact of multiple hits. Oa watched as Void beams tore through the floor, leaving holes as they ripped the vessel apart.

Oa was puzzled. Why wasn't the whole ship dissolving like the other Awoken? *Maybe it has to be alive*, he reasoned. Whatever the cause, he was happy the ship was not disappearing out from under them.

Then he heard the engine stutter as Kiri yelled, "We can't sustain altitude! The engine's losing power!" The Mark IV shook then dropped for what felt like an eternity. Kiri cursed loudly above; and the engines kicked back on but in reverse, jolting the damaged craft up and backwards.

Oa grabbed one of the handholds he had seen earlier, but Jad was thrown from his place in the back where he had just finished strapping down the wounded Marauder and the case of soul embers. Bota lunged forward and tried to grab hold of Jad, but he was too late. As Jad flew out of the front of the hold Oa acted on pure instinct. He dove to the edge of the platform and tried to grab hold of Jad, but missed. Oa's silver sphere rocketed over his shoulder and struck Jad in the chest, holding him suspended in midair. Then, as if following Oa's will, the sphere began to charge back toward him pulling Jad along. Oa had no idea what he was doing. All he knew was that it felt natural, and there was no time to think further because Jad was being hauled rapidly toward him. Oa flipped over and pointed his hand at the back of the hold. Jad and the sphere came flying over the edge together and smashed up against the grate at the back. Oa laid on the edge of the platform as the sphere dropped off of Jad and flew back to his hand. Oa laughed aloud, at the thrill of what he had just done. Then he looked at the two stunned Marauders before him.

"You're incredible! Thank you!" Jad exclaimed.

"We're not safe yet!" Bota barked, quelling the excitement. "It appears we're at war. Quick, Oa! Use that mystical power stuff you got there to fix this engine. We have to save the rest of … ."

Bota's words trailed off, and his head snapped back toward the Void. Oa heard a poisonous whisper. "Bota, you can redeem yourself in my sight. You can succeed where your cowardly leader has failed. Bring the anomaly to me, and you will be forgiven. Your ember offerings will bring peace again. Your sacrifices will grant you life."

Oa looked to see if Jad had heard Eol's voice, but Jad seemed unaware. Oa stared at Bota and noticed he was looking at him. Their gazes locked. Oa looked away not wanting to give away his mysterious knowledge of the message, which was clearly intended for only Bota to hear.

Oa felt the rush of imminent danger. His mind rapidly concocted a crazy plan. He stood up and replied loud enough for everyone in the ship to hear. "I am not fixing anything. You will fly just fine if you have a little less weight right?"

Kiri shouted back, "Yeah, but we got nothing else to chuck off; and if someone tosses poor Coop out the front, I will crash us all."

"That's not the plan," Oa responded. "This is where we part ways," he said as he took a step back standing right on the edge of the platform.

"Wait!" Bota shouted as he fired his boltspitter down at their attackers. "We stood up for you back there because you saved Coop, and now you also saved Jad. You aren't a Sleeper or some old coward hiding in ruins. You belong with us, fighting to stay free. We protected you as one of our own, now act like it!" Bota's words sounded convincing and sincere.

Oa realized that no one else on the ship had heard what had taken place below. He stared intently at Bota for a moment. The Lieutenant's true intentions were still unknown. Was he really ready to resist Eol? Or was he simply planning to turn Oa over and renew the Marauder's servitude to the monster?

"You can still save your crew from my wrath," Eol's voice hissed again in Oa's head. He watched as Bota stopped firing his weapon. The Marauder looked over at the metal case strapped to the deck, then he looked down below. Eol stood amid the horde of Void warriors. Bota nodded, then slowly turned and looked at Oa. The light of the battle glinted ominously across his goggles.

Oa had seen and heard enough. He made his decision and spoke, "I'm sorry, but I don't belong here. You just see me as a tool to help you keep Eol satiated. I don't understand the interest in me, and I don't want to find out. I'll find my own way."

"Why don't you stay? You haven't heard Bota's singing voice," Jad said mocking Oa's sudden dramatic tone. Jad was unaware of Eol's concealed message to Bota.

"Never going to hear it," Oa retorted. "Our paths shouldn't cross again."

He tried to will himself to take a step back; but to his embarrassment, he couldn't. His feet would not obey the lunacy his mind commanded.

Bota was pleased. His voice held the satisfaction of victory as he spoke. "Stop being melodramatic and fix this engine. You won't leave unless—"

Just then, the engine coughed, rocking the vessel ever so slightly. Oa lost his balance and fell, plummeting out of the dropship.

EPISODE 03

FRIEND

Oa was filled with a paralyzing thrill as he fell. His wild idea came rushing back to him all at once. He frantically flailed out, trying to spin around and orient himself toward the ground. The movement only sent him into a tumble. He spread his limbs out, flattening to reduce the spinning. Luckily he had not lost hold of the little silver sphere. Oa stuck out his hand, reaching toward the jagged stone far below. The rune covered orb launched from his hand. He tried to direct it downwards, but his world was still a wheeling plunge of confusion. Oa forced the fear and stress of the situation down. He only had one option and so he focused on his difficult task. Out of the corner of his visual receptors, Oa thought he caught a glimpse of a figure rocketing up toward him but he soon lost sight of the object.

I can't be distracted, Oa thought in frustration as he refocused on his highest priority—not dying. He finally oriented himself so that he was facing straight down. The metal sphere shot below into the rock. Upon its impact, Oa immediately began to push with his mind. He felt a strain throughout his body, and his fall began to slow.

This is going to work, Oa thought excitedly. Then to his dismay, he realized he was far too close to the ground and was still falling too fast. He strained, exerting all the will his mind contained, to try and arrest his descent. It wasn't going to work. Suddenly, Oa felt himself snatched out of the air as the arm of an Awoken caught him around the waist. They coasted down into the deep canyon below. Landing lightly on his feet, Oa's rescuer dumped him onto the ground. Oa was shaking slightly as he quickly glanced up into the sky, but he saw no sign of any Mark IV Reapers. Above the gorge, the roar of engines faded quickly. Oa spotted his silver metal sphere a short ways ahead on the stony ground. With his mind, he called the little object back to his hand. In response, the sphere came rolling to him but stopped at his feet instead of returning into his hand as it had done previously. Annoyed, Oa bent down and picked it up.

"That's the most innovative way to hit the ground I've ever witnessed. Don't you agree, Fred?" the cultured and slightly quirky male voice of Oa's rescuer exclaimed.

"Indubitably," a monotone voice responded.

"Aha! I do enjoy that word. When is the last time you used it?" the Stranger inquired.

Oa turned to look at the absurd conversation going on behind him. He saw that his rescuer was indeed an Awoken, tall of stature and lean. He wore a random assortment of sturdy looking cloths held together by buckles and straps. There were numerous tears and signs of age in the material. His left arm was uncovered, revealing the faded alloys of the metallic appendage. His right arm was heavily bandaged, and it ended in a stump where his hand should have been. The right leg was also covered completely in a pant leg held tightly by a bandage around the knee. The hood of his cloak covered the Awoken's head. Oa looked at the Awoken's face, the slanted arrangement of his facial plates made the him appear sharp and slightly imposing. Two features caught Oa's attention: the Awoken's right ocular plate glowed with a piercing blue light, and the left half of his face was covered by a mechanized mask. Oa could see a flickering blue light through the slits in the mask. Connected to the bottom of the mask was a microbur cylinder like the ones Oa had seen on Jad's chest.

Could it be the Traveler? he thought to himself.

"Who are you?" Oa asked, daring to hope that he had just bumped into the Awoken from Jad's story.

"My name is Ohm. And this is my loyal friend Fred," Ohm said, turning around to show Oa a metallic pack. The pack held a hefty looking tank of clear liquid.

"Greetings," the pack said. Oa recognized the monotone voice he had heard earlier. The blue panels on either side of the tank glowed brighter as the pack spoke.

"You're the Traveler!" Oa blurted excitedly.

"I am a traveler, yes. Fred and I have been tracking you since you were just a shooting meteor across the sky. We had to see you. No one has woken up in a very long time. I apologize for the discomposure of our meeting," Ohm explained, his voice cheerful and welcoming.

"Wait...what do you want?" Oa asked, warily curbing his excitement. "So far, everyone I have met seems to have motives I can't completely figure out."

"Well, allow me to change that," Ohm offered pleasantly, "Fred and I just wanted to prevent you from hitting the ground. Now that we have accomplished our task, I'm curious to discover what your immediate and long term goals are." The old Awoken arched back, stretching out his old joints nonchalantly.

"I don't have any plans. I don't even know what I'm doing right now," Oa said wearily as he sat down on a lump of rock protruding from the canyon floor.

"Ah, so you were hoping to hit the ground. Let us both offer our most humble apo—"

"No, I was trying to escape. I was going to use this silly thing to stop my fall," Oa said, interrupting Ohm's comically reverent apology. He waved the silver sphere for Ohm to see before he put it back in the bag at his side.

"Oh! Well then, it all worked out fantastically! The decision is yours, but you are welcome to come wandering with us," Ohm offered. "Fred can be ludicrously dull, but I have been known to say some interesting things from time to time."

Oa considered the offer for a moment. He was puzzled at the coincidence of meeting the Traveler from Jad's tale. He needed to be cautious and shrewd, but deep down he also wanted to simply meet someone he could trust. A kind old wanderer seemed close enough. Ohm turned and looked at the sky. The leading trails of light had passed leaving behind only a few weak winding streams.

"Another cycle fades. I wonder how many more are left," Ohm said quietly. He turned back to look at Oa. "You should resolve your direction sooner rather than later. Indecision is a luxury you don't have time for, with the world ending and all."

"The world's ending?! I just got here!" Oa protested in shock as his face plates flashed.

"It's unfortunate, but that's the word going around, isn't it Fred?" Ohm replied in a self- assured tone.

Fred's reply was monotone, yet it still managed to convey a sense of mockery. "You seem to have forgotten that we have not spoken to, or overheard conversation from anyone in over three million—"

"Ignore him. He exists solely to contradict me," Ohm interrupted with a dismissive wave of his good hand. He noticed Oa staring at the ground dejectedly. "What's wrong?"

Oa's shoulders slumped. "I woke up eager to explore and learn. But it seems everything is broken, and I'm surrounded by death. I have no idea what I'm doing here. Is this place supposed to be so …?" he let his words trail off into silence as he looked for a word to describe his first few cycles. All of the vague emotions he had experienced while healing now began to bubble to the surface of his mind; a primordial inferno of ideals waiting to be imprinted on his spirit.

Ohm sat down next to him. "The way I see it, you should consider yourself fortunate. You haven't yet made the mistake of asking Fred what he finds most interesting about the layering of soil." The old wanderer chuckled at his own joke, then grew more serious. "Living is like a journey, and journeys are a total mess of possibilities. It is impossible to predict exactly how things will turn out. It can be tiring carrying around too many grand expectations."

"Well, I thought I could help," Oa replied in frustration, "but then stuff got crazy," he paused, thinking before he continued. "I just need to figure this place out. There are things I need to understand. Then I am going to do something about all this."

Ohm took a moment before giving a response. "All begin their journey hoping for happier and more meaningful endings than they receive. Only a select few can hold onto that hope through the duration of the voyage, all the way to the end. Perhaps it's something unique in their programming."

In the following silence, Ohm's hand involuntarily drifted to his chest. His fingers brushed an unseen object hidden beneath his cloak. He quickly snapped out of his momentary daze and stood up.

"Total waste of effort in my opinion; but you seem to be that way Oa, so there is no helping it. I've always been curious about Awoken like you," Ohm said casually. He turned and started to walk further into the canyon.

Ohm's words piqued Oa's interest. The backhanded compliment lifted his spirits. Ohm was so very different from the other Awoken Oa had met. *If he also senses this inner drive I have, then maybe I am not just delusional*, he thought to himself with newfound determination. He made his decision and stood up to follow Ohm, speaking resolutely to himself. "Alright then. I will walk with this Traveler and learn as much as I can. I don't care if I'm at the end of this world's story. I will find a way to make a new story."

Ohm stayed silent as Oa walked up to join him at a fork in the desolate gorge. "Alright, I'm coming. It seems my time is precious, so this better not be boring," Oa teased.

"I am glad you are joining us! You have yet to disappoint me. Let us begin by going ..." Ohm paused for a long time. Oa grew impatient at having hurried his big decision only to wait on the ancient Awoken to make a seemingly simple one.

Ohm waited until Oa started to pace about in agitation, swinging his arms and glancing around in boredom. Ohm chuckled to himself and decided he had tested Oa's patience enough.

"That way!" Ohm exclaimed confidently as he quickly pointed to his left with a speed that implied a random decision. Oa perked up in excitement, rushing to follow Ohm as the old Awoken strode off.

Oa and Ohm followed the canyon, ignoring any smaller off-shoot ravines they passed as they ventured further into the labyrinth of rock. There was silence for a while as they walked in the dim twilight of the sky's cycle. Oa looked around in wonder at the stones around him. They were huge and faceted as if the canyon had been cut out of the stone by some ancient tool. The sides of the rock had bright veins of unknown minerals that shimmered, casting a soft light.

After some time, Ohm spoke up. "So, how do you use that shiny ball?"

Oa fished the metal sphere out of his satchel and handed it to Ohm as he responded, "I don't know. It seems to go wherever

I direct it, and it can attach to anything I want it to. But it's difficult, especially when I'm falling out of the sky."

"Understandable," Ohm replied as he turned the sphere over in his hand, studying it closely. He tossed it into the air a few times. "You just need to fiddle with it, so the next time you fall out the sky you can ... hold on just a weeble! What was your actual plan?" He looked quizzically at Oa.

"I don't know really. I thought I could maybe launch it so hard at the ground that I would slow down and land lightly on my feet or something," Oa admitted, laughing nervously at the absurdity of the idea.

"Well that's inventive, but nevertheless I still had to save you. I believe it's time for some much needed practice," Ohm replied jovially. "So how about this? I will throw this gadget as far as I can and then you will try to catch it." Oa shrugged and nodded in agreement. "Good. We start now," Ohm commanded.

Oa watched as Ohm wound his arm up once and threw the orb. His arm moved in a blur. Oa thought he had never seen anyone move as fast, but then he remembered Eol. *That would be a close match. Maybe I can move that fast,* he wondered as he watched the little sphere sail farther than he thought possible. Oa took off after it, running as fast as he could. *I am fast!* he thought happily. He quickly realized there was no way he was going to catch the sphere, though. He reached out his hand and focused on the little orb, willing it to return to his hand. The sphere started to curve from its flight path. Then the young Awoken tripped on a rock and sprawled out on his face, hand still outstretched as the silver orb rolled back to him.

"That's almost the idea," Ohm teased. He pondered something briefly. "I think I'm gonna name that gizmo. How does Seeker sound?"

Oa got back up considering the name.

"I know it's not terribly clever," Ohm admitted, "but it seems to fit."

"Seeker works fine," Oa said, pleased by idea. "Do you name everything?"

"No. Fred picked his own name," Ohm said. "Now let's try again."

Oa levitated the sphere over to Ohm, and they repeated the exercise numerous times. At first, Oa tried to overtake Seeker with speed; but as fast as he was, he was never faster than Ohm's throw. Oa revised his strategy, slowly shifting his focus from physical to mental strength. He gradually decreased the distance he ran until he was able to call Seeker back to his hand from wherever Ohm threw it. Three cycles passed during this training. Ohm watched Oa with growing surprise. He had seen Oa express the impatience and inexperience common in any Awoken so young, but something about working with Seeker made him different. The drive to bond with the strange silver orb separated the young Awoken from any concept of time or boredom.

"You are unique, Oa. I did not think you would pursue this so relentlessly," Ohm said breaking the silence and halting the lesson.

Oa returned from the intense focus he was in with a delighted laugh. "I got it, though. See, now when you throw it, I don't even have to move."

"Yes, your control is much more refined, not just an instinctive accident," Ohm congratulated. "Let us begin another lesson." He decided to keep silent about the unusual amount of time they had just spent on one exercise.

Ohm instructed Oa levitate Seeker and learn to control its movements in the air while Ohm tried to grab it. As he had before, Oa focused on the task until he had completed it, completely unaware as a whole cycle flew by. Ohm's final test was a game of chase. He launched from the ground on a geyser of liquid jetting from his pack. Oa was curious as to how the pack worked, but he was more focused on his mentor's test. He sent Seeker flying after Ohm. The old wanderer was quick and surprisingly acrobatic in the air. Oa had mastered his control of Seeker; and before another cycle passed, he had nailed Ohm in the shoulder. Ohm landed roughly from the impact and jogged back toward Oa.

"This gizmo really does stick. I can't get it off," Ohm said impressed as he tried to pry Seeker from his shoulder.

"I got lucky and discovered that ability when I used it to rescue someone," Oa said as he called Seeker back to his hand from Ohm's shoulder. He placed Seeker back in the bag at his side.

"Now you know how to control Seeker. You'll be able to apply the skills you've learned to whatever zany scheme you come up with in the future," Ohm said encouragingly.

Overhead, the roar of an engine surprised the pair. They quickly ducked under an overhang in the rock wall. Oa peeked his head out from under the cove and located the source of the noise; a Reaper. The vessel careened over the canyon, trailing dark ugly smoke. Oa ducked back under the overhang as it passed.

"It's one of the Marauder dropships. It's been damaged. It must be from the group I was with," Oa reported. "I thought they were gone."

"Probably returning to their camp," Ohm muttered.

"Here?" Oa asked in disbelief.

"These ravines have numerous caverns and crevices they could hide in," Ohm explained. "The question is: are they limping home or out searching for something?" He looked meaningfully at Oa.

"They might be looking for me," Oa admitted, after a moment of deliberation.

"Marauders fear the Legion, but they serve obediently. I witnessed a little of the conflict just before I caught you. What exactly happened?" Ohm asked.

"Legion? You're referring to the soldiers with the single red eye right?" Oa asked for clarification. Ohm nodded in response.

"The Marauders were delivering a case which I believe contains soul embers. Then there was a disagreement; over me I think. The Marauders resisted at first, but the Legion put them on the run. I sensed one of them was going to give me up, so I jumped—or fell rather," Oa explained while Ohm listened closely. "So who are the Legion?" he questioned, taking advantage of Ohm's silence. He did not want to give Ohm the chance to pry further. He liked Ohm, but he did not feel ready to bring up his lack of a soul ember or the possible reasons why the Legion would want him.

"They are creatures of the Void, the physical embodiment of Eol's will," Ohm replied somberly.

"The one shrouded in rags—he was very dangerous," Oa said, remembering the demon.

Ohm grabbed Oa's shoulder in shock. "You have seen him?!"

"Yes, and so have the Marauders. They seem to have met him several times recently," Oa replied, taken aback by the sudden outburst.

Ohm turned away and stepped out from under the outcropping as he explained his concerns to Oa. "Eol has never had a physical form that I know of. His Legion never strayed too far from the edge. Eol was just a shadow, the voice of his minions … Something is not right. The Legion is getting stronger if Eol is now killing Awoken himself. Maybe he no longer needs to manipulate them to fight each other. It worries me."

Oa stood next to Ohm as he stared off into the sky. Oa followed his gaze. He saw the damaged Reaper off in the distance, still flying over the canyon.

"I'm certain that case contained embers for Eol. They accept his word as law. It's why the Marauders were crushed so easily. I wish I understood their situation more. There has to be a way for them to be free," Oa reasoned pondering his brief time with Jad.

"I do not think you completely understand Eol's madness, Oa. The soul ember is an Awoken's consciousness. When life leaves the Awoken, an echo remains. All their experiences and memories, who they were, is preserved by the ember. Nothing remains in this world that could destroy an ember. Nothing except the Void. Eol is devouring our past while his Legion slowly eats away at the edges of this world, obliterating our future," Ohm said grimly.

"I see," Oa muttered quietly. He was perplexed. *How would Eol know to single me out? I should have just been another Marauder to him—*

"It's intriguing that there would be an entire battle over you," Ohm said cryptically, interrupting Oa's thoughts. He turned to Oa. "It was incredibly difficult to locate you because there was no ember trail for Fred to track from your birth cell."

Oa froze, realizing that Ohm knew. He decided that he had to follow his instincts and trust the Traveler if they were going to continue to journey together. He lifted up the cloth covering his chest.

"Are you seeing this, Fred?" Ohm asked.

"Scanning …" Fred said. "Oa's lack of a soul ember disproves his existence. Despite this impossibility, my readings do not lie. He is somehow conscious and functioning. My working theory is that your malarkey has bled into my circuits, Ohm, and we are both hallucinating."

"He most certainly does exist, Fred, old buddy," Ohm said, trying hide his amusement. "So stop complaining about it and start theorizing."

"Since my extensive quantitative and qualitative capabilities have been reduced to conjuring up malarkey, I theorize that Oa is powered by everything and nothing at the same time while suspended upside down in seven points of time through another dimension," Fred retorted sarcastically.

"Stop being cranky," Ohm chuckled. "You are just mad I found something else you can not make sense out of."

Ohm patted Oa on the shoulder. "I would assume that Eol wants you for the same reason we can't explain how you are alive. You are unique, Oa, in more ways than you or I can understand. Somehow it is linked to Eol, I am sure of it."

The idea of the shrouded fiend seeking him out did not terrify Oa as much as he thought it would. Instead it conjured up a new emotion within him, defiance. For a moment the various abstract feelings of purpose he had experienced when using Seeker now had a focal obstacle. Perhaps the problem wasn't all that complex. Perhaps only one symbol was out of place in the universe. *Fix that and everything else falls into place...*

Oa emerged from his contemplation, realizing he had created an awkward lull in the conversation. Ohm was looking expectantly at him as if awaiting a response.

"That's great; maybe Eol and I should be friends," Oa said sarcastically. He continued in a more serious tone. "This information only gives me more questions. I must have a reason to exist if I'm so different. You've been very helpful, but your main trait seems to be meandering. You haven't offered up any solid direction yet, so I'm going to create my own."

"Fantastic," Ohm said enthusiastically. "Fred and I just wander, learn, and teach; but we are always open to new ideas."

"I want to steal that case of soul embers," Oa said determined. "No one seems to be willing to go against Eol, so I will. I am going to start by taking the embers from his servants."

"Are you sure the Marauders are still working for Eol?" Ohm asked incredulously. "Last I saw, they seemed to be trying to kill one another."

"I heard Eol's voice tempting one of them. All they had to do was turn me over, along with the embers. They have accepted killing to survive and don't seem strong enough to resist their master. Either way, I'm not going to give them the chance to feed him anymore," Oa said with conviction.

"Well it seems you have judged the situation. I only saw from afar so I will not question you further," Ohm replied, skeptically.

Oa paused and reconsidered his judgment, then he spoke in a softer tone. "I don't really know what their motives are anymore, but I do know they will never be able to change while trapped in Eol's shadow. If I take the embers, then he will come for me. I am going to distract him from whatever sick game he is playing on the Great Planes. Then I'm going to figure out a way to stop him. It's going to be dangerous so if you don't want to help, that's fine." He motioned to Ohm's bandaged arm.

"That does sound risky," Ohm said, feigning worry. "But even if you do manage to sneak through hordes of Marauders and rescue the lost embers—thus angering the demon—what do you plan to do next? Where will you go?"

Oa shrugged. "I don't know yet. Do you have any ideas?" He looked up at his newfound mentor for guidance.

"I am relieved. I was afraid you had no further need of my company, since you seem to think my wounded arm makes me an invalid," Ohm exaggerated teasingly. "I will help you. I have heard of a place where Awoken worship the embers and keep them safe. On the way, I will teach you and help you understand all that I know of the Great Planes. Somewhere out there, we will find a way to deal with Eol," Ohm said, spreading his arms wide with a flourish, to encompass all that laid before them.

"Well, I'm glad that stealing soul embers and fighting monsters isn't too radical for your wandering lifestyle," Oa said, chuckling slightly at Ohm's antics. "Anyway, I don't see that dropship anymore, and the smoke is gone. But it was headed away from the edge, like us."

"Judging by the color of the skylight, the windspeed, and the velocity of that dust mote we passed two cycles ago, the Marauders should be hiding in this canyon. Fred's trained sensors will be able to locate the entrance to their camp. It will be difficult for you or I to spot," Ohm explained.

"Will we find it faster if we run?" Oa asked, eager to use his legs again. Ohm nodded in affirmative.

"Then let's go!" Oa said impatiently, taking off in a sprint. Ohm followed, catching up easily. The two raced up the canyon, dodging through boulders and spires that littered the canyon floor. Occasionally, Ohm would jet off to the side of the gorge to inspect a random crag or fissure briefly before returning to run with Oa. The young Awoken enjoyed the speed of running. His legs were a blur, and his reflexes had been trained chasing Seeker. He only tripped once on the uneven ground. Oa was enjoying himself so much he momentarily forgot about finding the Marauder camp. Ohm ended the moment as he reappeared from another scouting trip. Running alongside of Oa, Ohm revealed a discovery. "I think that fissure in the rock might be the entrance.

"What fissure?" Oa asked, turning to look at Ohm for a moment.

"That one," Ohm said as they rounded a bend and came upon a gaping crack in the canyon floor between several towering rock spires. Oa dug in his heels and skidded to a stumbling halt at the edge of the chasm.

"Thanks for the warning," Oa said in mock gratitude.

Ohm ignored the jibe as he peered over the edge of the precipice, a small ledge jutted out from the rock face about an arms length below them. "I see burn marks on the stone, probably from their ship's thrusters. Also, there is a faint glow coming from a platform way down there." He paused for a moment. "I completely forgot: Fred's the expert Marauder-cave detector. What do you think, Fred?"

"It appears to be a cavern," Fred replied evenly, clearly annoyed at being overlooked.

"Insightful as ever," Ohm nodded sagely. He hopped down onto the ledge and sat.

"Ohm, it is unwise to aqua jet into the cave. The noise will be amplified by the cavern, and the Marauders will immediately be alerted to our presence," Fred droned in his robotic voice.

"Too true, Fred," Ohm admitted, temporarily puzzled as he thought up a solution. "Oa, what if you use Seeker to lower us down to that platform? You can anchor it to this berm."

"It should work," Oa said. He stretched out his hand toward the ledge. Seeker darted from his satchel and affixed itself to the stone. He carefully stepped down next to Ohm. Oa rested his feet on the rim of the sill and leaned back over the abyss. His arm still pulled toward Seeker as if an invisible line connected the two. Ohm scooted over next to Oa. He grabbed Oa's ankle with his good hand and pushed off the ledge with his bandaged stump. Swinging from his one hand, Ohm dangled over the pit.

"You can jump now," Ohm said. Oa shut off his visual receptors and drew within himself to find the courage. He let the invisible line between his hand and Seeker lengthen, and he felt himself fall backwards. Ohm's weight on Oa's ankle pulled his feet off of the ledge. The two fell a short distance before Oa recovered from the shock of the drop. He slowed their descent to a steady pace. They swung back and forth lightly as they lowered further into the darkness. The odd-looking pair dropped down into the cavern, edging out of the light's reach.

Oa turned his visual receptors back on and looked around. They were still traveling through the fissure in the rock. Eventually it opened up; and they were underneath the foundation of the world, in a cavern that seemed as infinite as it was dark.

He could make out streams of light coming down from other openings in the ceiling far off in the distance. There were huge slabs of rock hanging down from the bedrock, almost mirroring the spires that they had seen on the surface. Oa noticed that they were descending next to an especially gargantuan, smooth faceted spire. The shimmering veins within the stone shone brilliantly in the sparse light. He reached out to touch one as they passed by. Ripples of energy flowed through the vein as his hand brushed against it. The allure of the lights captured his attention briefly. Oa looked down and spotted a round balcony protruding from the stone. It was still far below so he sped up their descent, closing the gap quickly. He could hear a strange sound floating up, echoing off of the rock. It was sad and melodic. *Rather haunting*, Oa thought to himself.

As they neared the platform, Ohm whispered, "Stop us here. I can see a glow in the center of the platform. We are headed straight for it. We need to land on the edge where there is less light."

"Understood. You start swinging us. When we are over the edge of the platform, I'll retrieve Seeker, then reattach it to the deck as we fall past it," Oa explained, quickly outlining a plan.

Ohm began to swing his legs; and soon the pair was swinging in an arc that took them past the edge of the terrace. "Alright, we had better do this before we have time to think about the odds of failure."

"Get ready," Oa whispered. His voice faltered slightly but he put faith in his recent training. He called Seeker back. The instant Seeker detached from the ledge, they plummeted downward. Oa focused on retrieving Seeker. After what felt like an eternity of falling, He felt the silver orb strike his awaiting palm. The edge of the platform flashed past his face, just a few finger lengths away. He looked back up and threw Seeker toward the metal deck. Their fall came to a jarring halt as Seeker latched onto the rim of the balcony.

"That was close," Oa said in relief, his voice shaking.

"I'm glad I made you practice so much with that gizmo," Ohm agreed. Oa quickly pulled them up to the deck and held onto Seeker as Ohm awkwardly climbed up over him with his one good hand. Ohm got a boot up on the platform and launched himself over the railing. He picked himself up and reached back over the railing to grab Oa. Once on the platform, Oa retrieved Seeker and crouched next to Ohm behind a stack of crates. They peeked over the crates to see that the half-circle terrace had several raised sections along its fringe. Oa assumed these sections were meant to be landing docks for the dropships he had seen earlier, yet only one remained. A plethora of tools, equipment, and raw goods were strewn about the landing decks. Crates were stacked haphazardly around the docking stations. In the center of the platform, the Marauder camp rested beneath thick support beams bolted to the stone and deck. There were cloths draped over poles to create makeshift shelters, and at the center of them sat the source of the exposing light. It appeared to be a pile of red and yellow glowing stones. They cast a warm light on three figures sitting around them. The figures were the source of the strange sound Oa had heard earlier.

"What is that noise?" Oa whispered to Ohm.

"That is music—well-crafted music," Ohm replied.

"Sounds nice, but I don't see the soul ember crate," Oa said worriedly.

"They probably just put the embers in another container. Don't fret. The Marauders will be keeping them close," Ohm muttered as he scanned the camp. Then he pointed excitedly. "Look closely next to the pile of warmth shards. See that small bag? It is very old, I can tell by the markings. Old means valuable. The soul embers must be in there."

"The noise you are emitting is loud enough to revive one of those soul embers," Fred chided in a lowered voice.

Ohm's head cocked back for a moment. Then he reached down to his hip and fiddled with something for a moment before jabbing Oa in the side with his elbow. Ohm leaned in close and whispered, "I reset Fred's voice emitter. He is insanely loud now."

Oa turned, startled. "Why would you do that?"

"Because it's hilarious, and will serve to get their attention," Ohm replied. Then turning his head slightly, he whispered back, "Hey Fred, remind me. What is that word you like so much?"

"MALARKEY!" Fred's voice thundered throughout the cavern.

The three Marauders abruptly stopped playing their music and sprang to their feet, reaching for weapons. Startled, they scanned around looking for the source of the deafening voice.

Oa looked down to see Ohm rolling on the deck in muffled laughter, quite amused by his own antics.

"Very clever," Fred said, his voice returning to normal. "A simple resetting of my vocal emitters—"

"What do we do now? I didn't want their attention," Oa whispered urgently, cutting Fred off.

Ohm immediately ceased his mirth and rolled back up into a crouch next to Oa. He outlined his plan conspiratorially, "I will distract them while you stay out of sight. Circle around to the right, grab the bag, and use Seeker to get back out. I will be right behind you." Ohm's voice was determined and focused. "And don't get shot by their boltspitters." he warned as he scuttled away.

Oa ducked low and waited in position while Ohm ran off to his left. As Ohm ran, he knocked over several crates making enough noise to attract the attention of the three Marauders who slowly started stalking toward Ohm, boltspitters held ready. When Oa heard the sounds of Ohm's distractions, he sped around the platform in the opposite direction. Oa raced through stacks of crates, taking care not to stumble over the random gear strewn about. He heard the familiar pop and hiss of the boltspitters going off. Some fired in quick bursts while others were long drawn out crackles. The light from each shot reflected off the metallic crates and filled the dim cavern. *I hope Ohm knows how dangerous those things are*, Oa thought to himself as he remembered the gaping hole a boltspitter put in Birk's chest.

Oa reached the rear of the balcony where metal met rock. He scrambled over a stack of old junk and knelt down behind a heavy crate. Peeking out from behind the box, he could see that he was now very close to where the Marauders had been sitting. Oa spotted the bag next to one of the seats. He rolled out from behind his hiding spot and crawled over to the bag. He flattened down and grabbed the bag; there were many strange markings on the ancient fabric. He could not read them, but he pulled open the top of the bag and looked inside. Sure enough, Ohm had been correct: in the bag laid several glistening soul embers.

Elated, Oa hopped to his feet, but he saw one of the marauders returning to the camp. Oa backed up in haste, trying to get to the shadows. He tripped backwards over a piece of equipment, making a muffled clang as his body hit the floor. The Marauder spotted Oa and raced forward. As he came into the light, Oa instantly knew who these Marauders were. It was Bota, Jad, and Kiri.

Jad stood in front of him. He pointed his boltspitter at Oa, speaking in a surprised voice. "Oa? But you fell. How?"

"It doesn't matter," Oa interrupted as he stood up. "I have to do this. Leave a message for Eol, tell him I stole the embers. He can come after me himself if he wants them."

Oa held Seeker hidden behind his back. With a simple thought, he sent it shooting up toward another hanging spire of rock over the other side of the platform. He held the bag up with his other hand. "I am going to keep these embers safe and deal with Eol. So go find another life to live."

"Wait! Oa, you don't understand," Jad said taking a step forward but it was too late. Oa's impulsiveness overrode his willingness to listen. Seeker had attached to the rock. Oa reached out with his hand, made the link, and flew up off the deck toward the hanging spire. As he flew over the terrace, Oa saw Bota and Kiri firing at Ohm as he ran toward the edge of the platform. Ohm dodged through the mess of crates, contorting his body to avoid the deadly bolts that filled the air. He was agile and quick, but one of the bolts cleaved through his left leg. Ohm skidded on the ground as his next step landed him on the stump where his knee had been. A stray shot from Kiri hit a tank next to him. It exploded spectacularly. The shock wave knocked Bota and Kiri over and sent Ohm rolling backwards.

Ohm vaulted up off his good leg and somersaulted backwards over the railing. He reappeared a moment later, aqua jetting up to follow Oa. As he flew through the air, Oa watched Bota push himself up into a firing position. The Lieutenant took aim and fired at Ohm. The shot was deadly accurate. Ohm raised his hand as if to block the bolt. Liquid jetted out of the Traveler's hand shaping into a shield. It hardened instantly, stopping the energy bolt cold. Oa tore his disbelieving visual receptors away from the chaos, looking forward in time to see the rock spire rushing at him. He hit the rock at an angle and with enough momentum to skid up the smooth stone face.

Oa recovered from his blunder and sent Seeker speeding back up to the ledge. He felt Seeker attach just as he started to fall. He pulled as hard as he could, sending himself flying up the remaining length of the shaft. He looked back to see Ohm right behind him; the strange shield gone. Ohm's bandaged arm was now encased in a long clear blade extending from the stump. Below, Oa could see the light of an engine as the Marauders fired up their Reaper in pursuit.

As they approached the opening to the cavern, Oa heard Ohm yell, "Fred, I need to see the fracture points of those two spires, now!" The next instant, Oa flew out of the fissure, tumbling to the ground roughly. Behind him, Ohm rocketed straight at one of the rock spires on the edge of the pit. He crashed into it, stabbing his blade all the way into the hard mineral. He leaped off the rock, aqua jetting to the slab on the other side. Both steeples began to crumble as cracks spread from where they had been stabbed. Ohm coasted to a landing beside Oa, where he collapsed on the ground. They watched as the weighty stones toppled over, sealing the rift's entrance.

Oa looked over at Ohm. The strange blade was gone now.

"Did we get the embers?" Ohm asked, his voice slightly betrayed the pain of his injury.

"Right here," Oa said. He retrieved the sack from his satchel and opened it to show Ohm the glistening soul embers within.

"Fantastic," Ohm said in a strained voice. "Just as we planned. Oa, you were brilliant. And thanks for preserving my life again, Fred. That Marauder was the best shot I have ever seen."

"It is my purpose to provide assistance," Fred replied.

Oa's face plates pulsed in shock as he stared dismayed at Ohm's sparking stump of a leg. It was leaking water out onto the rock. Ohm noticed Oa's worry and quickly reassured him.

"I'm not going to die. You can help patch me up. Then we will be on our lively way. We have too much to see to let this slow us down."

EPISODE 04

THE TIRED STORYTELLER

Oa knelt over Ohm's wound. "You should have followed your own advice and not gotten shot! Those boltspitters destroyed your leg," he said, distraught at the damage.

Ohm shrugged. "I can patch this up. We should be able to find some parts to rebuild the rest of the leg in the next town." There was fatigue and discomfort in the Travelers voice, despite his casual tone. "Fred has some tools we can use to stop this leaking and close these broken circuits." He reached over his shoulder to pull Fred off his back. As the robotic pack detached, Oa heard a click followed by a slight hiss as pressure was released from unseen connectors that linked the pair.

The canister attached to Ohm's mask blinked red. Then the flickering blue lights within the mask went dark. "Impeccable timing," he said wearily, pausing for a moment. He looked at Oa. "Will you patch up my leg? I must replace this infernal microbur canister on my face." When Oa nodded, Ohm opened a panel on Fred's side and pulled out a glove and a few medical cylinders. He offered the glove and one of the canisters to Oa. "Here. Attach this to the glove. It's got a supply of microburs inside that you can use to patch up my leg. Nothing elegant, just some cheap alloys to gum up the bleeding. I can show you how to use —"

"I've seen these tools before. I won't need them," Oa said, interrupting Ohm as he waved the glove and microbur canister away. He held out Seeker in his right hand. "Watch this." The young Awoken sat back and withdrew into himself.

The Traveler had helped teach Oa how to control Seeker, and now he was confident that he could use the device to heal his new friend. Ohm sat, watching Oa levitate Seeker between his palms as he silently meditated. After a moment of observation, Ohm shrugged to himself and got to work. He swapped the old microbur canister in his mask for a fresh one; taking care to align the connectors properly. The blue lights behind the mask sparked up once again, as the canister connected. Oa was vaguely aware of the exchange as his inner sight began to take hold. He quelled his curiosity about the mask, narrowing his gaze on Ohm's wounded limb.

Gradually, Oa's mind cleared and his world exploded forth into a maelstrom of strange symbols chaotically racing through existence. In the midst of the torrent of information, Oa glimpsed the aura of Ohm's limb. He pushed through the chaos around him until the visage was resolute and unwavering. The appendage was severely damaged; but Oa could see every alloy, vein, and spark of energy as they were meant to be. He drove toward the goal, grasping at it with his mind. Seeker spun slowly, glowing white-hot as energy flowed around it. The design grew brighter and clearer to Oa as Seeker began to spin faster and faster, humming as its energy spun out to thread together a new leg of solid radiance. The light grew to a blinding brilliance, dancing across the smooth stone.

There was a loud crack that echoed through the gorge. The light dimmed and the echoes faded. Oa felt himself tire; but he held onto the vision, willing Seeker's power to remain at the ready. He looked up toward Ohm's missing right hand and face and was shocked to find a familiar murky shadow hovering over Ohm's mysterious injuries, blinding his vision. Oa was troubled; then he felt his strength slip away, replaced by a ravenous weariness. Seeker stopped spinning and plopped back down into his hand.

Ohm sat staring at his leg, new as it had been the moment he awoke, every speck of matter in its proper place. There was no sign of damage. "What ...?" he gasped in disbelief. He moved his leg hesitantly, rotating his foot and tapping it on the ground. "Impossible! I can feel—I can move it." His head snapped up toward Oa. "I must inspect that gizmo!" Oa tossed Seeker to the old Awoken then sat back exhausted by the inexplicable strain he felt after mending Ohm's leg.

Oa was still upset by his inability to heal Ohm's hidden wounds. He tried to recall the mysterious force that had hindered him when suddenly his vision darkened. A pair of red eyes burned into his consciousness with a ghastly shriek. As quickly as the trance took Oa it left. *Wait, what wounds?* Oa thought to himself as he looked at Ohm. There was nothing wrong with Ohm. The Awoken was missing a hand but Oa did not think it strange anymore. He realized with a tired shake of his head that he had forgotten something important. His mind told him he had fixed Ohm, but a hint of a memory whispered that he was missing something. Oa tried to chase the whisper through his consciousness, but he gave up and accepted the fuzziness in his perception as a side effect of the effort he had exerted.

Ohm snatched Seeker out of the air and shook it, listening for any noise. Then he held it up to his one good visual receptor, inspecting the orb closely. The blue light from his eyeplate reflected off the shiny metal. Ohm found nothing and started to bang Seeker against the ground. He listened to the hollow ring that it made as it hit the rock. He returned to intensely staring at the rune covered sphere.

After some silent pondering, Ohm spoke. "You didn't happen to get any readings on what just happened, did you Fred?"

"I was only able to observe the event through your visual receptors. Since we were not directly connected, my full analysis spectrum was unavailable," Fred replied

Ohm flopped onto his back, throwing his arms out as he sighed, "Of course it would be one of the few times we aren't connected that this happens." He looked up at the sky. "That most certainly factors into Eol's interest in you, Oa. I have never seen anything like what you just did. Next time you do that, I will be ready with Fred and his *full analysis spectrum*."

Oa climbed out of the lethargic stupor he was in and replied, "I'm unusually tired; but if you can find someone else reckless enough to get their leg blown off, I will fix them up."

Ohm laughed and said, "That could be easier than you think. We Awoken can be a stupid crowd. Let us go gather data and start unraveling this mystery! I have a hunch it will help us sort the Eol problem."

The Awoken rose to their feet. Oa put Seeker back into his satchel, while Ohm repacked the remaining medical canisters and loaded Fred up onto his back. Oa heard the click of connectors as Fred and Ohm's systems were rejoined. The Traveler then turned and led the way further into the canyons, moving away from the Void until they could no longer see the black horizon. Oa followed, walking beside Ohm.

"So who are we taking the soul embers to?" Oa asked, patting the satchel that now held the precious stones.

Ohm's reply was more of a lecture, educating Oa as they walked. "We will journey to the Enlightened City. I have heard that the Awoken who reside there, or the Enlightened as they prefer to be called, study the soul embers. They are supposed to be great warriors who protect the embers and honor the memories they hold. Stories even tell that the Enlightened meditate deeply enough to feel the past lives contained within each ember."

"That's possible?" Oa asked in disbelief. He took the bag of soul embers out of his satchel to stare at it as he walked.

"So they say. The soul ember contains everything an Awoken ever was or could be. Their essence is stored within the little crystal. Through focus and meditation, an Awoken may access the ember. Some only feel slight emotions, hints of the past. Those of great will and depth are said to hear the echo of the Awoken's existence. Communing with the lost as if they had never died," Ohm explained reverently. Oa noticed Ohm absentmindedly brush at the spot on his chest again. The young Awoken discreetly glanced over and noticed for the first time a thin strand that ran around Ohm's neck, beneath the hood he wore. Oa reasoned that the necklace must be holding something, but it was hidden beneath the cloak. *Ohm clearly cares a great deal about it. His hand constantly returns to hover over that spot on his chest,* he thought to himself. He considered inquiring about the necklace but decided against it. Ohm obviously did not want the mystery object to be seen so Oa chose to respect his new friend's privacy.

The ragged storyteller did not notice Oa's curiosity as he lectured on. "The fabled City of the Enlightened sits high upon the great mountain, somewhere close to the peak. It will take us many, many cycles to reach it. We will have plenty to explore on the way. I want you to see and understand the value that this world has left to offer."

The lecture was concluded. Oa nodded to show he understood, even though his mind was focused on the hidden object Ohm wore around his neck. As they walked together in silence, Oa watched the shadows of the canyon walls gradually shift as another cycle passed.

At one point Oa dropped back, allowing Ohm to take the lead. He took out the ornate bag and removed one of the embers from inside. *I hope I made the right choice by taking these. I wish I had taken the time to listen to Jad. If only Bota wasn't trying to blast Ohm into oblivion,* he thought in frustration. Accepting his choice, Oa peered into the depths of the glistening shard. *I wonder what would happen if—* He placed the ember into the empty socket of his chest, taking care to make sure Ohm didn't notice his weird experiment. Nothing happened and feeling quite foolish, Oa placed the ember back into the bag. He moved back up to join Ohm.

Eventually the gorge began to widen and slope downward, revealing a sprawling valley. There were numerous spires of stone that rose up from the valley floor to create a labyrinth of mineral. A web of other ravines split off from the valley and headed in all directions. At the center of the valley, Oa could see a city. The lights were bright and contrasted with the dim sky of the fading cycle.

Oa pointed. "Have you been there before?"

"Yes, many times," Ohm replied. "That is the town of Bolleworth, and it has become quite disheveled in recent weebles. Still, there might be incidents of the intriguing nature to see. Let's stop by. It will be good for you to experience at least one of the few remaining Awoken cities."

They exited the canyon, moving down into the valley at a brisk pace. As they trekked toward Bolleworth, Oa could not help but pry. "Ohm, can you explain what happened at the Marauder's camp? How do you fly around with a talking backpack and create shields and blades out of thin air?"

"Not air, but water; the secondary blood of all Awoken. It cools the fire of the sky that flows through us," Ohm replied, comfortably settling into his teaching persona. "Fred is a fusion pack, but all he makes is water. Every Awoken has a much smaller fusion pack built in them, to replenish the liquid in their veins. It is quite dull. Fred is special though, he can hold a conversation. We have been together for as long as I can remember. I learned to manipulate the shape of water early on in my adventures. The training also revealed an innate ability I had to drain all energy and heat from the liquid. I can create an unbreakable ice. It is what I protect myself with."

"How did you learn that? Can you teach me?" Oa asked excitedly.

Ohm chuckled. "No. It's a dull story involving lots of repetition, and there is no need to burden you with the past. Besides, there are none left who can teach such a skill. Be content with your gifting."

"I see," Oa said, slightly disappointed. "Do a lot of Awoken have weird abilities like ours?" He was excited at the thought of a world of ultra-Awoken.

"No. We are the only ones left that I know of. Things used to be more interesting around here, but that was a long time ago," Ohm replied, squashing Oa's dreams of fantastically powered Awoken. He noticed the young Awoken's disappointment. "Perhaps some of the wild stories about the Enlightened will prove to be true. These are exciting times. After all, Fred and I found you—number One. When we reached your crash site we could hardly believe it. A second Awoken with that number. Your gift outweighs anything I have seen thus far."

"The number on my birth cell? You saw it?!" Oa asked in surprise.

"Yes I did. You have little perspective on the significance of that number, so I will try to explain. You would have been worshiped as a hero by now dead civilizations. They would have sought your advice and even gone to war for you. You see, Oa, each Awoken was born with a number; and while its full meaning remains unknown, lower numbers have always been treated with more importance. Awoken have theorized that the numbers are the order in which the creator made all of us. Up until now, it also represented the general order in which our birth cells emerged from the ground. It is curious that you should wake so late," Ohm explained, glancing over at Oa.

"Anyhow, you are stuck with us; and even though I am impressed by you, I will not worship you or go to war for you quite yet," Ohm lectured in mock severity. He pointed over his shoulder. "Fred, on the other hand, isn't impressed by anything. He has never complimented my abilities, no matter how many times I save us with my ice shield."

"I don't think I could ever be ready for a bunch of Awoken to go to war for me," Oa said with relief. He turned to Ohm as curiosity temporarily diverted his attention away from more pressing questions. "So you can control water's shape, but all you ever make is a sword and shield? I can think of a bazillion other ways you could use that water." He let his mind wander to all the amazing things he could picture Ohm creating.

"I agree with Oa," Fred chimed in. "You used to be much more liberal with your skills. Limiting yourself to use a mere sword and shield is grossly inefficient. For instance, when facing the Marauders, we should have fired the water in the form of ice project—"

"I resent that!" Ohm interrupted haughtily. "It's my skill so I will be the one deciding in what way I will use it."

"It is pointless to try to change his mind, Oa," Fred said.

"Fine, I will keep my amazing ideas to myself," Oa teased. He returned to the topic of his number, bombarding Ohm with his questions. "So if I am number One, how come I took so long to wake up? Hasn't there already been a number One? Also, what's your number? How long have you been around?"

Ohm slapped his palm against the side of his head. "I forgot how many questions young minds can conjure," he complained. "I am not sure why it took you so long to wake. It could have something to do with your power or Eol's power. Perhaps it was just some insane weather. Your number might not even be *One*. Maybe it was misprinted when the Creator made it. Who knows?" He gave a flippant toss of his hand. "As for me, my number probably has a *One* in it somewhere; and it has been a very long time since I woke up."

"But, do you even know how long? The Marauders measure time in cycles. I heard you use the term 'weeble'. Are you referring to the cycles as well?" Oa asked, pressing for answers.

"No. Cycles are too simple. Who can say that a cycle's duration is constant? What if the mind moves through time at varying speeds? So I invented the weeble. Well, I suppose Fred helped a bit. Weebles are much shorter than cycles. They measure time as your mind perceives it. Thus the number of weebles in a cycle generally fluctuates, but I don't keep track of how many I go through. Fred does. You can ask him," Ohm said, bored with the topic.

"Since the invention of the weeble, 9,564,353,343,324,432 weebles have passed and 54,345,843,492 cycles have occurred," Fred recited.

Oa was silent for a moment as he tried to comprehend the amount of time Fred's numbers represented. "I'm not quite sure I understand how your weebles relate to cycles," he said, giving up.

"Don't try to figure it out, Oa. Accomplishments can be made in one weeble that would outweigh all the cycles I have lived through," Ohm instructed. "Although I just remembered a trend worth noting. Fred likes to measure my weebles per cycle. According to his data, cycles are getting shorter; or time is moving faster, as if it is accelerating toward something …" he trailed off, pondering his old findings with renewed interest.

Oa nodded, trying to process all the new information Ohm was feeding him. "I must be one of the last Awoken to wake up. I've got to have a purpose with all this significance surrounding me. Besides, Seeker is way more interesting than your ice nonsense."

"I will grudgingly concede on that last point, but don't get too excited. Being a lower number is not *that* great; too little of this world remains to worship you," Ohm joked.

"That's not what I meant. I just think that we can do something impactful. The coincidence of our meeting and the fact that we both are unique makes me believe all the more that we are meant to change things in this world for the better," Oa said, turning serious.

Ohm turned to look at the young Awoken. "Try and hold onto that belief, Oa. I seem to have misplaced mine in the endless line of weebles I have been stumbling through." He toyed idly with the dressing on his damaged arm.

"There are still a few more things I'd like to have explained," Oa said. When Ohm remained silent he continued. "You have been around a long time, so tell me more about this world where we come from. What's your exact number? Who is the Crea—?"

"No time for that now," Ohm interrupted as the two rounded a spire of rock and arrived in a wide clearing at the center of the valley. As the city of Bolleworth rose before them, Oa gazed up, taking the city in. Bolleworth was a giant dome. The outer shell of the dome was split into many pieces, with each piece held in place by a tower that ran through it. Lights shone out from windows in the towers and through cracks in between the dome fragments.

"We're here. It's time to show you the world as it is; we can discuss what it was later," Ohm said, deflecting Oa's questions.

Together they strode into the city. There was no main entrance to Bolleworth, since it could be accessed from any point under the edge of the dome, which rested several body lengths off the ground. Once inside, Oa and Ohm found themselves in a maze of towering structures. Down at the ground level, there were no signs of activity. The walls and lanes were dirty from all the dust that blew in from the surrounding desert. Oa looked up above him, his view of the top of the dome was obstructed by the numerous crossways set between the towers. From the glow above he could tell that the lights of the upper levels were crisp and clean. They didn't flicker the way the dim lighting did down where he stood. Oa had a hunch that the upper lanes were cleaner as well.

"I bet all the amazing stuff is up there," Oa said wistfully gazing up.

"In a weeble. There are things to see down here, I am sure," Ohm chided.

"Where is everyone?" Oa huffed, slightly impatient and bored with the empty city streets.

"Not many Awoken are left. There are many friendly dust piles, though," Ohm replied leading them further into the city.

As Ohm navigated the streets, Oa was distracted several times by figures scurrying just out of sight. At one point, he saw an Awoken walking toward them from a connecting lane.

Excited, Oa waved his arm high. "Hello there," he called. His words hung dead in the air as the Awoken passed by without any sign of acknowledgement. The silent figure continued shuffling down the avenue.

"Most Awoken keep to themselves these days, passing the time in various forms of solitude," Ohm said quietly.

Oa looked back, the dismal Awoken had already disappeared from sight. Turning forward again, he caught sight of markings on the side of a building just ahead. Oa was eager to find something interesting, so he darted ahead of Ohm to inspect the markings. There were several symbols burned into the wall. The most interesting symbol, and the focal point of the strange art, was a circle split at an angle by a deep gash. Next to this glyph was a series of smaller symbols all lined up in neat columns. Oa gazed intently at them for a moment. His sight blurred then cleared rapidly, causing his head to snap back in disorientation. He leaned in again. As his vision cleared, he found that he could read the words inscribed on the wall: *He is inevitable, our destruction is near.* Oa looked around the wall as the same words were scattered all around the slashed circle. He recalled the strange discussion he had overheard Swift's gang having. Ohm stood next to Oa, looking at him.

"That was the first time you ever read something, wasn't it?" Ohm asked knowingly.

"Yeah, it was. I couldn't read these glyphs, and then suddenly I could understand them," Oa said, surprised.

"It is pre-programmed into you like your ability to walk and speak. You took to it gracefully. It is usually jarring for young Awoken when they realize they have programming they did not previously know about," Ohm explained.

"Programmed?" Oa asked.

"It is how I see it," Ohm stated vaguely. He leaned in to look at the glyphs. "I saw these the last time I was here. Hmm ... Nothing new." Disappointed, he glanced down the avenue, looking for more of the markings. Finding none, he straightened up and headed further into the city. Eventually, they came across a spacious amphitheater in the center of the city. A single beam of strong light descended from the upper levels to illuminate a round stage at the center of the arena. Dust motes wafted lazily through the beam.

"What is this place for?" Oa asked.

"It is a forum for discussion and sometimes pointless bickering. It was also used for music and performances, even storytelling. I have told a few good ones here," Ohm explained as they walked down into the center of the amphitheater, past rows of seating carved into the rock. Oa sat down in the front row as Ohm walked up onto the stone stage. Towers spiraled up all around them, and the light from above spotted him perfectly.

"Alright then tell us all a story, Traveler," Oa demanded as if an imaginary crowd sat with him. "The one about the Destroyer." Since meeting the Traveler, Oa had been patiently waiting for an opportunity to hear Jad's tale completed.

Ohm turned sharply to face him. "Very well then, if only to please the crowd." He let a dramatic pause hang in the air before launching into his story while Oa sat back in enjoyment and listened.

"Thus follows the tale of the Destroyer as researched by Ohm the Traveler, with the assistance of Fred the Pack. Long before our time, before our light and our life, there was nothing. We resided in a pocket of nonexistence for all of eternity. Then something happened upon us in the form of a light; it was the Creator. This light shone into the Void battling back the darkness to reveal the Great Planes—a world teeming with chaos and beauty, with a broad expanse of rock beneath it and a roaring sky above. The two sides of the world were connected in one singular point by a great peak that stretched up to reach the sky. Between these limits raged a maelstrom of ice and fire. The never-ending war between heat and chill produced an energy that flowed through the ground and up into the sky. The energy of life. These three elements—Ice, Fire, and the Lightning of Life that they fuel—made up the universe in a glorious storm.

"The primordial tempest raged on for eons, until one cycle when the Creator saw fit to fashion mechanized beings to bring order to the chaos. The automatons were constructed of alloys from the earth and fueled with the energy of the sky. The Creator gifted the beings with intelligence and consciousness and placed them in the ground to wait. The first of these beings that the Creator made was placed atop the great peak, high in the midst of the sky. The Creator awoke him, gifted him with a name, and tasked him with waking the others. The Creator granted the First One with power and a choice: within his right hand rested the gales of destruction, and in his left hand, the whisper of life. With these powers, the First One was to guide and protect all the Creator had made. He was to bring order, beauty, and ultimately growth to the world.

"After delivering these guidelines, the Creator left, never to be seen or heard from again. The First One vowed never to use the power of death, seeing it as evil. He spent an age battling through a maelstrom of blizzards and molten magma to reach the base of the mountain. There he found the first generation of Awoken. Seeking to use the power of life to bring them out of their sleep, the First One placed his left hand on them. They did not stir. No life flowed from him. After countless attempts, the First One realized he had been deceived. With no other choice or options, the First One broke his vow. In bitter anger, he called upon the power he swore to never use, unsure of what to expect. To his great surprise, the touch of his right hand caused his brothers and sisters to wake.

"The First One was overjoyed. Under his guidance, the Awoken calmed the storms of the world. The three elements evolved into mysterious beings of beauty, giving the raw power of nature a form. In total balance, the world flourished. Life grew in numerous ways, colors, shapes, and sizes; and the Awoken saw fit to preserve and care for them all.

"It would have remained that way forever if not for the curse of the First One's right hand. The power of death grew in each Awoken's soul ember, stemming from the One who woke them. Caretakers and stewards became conquerors and tyrants. Evil overtook the Awoken, and war followed. The First One became Peacekeeper. He settled all conflicts with the might of his right hand. His head was turned away in sorrow each time he was forced to return the Creator's children, whom he had brought forth, to nothing. The Peacekeeper's hands were stained with the dust of countless soul embers he destroyed to protect those still faithful to the Creator's task. The day came when the Peacekeeper's name changed to Destroyer. The remaining Awoken no longer trusted him; they feared him and the monster he had become in trying to keep them safe. The Destroyer secluded himself in exile amid the icy cold of the mountain.

"Gradually, the Awoken forgot their duties; and while the peace among them lasted, the curse of the right hand found new ways to express itself. The Awoken began to abuse the land, seeking to tear down the Creator's work and replace it with their own constructions and abominations. Nature struck back. Packs of fire beasts burned through the Awoken and their cities seeking to restore balance. The Awoken chose to war against the world itself rather than see the error of their ways and remember their purpose. Their leader, one of the first woken by the Destroyer, called out to the mountain.

"The Destroyer responded; and remembering his duty, he descended from the mountain with the cold storm at his back. He sought to protect his kind while restoring order to the world, but the curse of his broken vow betrayed him. His wrath was so great that he snuffed out the elementals of fire. With the balance forever broken, the beings of ice faded from existence. Only the beings of the sky remained. They continued to fuel the life of the Great Planes, but their energies gradually decreased without the other two elements to sustain them. The world began its unstoppable descent into decay. The Destroyer spent his remaining cycles exiled in the mountain where he allowed himself to die with the beasts of snow, full of regret and despair."

Ohm paused, cocking his head to the side and listening to some faint noise he heard echoing through the city. "And thus concludes the tale of the Destroyer," he said, abruptly finishing his story.

Oa stood up. "I liked it. Sort of depressing, though," he admitted.

"It's the overarching lesson that matters—well, mattered," Ohm replied. "A long time ago, I tried to bring this message to those who could make a difference; but as you can see, I had little effect. Now this world is dying as it is slowly consumed by the Void."

Oa nodded deep in thought. "So how much of that story is true?" he questioned skeptically.

"My research was pretty thorough, but I keep the story a bit vague so I can embellish if I want and gloss over the parts I'm not too sure of. I am old enough to have seen some of it first-hand, though. How do you think I learned my little ice trick?" Ohm asked mischievously, his blue ocular plate glinted in the light.

"Did you ever meet the Destroyer?" Oa asked, following Ohm up out of the amphitheater.

"Who do you think I learned it from?" Ohm replied, as he led them down another alley.

"Wow, you are pretty old to be in your own legends" Oa joked.

"Alright, enough about my age. Let's go up and see what wonders the upper levels of this city are hiding," Ohm replied with a chuckle.

"Finally," Oa said excitedly. He snatched Seeker from his satchel and sent it flying up toward the web of crossways high above. Oa turned away as Ohm jetted off, spraying a trail of water behind that soaked Oa's cloak. He shook water droplets off his face, laughing a little. Then he sensed Seeker latch onto one of the walkways. He pulled himself up after Ohm, flying through the upper levels of the city. The glossy gray walls of the buildings flashed by in a blur along with several colorful panels. Oa figured they were signs marking the structures, though he was moving too fast to tell. He sailed past the highest walkway, retrieving Seeker as he passed. He arced smoothly over the rail to land lightly on his feet next to Ohm.

One of the first things that Oa noticed was just how clean everything was. The ample lighting, which was both soft and warm in color, gleamed on the smooth white metal of the crossway. Not a speck of dust could be seen. He looked up and was surprised to see that there was art on the underside of the dome. He had not noticed the art from the floor of the city. The shell's interior was decorated with images of strange figures etched into the metal. Somehow, each line glowed with light, creating a beautiful depiction of what appeared to be a great battle. He began to make out several figures in the chaos that looked like Awoken. In fact, one of the figures in the focal point of the scene appeared to be wielding a round shield.

"Oa, come look at this," Ohm called, before Oa could interpret the art any further.

Ohm was next to a nearby tower. He stood gazing at it. Oa ran over to him, his boots making light pings as they hit the walkway. When he reached the building, Oa realized that the walls were transparent, revealing a sparse, yet beautiful interior. The architecture was simple and smooth. What caught Oa's attention were the objects on display in the room. They were exotic and clearly ancient. Some sat on stands while others were so big they just rested on the floor.

"What is all that?" Oa asked Ohm.

"Memories, relics of our past. Artifacts like these used to be of great value and were obtained by the wealthy; but all things decay, Oa, including value. There are few left to envy such wealth, so there is little joy in it for the owner," Ohm explained.

"Someone lives here? So do they just sit around and stare at this old stuff?" Oa asked, demoralized slightly by the notion.

"Actually, that's exactly what they do. There is so much history to wallow in. Over there is a petrified tree," Ohm said, pointing, "and there is an old lighting etch. Hmm … It's a piece I'm not familiar with. Perhaps we could get a tour. Fred's fiery spirit might brighten the mood of the owner." He reached out and knocked on the glass. Instantly, alarms rang out from inside the tower and red lights began to flash inside.

A panel opened up above them and a segmented mechanical arm slithered out. A bulky boltspitter was attached to the end of the appendage. The sentinel waved around for a moment before snapping back to point at the intruders.

"Tight security," Ohm stated. He tackled Oa over the side of the walkway as the sentinel blasted the space they had been standing in.

Ohm arrested their fall with Fred's trusty aqua jet. They coasted to a safe landing in the lower levels, several avenues away from the tower they had disturbed. Their landing startled an Awoken out of its quiet shuffling. The skittish Awoken ran into a nearby building, slamming the door.

"Nobody likes you, I guess," Oa teased, darting forward to look at some more glyphs he spotted up ahead. "Wow! Ohm! Look at these. That same symbol is here, but there's a lot of different writing."

Ohm inspected the work as he responded, "These are new. The writing is definitely the ravings of an oracle." Ohm glanced over to see Oa staring at him. Sensing a question, Ohm proceeded to explain the term. "Oracles are lunatics that tried to climb past the Sacred Temple of the Enlightened to reach the forbidden peak of the mountain. Their programming gets scrambled by the power of the sky. If they survive to return, they will just scrawl lunacy in places other Awoken will see it. Look, here is some nonsense about laser porridge."

Oa digested the information but didn't respond. Instead, he began to read the script before him aloud, "First to sleep, last to wake, brood of death, our souls to take." Ohm's head slowly turned to look at the words. Oa continued reading, "Destroyer once broken, but the piece has been found. In Destroyer's completion, all existence shall drown." They stared in silence for a moment. "Below that, the single word Eol is repeated over and over and over," Oa said, kneeling to trace the glyphs that trailed down the wall.

"Impossible," Ohm muttered. Then he regained his composure. "Fred, I need an analysis of these scorings. Are they recent enough to imply the writer is still in the city?"

"They are recent enough," Fred replied. "In fact, whoever wrote this can't be more than a couple avenues away."

Ohm spun on his heels and set off running down the lane as Oa rushed to keep up.

"What's wrong? You said oracles just write gibberish. You said that the Destroyer is dead, right?" Oa asked, disconcerted by Ohm's sudden urgency.

"I don't think it's gibberish. Not this time, Oa. The Destroyer is dead but the legacy of his broken vow still lives on," Ohm snapped back, his voice rising as they raced through the maze of the city. "Every once in a very, very long while, one of those poor idiots gets scrambled the right way. Somehow, they catch a glimpse of the universal programming; and when that happens, secrets are revealed. Secrets that could help confirm my suspicions to the nature of Eol." They rounded a corner into a dimly lit courtyard with no exit, save the one through which they had come. "Aha! Gotcha!" he exclaimed.

Before them, in a beam of light cast down from the upper levels, hunched a trembling Awoken. It was the oracle. The oracle's clothes were scorched, and its alloys were rusting away. Sparks escaped from the oracle at random spots. The oracle stood, finger to the wall, writing with sparking energy. The energy darted from its fingertip into the wall, leaving a deep scorch.

Ohm ran up to the Awoken and pulled it from the wall, spinning it around to face him. "What do you know of Eol's connection to the Destroyer?"

The oracle let out an eerie shriek; and its whole body sparked up, knocking Ohm back. The mad Awoken scuttled back to the wall, arms hanging limply at its side. Ohm stepped forward again and then froze; his head snapped toward the shadows at the edge of the courtyard.

"Ohm, we are not alone," Fred spoke.

"I see them too. How far gone are they?" Ohm asked, his voice tense. Oa looked around trying to see what Ohm and

Fred had spotted. Then he saw them, ominous shifting shapes in the shadows all around them.

"They are in the final stages of sleep; and even though pacifism is your best hypocrisy, I suggest we run. It would not be advisable to trust your new leg in combat this soon," Fred answered.

"Just back away slowly, Oa. If we head out the way we came, the Howlers won't bother us," Ohm instructed calmly, heeding Fred's advice.

Just then, the oracle sparked up and let out another eerie shriek as it started running toward the exit. Instantly, Howlers surged from the shadows, wailing and screaming as they tackled the oracle.

The Howlers were ghastly life forms, hardly recognizable as Awoken. Nearly all of their alloy skin had peeled away, leaving tubes and joints bare. A thick black ooze coursed over their exposed veins. The few remaining faceplates each Howler had flashed frantically in the dim light.

Oa snatched Seeker from his satchel as several Howlers lunged toward Ohm and himself. Oa recognized the familiar oily splotches on these Awoken that he had seen on Swift and her gang, but these Awoken were completely covered in the murk. He concentrated and sent Seeker zooming toward the oncoming Howlers. The orb pelted through the attackers, knocking them off their feet.

Ohm ducked under a charging Howler. He drove back up, using the Howler's own momentum to send it tumbling over his back. The Howler was thrown into the air and fell to the ground, stunned.

Ohm turned to Oa. "Get out of here! Use Seeker to get over that wall. I'll follow you. I just have to get that oracle before the Howlers tear it apart!" He ran forward and dove into the pile of rabid Awoken, chucking them out of the fray one at a time.

Oa turned from the chaos and sent Seeker to the top of the nearest wall spanning the gap between two buildings. He pulled with his mind, launching himself over the barrier while retrieving Seeker as he sailed over. He landed hard, tucking into a roll as he hit the ground. Oa sat back against the partition and listened to the noise of the melee. After what felt like an eternity, he heard the familiar sound of the aqua jet. The screaming had not stopped, but Ohm came sailing over the wall carrying what was left of the oracle in his arms.

Ohm lay the poor Awoken's remains on the ground and sat down next to Oa. "I was unable to save the oracle," he grumbled moodily.

"At least you made it out alive," Oa said relieved. "This is a good time for me to use Seeker. Now Fred will be able to see how it works."

"Of course! Brilliant idea," Ohm said enthusiastically, his mood brightening.

"First, I need to know what the Howlers are. I met some Sleepers but they weren't this rabid" Oa said.

"That is because they were not as infected as these ones. The Legion has been distributing Void capsules for quite some time. The capsules allow Awoken to immerse themselves in the

Void. The experience is addictive because it allows Awoken to experience memories of those already dead. A side effect is the infection that covers their bodies. As it progresses, the Awoken start to sleep. The time spent sleeping gradually increases. Those Howlers are near death; and now the few times they wake up, they are driven mad by this world so they tear it apart trying to return to the bliss they felt in the Void," Ohm explained.

"Are they really experiencing memories of dead Awoken?" Oa asked.

"I am not sure. Their madness is nothing like an oracle's. Sleepers I have spoken to say that they see and hear lost Awoken all around them, reliving memories as if they were still occurring. It is similar to the stories of the Enlightened meditation, but it seems much more visceral. The addiction has consumed what was left of civilization out here in the edge-lands. That is why this place is so empty," Ohm replied somberly.

Oa mulled over his past experiences. "So the Marauders do resist the Void in their own way, rather than drowning in the past—"

"Perhaps you see some truth in the convictions of a Marauder. Let us fix this oracle before the Howlers attract unwanted attention," Ohm interjected, refocusing Oa on the task at hand.

"Not enough truth to escape Eol's Law," Oa said sadly as he got up and knelt down next to the oracle.

The limbs were gone and the oracle's torso was shredded, leaking water everywhere. Oa could sense Ohm watching him closely as he began to quiet his mind. Oa let go of his uncertainty about the Marauders and his confusion toward Eol's Law. His mind opened once more to the sea of symbols. *Could this be the universal programming?* Oa thought in wonder. He felt the familiar rush of awareness, but he did not let the storm shake him. He soared through it to a place where the broken oracle stood strong and tall, with a mind that did not have to chase sanity. Oa saw more clearly than he ever had. He found the point which the oracle's aura emanated from, the soul ember, a pure singularity. As he gazed into the ember, pieces of information caught hold of his mind. He realized that the oracle was *she* and that she had a name, *Ibra*.

Ibra will be whole again, Oa thought to himself. Seeker rose from his hand, glowing white-hot. Its deep hum resonated through the air as it spun faster and faster. Strands of glowing energy shot out from the Seeker, forming the image in Oa's mind. Oa knew what Ibra should be, and he let his will stitch together the broken pieces before him.

Ibra was nearly too bright to look at, as new limbs and body were forged in Seekers blaze. Oa was lost in the bliss of reaching his potential. His focus was completely on healing the broken Awoken, when a voice edged its way into his mind, jarring his focus.

"Oa! You have to stop! Oa!" the voice said.

Oa was snapped out of the moment as Ohm grabbed him by the shoulders and hauled him away from Ibra. The new Awoken was sitting up and looking around as the glow around her began to fade. Oa was dazed for a moment, until he spotted them: two figures at the end of the lane, standing in the dim flickering light, tall and ominous. Fear struck Oa as the figures' heads lifted revealing a single glowing crimson eye that peered out from under a brimmed helmet. It was the Legion.

The two Legion soldier's bodies remained perfectly still as their right arms raised pointing at Ibra, Ohm, and Oa.

"Fred! Aqua jet!" Ohm yelled, wrapping his arms around Oa. Fred activated the aqua jet, sending them rocketing up and over the heads of the Legion soldiers just as they fired their weapons.

Oa had never been close enough to the Legion to feel the deadened air around the black bolts that fired from their pistols. He looked back and watched, horrified as the Void bullets rammed through Ibra's chest. She stood, sane and alive for the first time in many cycles. She stared down in confusion at her hands, watching them dissolved away into nothing. Sound returned, and Oa could hear the end of his own cry of frustration.

Ohm flew them to the end of the lane where they landed at a crossroads between several towers. The Legion soldiers spun around and walked calmly after them, weapons raised.

"Run!" Ohm commanded, and they took off around the corner as the wall exploded behind them in a deafening silence.

"I hate nihilistols," Ohm grumbled, referring to the strange pistols the Legion carried. "Always disintegrating important things and making it impossible to hear anything," he complained, as they sped through the streets of Bolleworth.

"Why are they here?" Oa asked, still in shock at the Legion's sudden appearance.

"You're the one who wanted Eol's attention. It appears you have it. I might have a theory as to how they found us, but you're not going to like it," Ohm replied somberly.

They rounded another corner and found themselves running out of the city and back into the maze of the surrounding canyons.

"We will lose them here; just follow me" Ohm commanded. Oa followed as Ohm wove through the tall spires of rock at a breakneck pace. Ohm's step faltered; and he halted suddenly, ducking into an outcropping in the stone wall. Oa rushed in behind him.

"Oa, there is something I have to tell you," Ohm said with urgency in his voice as he grabbed Oa by the shoulders. "You need to kn—" Ohm's voice cut out. Then he went limp and fell to the ground.

"Ohm!" Oa exclaimed, kneeling next to him to see what was wrong. Getting no response, he tried something else. "Fred?"

"Yes, Oa?" Fred replied in his curt monotone voice.

"What's wrong with Ohm?" Oa asked.

"He has fallen asleep," Fred replied bluntly.

Oa was troubled. *How can Ohm be asleep?* he thought to himself. *He had no Void infection, unless ...*'

Oa grabbed Ohm's handless arm and peeled back the bandages. To his dismay he saw that the appendage was infected with the oily black splotches of a sleeper. Suddenly Oa remembered the murkiness he had seen before, when he had tried to heal Ohm. It had not just been fatigue. Why had he forgotten such a vital piece of information?

"Explain this, Fred," Oa demanded, upset and startled.

"It is not my place, Oa. You will need to wait until Ohm re-awakens," Fred replied cryptically.

Oa grunted in frustration as he gripped Seeker and knelt down. He reopened himself to the universal programming and gazed upon Ohm's injuries with his inner sight. A fierce presence lashed out from within the murky depths of the virus. The attack knocked Oa back and threw Seeker from his hands. He instantly rolled over and retrieved the orb. He scuttled back into the outcropping, shocked at what had happened. *I can't heal this infection; I couldn't do it with Buri either. Why?* Oa thought to himself in confusion.

Oa peeked out around the edge of the outcropping, whispering to Fred in agitation, "Well, I can't heal Ohm; all that's left to do is be patie—" He was silenced by the sight of the two Legion soldiers rounding the corner. They were headed toward his hiding spot. Oa pulled himself back so sharply that he lost his balance and fell against the wall.

"They found us!" Oa whispered urgently to Fred.

He looked up; and across the narrow gorge they were in, he spotted a slim ledge. He wondered if they could hide on the ledge as the Legion passed by underneath.

"I have a plan, Fred," Oa said reassuringly to the pack, though the statement was truly to reassure himself.

I have to be quicker than I have ever been, Oa thought to himself as he sent Seeker up to the ledge. Grabbing on to Ohm with one arm, Oa reached out his other hand toward the ledge where Seeker was attached. *Now!* Oa thought to himself. They burst from the outcropping, zooming toward the ledge. Oa kept a mental hold on Seeker as they passed over it. The invisible tether between Oa's mind and Seeker slingshot them straight down onto the cliff mantle, landing with a hard thud. Oa felt as if he had crushed every alloy in his body, but they were safe. He looked down to see if the Legion had noticed them. They had not. *So far, so good*, Oa thought.

He rolled over and looked around the stone sill they were on. It was small and barely had enough space for the trio to lay on. Suddenly, the rock wall they were up against disappeared revealing a long dark tunnel cut into the stone. There was a crackling bark from inside the tunnel, followed by a harsh shushing. A female voice whispered "Quick! Hide in here!"

Oa didn't know if it was his fear of the Legion or a sincerity he heard in the female voice that convinced him to trust the mysterious tunnel. He grabbed Ohm and dragged him into the cave. The wall re-materialized behind them, returning the ledge to its former obscurity.

EPISODE 05

THE HEIST

Oa dragged Ohm through the tunnel opening in the side of the cliff. A second pair of hands reached from the darkness and grabbed Ohm, helping Oa carry the weight.

"Here, let me help. You don't want to be outside when those red eyes are around," the female voice advised. There was a short pause. "Don't worry. There's no need to thank me; but if you want to, my name is Kai."

"Thank you, Kai," Oa blurted, remembering the importance of being polite. "You rescued us from quite the predicament. My name is Oa, and this deadweight here is Ohm." He was relieved that the stranger seemed so friendly.

He could not see Kai in the dim light of the tunnel, but together they dragged Ohm down into the corridor.

"This guy wouldn't be so heavy if he didn't have this mega-dense pack," Kai grunted.

"That's Fred his water fusion pack," Oa replied.

"Ohm and I have always been together," Fred spoke up.

"Oops, it's alive! Well I hate to be the one to break it to you, Fred; but you're heavy. This guy's a champ, lugging you around all the time," Kai said humorously.

"It's how we were created" Fred replied curtly.

"How did you know we were out there?" Oa asked, cutting into the conversation before Kai could rattle Fred any further.

"Susan was getting antsy, so I knew something was up," Kai replied casually.

The corridor brightened slightly as they turned a bend, arriving in a room lit by soft yellow light.

"Let's put the big guy over there on Susan's cot," Kai instructed. The pair dragged Ohm to a mound of glimmering fabrics piled by the entrance of the room and set him down on it. Oa turned to look at Kai and the room they were in. Before he had a chance to take in his environment, a large beast pounced from the roof of the cave, bowling him over. Oa struggled instinctively as the weight of the creature flattened him on his back. The beast barked, a happy yip that crackled and popped like far off rumblings in the sky. Oa couldn't see anything around the creature that had pinned him to the ground. A gaping mouth opened in front of his face; and a broad tongue of stormy vapor lolled out. It dragged across his faceplates, sending purple sparks of energy flying. The feeling was quite unusual and caused Oa to laugh.

"Susan, get off of him," Kai commanded sternly from the other side of the room.

The strange creature gave a reluctant growl and bounced back off of Oa, floating lightly to the floor. She lay her head between adorably big paws and stared at Oa with eyes of blazing violet light. A long, billowing tail snaked across the ground behind her, wagging softly.

"Sorry about Susan. It looks like she can't contain herself around strangers. We never get visitors," Kai called over from a work table she was sitting at. Oa realized that his crash into the tunnel entrance must have interrupted her work. She had already refocused on a task he couldn't see from his spot on the floor.

"She's fine," Oa said, bewildered but still grateful to be out of danger. He looked at Susan "What is she?"

As if noticing his gaze Susan propped herself up on her paws. She puffed her chest out proudly and looked away with aloofness. She was a wispy creature; made entirely of cloud and energy. *Like the sky*, Oa decided. A lightning of deep violet crackled about her edges, containing her body of roiling grays and dense clouds. He looked closer and the shape of the strange creature became clearer. She had a pointed snout and features that carried a wild beauty. Above her strong jaws, two pointy ears stuck up. One of the ear tips bent slightly, making her face less intimidating and more endearing to Oa. Behind the fluffy head, an equally downy neck curved down to thick shoulders. The shoulders carried a pair of blunt round paws. The remainder of her body wound gracefully into a bulging tail. Susan's body and tail filled half of the room as she posed nobly, floating lightly above the ground. The tail was the only part of her body not surrounded by the purple energy, and it billowed out in curly tufts. Violet light pulsed from deep within Susan's chest. Strands of lightning snaked out of her core to light her eyes and mouth. Other tendrils wound through her shoulders and down to her two paws, while a thick spine of light flowed down through her tail.

Susan's mouth opened in a yawn. Her smoky tongue rolled out, sparking with her purple essence. Concluding her yawn, she looked over and released a loud bark in Oa's direction. The noise was accompanied by a compressed explosion of violet sparks inside her mouth. The energy holding her body together brightened briefly.

"Susan is a lightning varl," Kai replied cheerfully, still working diligently on the project up on the table. "I've heard some wild stories about other varls that used to exist, but I think Susan is the most special. She's the only one left, and she's my best friend ..." her voice trailed off. The slightest hint of melancholy filled the air. "Come here you!" she called lovingly to the beast.

Susan paused to stare at Oa briefly. Her wild eyes enraptured him. He had never seen anything like her. Susan was a dichotomy between the terrifying power of nature and the adorable spirit of a loving companion. The young Awoken wanted to hug the varl, but he kept his distance. He did not want to overstep his bounds in the creature's territory. She curled her paws in close to her chest and bounced lightly through the air as she floated over to Kai. *She is immensely heavy, yet she floats everywhere she goes*, Oa observed as he sat marveling at the varl. Susan's undulating body swelled then compacted as she narrowed her frame and shrunk down to lay just off the floor, encircling Kai and the table. The varl's body hemmed Kai in like a protective wall. *She is able to conform to whatever size she needs*, Oa realized with awe.

He looked up from his seat on the floor to survey the room. Light drifted down from strips of glowing white panels inlaid in the smooth high arching stone ceiling. He reasoned that the ceiling's highest point must be at least three of his body-lengths tall. The light reflected off of golden yellow veins in the smooth stone walls, casting the soft glow he had seen upon entering. In the warm light, Oa could take full measure of the room. Ohm lay on Susan's cot next to the entrance. The work table Kai was at, sat towards the far end of the chamber. A myriad of tools and machine pieces hung from racks bolted to the walls. Directly across the room from the entrance, an opening led to a second tunnel. A collage of papers had been pinned across sections of the walls; diagrams and charts of all sorts were drawn on the sheets. Oa quickly realized that the drawings were designs of various machines and structures. He stared at several, trying to decipher their purpose. With his curiosity fully piqued, he stood up and walked over to the table Kai was working at.

Oa took a brief moment to observe his rescuer's appearance. Kai had a slender white head divided into three sections by a Y-shaped, rust-colored face plate. Her alloys were scratched and scuffed. They gleamed dully in the light. Two round visual receptors glowed softly from the faceplate. Bolted to the top of her head was a tattered piece of purple cloth that hung down to one side, framing half of her face. From the chest down Kai wore a baggy brown jumpsuit. The drab colored fabric was stained and patched in places. Over the jumpsuit. she wore a fitted gray jacket. The front of the jacket was open to reveal the gleam of a soul ember as well as the dented and scored plates of her upper chest.

Kai looked up at him abruptly, halting her work. Their gazes met.

"So your friend's got some serious bandages. You must have put a stasis ring on him to deal with the wounds, huh? Kai asked, staring intently at Oa. "I just ask because I almost mistook him for a Sleeper. Susan tends to get a bit rough with Sleepers when they go rabid." There was a sharp undertone to her casual words.

Oa paused before responding. Kai's warning was clear, but he decided that he would not lie to her. "I wish it was a stasis ring. Ohm collapsed just before you rescued us. I found the Void infection underneath those bandages. He is my friend, though; and I trust him. He isn't like the others. Fred won't say anything, but I will demand answers from Ohm when he wakes up." He took a half step back towards Ohm as he finished speaking, nervously looking at Susan.

Kai laughed. "Don't worry Oa. Friends are safe here. Susan will wreck whatever tries to hurt us." She shifted her gaze back down to the table.

Oa was relieved and slightly taken aback at the response. Kai was clearly confident enough in her companion to not be bothered by Ohm's condition. Oa accepted the good fortune and leaned over Susan to see what was on the table. It was cluttered with sheets, most of which were blank. Kai was drawing on one of the larger parchments with a slender needle-shaped tool. A bright red light at the end burned her strokes into the parchment. Oa examined the drawing. In the center, Kai had drawn what appeared to be the layout of a dwelling. Around the central layout, more detailed drawings depicted the rooms from various angles to better display the architecture and design of the structure. There were figures drawn into some of the rooms. He quickly spotted depictions of Kai and Susan. There were two other figures as well in the drawings that he did not recognize.

"It is very detailed. What is it?" Oa asked politely.

"This is home, or at least it will be when I get Cale and Jess to help me build it," Kai responded. She tapped the end of the drawing utensil idly against the table as she considered how to finish her work. Picking a blank spot on the page her hand began to rapidly draw in the final room of the dwelling.

"Who are Cale and Jess? Do they live here too?" Oa asked looking over at the tunnel that led further into Kai's home. "Will they mind Ohm and me hiding here?"

"No they are back in …" Kai paused in her drawing to contemplate something. "I just have to find them again," she sighed. "It's been so long that I don't remember where they are. It was a big place with lots of tall buildings, almost as impressive as mine." She motioned to the drawings hanging from the walls.

"Ohm and I were just in Bolleworth. Maybe your friends were there?" Oa offered helpfully.

"No, no, that's not the right place," Kai said after mulling the city name over for a moment. "Who cares what the name of the place is, though? I have a ship now. It will help me find them. Come see."

With a flourish of her wrist, Kai finished her drawing. She jumped up onto the chair, drawing in hand. She hopped over Susan to stand next to Oa. He noticed that he was just barely taller than Kai. Susan had been napping and was startled awake by Kai's sudden movement. The lightning varl uncurled from around the table and rolled onto her back. She stretched out, sparking slightly as her tail uncurled across the room. Her body expanded then contracted down to the size of an Awoken. Susan floated up next to Kai. The inventor turned and picked an empty spot on the wall, then slapped her drawing up in the blank space. The picture stuck to its new home, held by unseen adhesive.

Kai grabbed Oa by the hand and hurried him down the other tunnel. This tunnel was shorter than the first one; and when it opened up, Oa could tell he and Kai were in a much more open room. Kai punched a panel on the side of the wall, activating strips of white lighting panels in the ceiling. The same familiar warm yellow glow filled the space as the light reflected off of the veins in the rock. The room was more of a cavern. There were many tools and pieces of equipment scattered about the area. Shelves and cabinets lined the walls, holding more of Kai's odd trinkets. What caught Oa's attention most though was a large ship, resting in the center of the cavern.

Oa reasoned that he must be staring at a vehicle meant for flight. The vessel's main structure was a thick disk bisected by a central hub, which sat at the forefront of a powerful engine cluster. The upper right side of the ship was enclosed in scored, gray-metal panels. Oa could tell that the craft had once been adorned with a deep matte-blue and glossy-gray color scheme. Several rough patches of the colors remained in various places along the hull. A gleaming cockpit window made up the forward edge of the ship's right side. Behind the cockpit, the structure cut inward, making space for a broad wing. The wing was folded back behind the cockpit next to the engines. The other side of the vessel was a half-circle, open-decked platform with only a skeleton of support beams. There was no metal paneling on the left side of the ship, but there were a few translucent panels covering the front of the deck. A rectangular piece of the deck lowered down through the bottom of the floor, serving as an entry ramp.

Oa and Kai walked up to the ship, but Susan did not follow the pair. Instead she began nosing about the room. She inspected the familiar floor and corners as if to make sure the chamber had not changed in her absence. Standing beneath the vessel with Kai, Oa got a better sense of its scale. The ship rested a body-length off the ground on three sturdy landing pads. Oa ducked slightly as they walked under the craft. The underside of the vessel was covered with the same worn metal panels that clothed the upper half of the ship. The hull curved down into a broad flat underbelly. Several blue glyphs had been recently painted on the bottom of the ship, right next to the landing ramp.

"ARI," Oa said, reading the glyphs aloud.

"Yup! That's it's name—ARI," Kai agreed energetically. "I found it scratched into the pilot's console. I think it's a great name for a ship like this." She ran her hand across the underside of the hull and leaned up close to peer at the seam between two of the plates, inspecting it.

"Did you build this?" Oa asked.

"No, I rebuilt it," Kai corrected as she grabbed a nearby tool from a cart, using it to patch the weld she had been inspecting. The instrument blazed white-hot as its pointy tip sparked and burned. Kai finished her work and tossed the device back onto its tray.

"I found the wreckage of this hunk of junk scattered in the canyons; most of it buried. Susan and I hunted down all the pieces and dragged them to this cave. Then I rebuilt it. The blasted thing took a billion or so cycles to reassemble. I'm still missing a piece, so it doesn't work yet. Come here; I'll show you," Kai explained as she grabbed Oa's hand, pulling him up the ramp after her.

Oa allowed himself to be led up the ramp onto the open deck of the vessel. He had little time to look at his surroundings, but he scanned the deck as quickly as he could. There were two thick metal struts overhead that ran out from the central hub of the ship down into the railing that bordered the edge of the deck. A hefty metal track was bolted above the railing. Several broad metal panels were stacked up at the end of the track next to the ARI's bulky thrusters. Two metal pillars supported the overhead struts and held a peculiar piece of machinery up on the roof. The machine appeared to be a collapsed metal appendage with four digits hanging limply up at the end. Oa spotted several controls on the panels bolted to the support pillars. He didn't have time to look further because Kai had pulled him through the first of the two doors leading into the enclosed half the ship. They walked into a circular room that was dark except for a dim light coming through a viewport in the front of the hub. Oa turned and looked out of the window. He was staring out into the large hangar. On either side of the viewport, both halves of the disk-shaped ship extended forward like a pincer. Kai let go of Oa's hand and hit a panel in the wall. Orange lights in the roof activated with a slight flicker. Oa turned and looked at the room. The first thing to catch his visual receptors' attention was a raised half-dome platform in the center of the chamber. He reasoned that the platform also sat in the center of the whole structure.

"This is the central power hub. The whole ship is functional but there is nothing to power it," Kai said, walking up to the platform. She pointed to a missing section at the front of the power hub. "I think a fusion drive gets plugged in here."

Oa looked where she was pointing. There were two empty sockets for the fusion drive to plug into. The spacing and layout of the depressions in the platform seemed familiar, but Oa could not figure out why.

"Silly question; but you don't happen to be carrying a fusion drive in your bag, do you?" Kai asked.

Oa shook his head and shrugged. "Sorry, I don't know what that is—back in Bolleworth, I saw a lot of strange artifacts. Maybe one of them was a fusion drive."

"No," huffed Kai. She slouched down into the empty power hub. "Susan and I have already checked there. Nothing but useless junk and Sleepers." The perky Awoken sat up and pointed at Oa. "You seem comfortable enough dodging around the Legion. Their fighters have to be powered by fusion drives. I spotted a Legion outpost a few cycles ago. It's not too far from here. It's tucked high up in the canyons. They have been monitoring Bolleworth for several cycles now, probably waiting for something."

Oa could sense where the conversation was leading. He wanted to help make the ARI fly again. A ship would certainly speed up his and Ohm's travels. So he decided that they needed Kai as an ally. He was also growing fond of Kai and her strange comrade.

"Can you take a Legion fighter apart fast enough to steal a fusion drive before anyone notices us?" he asked.

"Of course I can!" Kai exclaimed enthusiastically, jumping up out of the power hub. "All we got to do is track down the outpost and infiltrate it. You can watch my back while I nab us a fusion drive. So what do you say to that plan, Oa? If you help me get the ARI flying, I can get you and your friend far away from those goons."

Oa considered Kai's proposal. He wished Ohm was awake so they could talk things over. So far his strategy had worked. He had stolen the soul embers, and now he had the Legion's attention. He needed help though, and Kai's motives seemed honest. Oa felt that her ship was his best chance to stay ahead of the Legion while he searched for answers in his quest to stop Eol. The young Awoken's curiosity also urged him to accept Kai's offer. He wanted to try his hand at piloting the ARI. It was much more interesting than the crude Reapers the Marauders flew.

"Your plan seems as good as any. I will help you fix your ship in return for a ride," Oa said, accepting Kai's offer. "But only if you teach me how to fly ARI," he blurted impulsively, slipping the proviso into the agreement before the deal could be sealed.

"There's the catch," Kai said, punching his arm teasingly. "We have a deal then. Let's get this thing into the air first, and then I will do my best to show you how to pilot it."

Oa followed Kai as she walked back onto the open deck and off the ship. Susan was hovering by the bottom of the ramp, gnawing at an unruly clump of lightning in her tail. Kai patted the varl's head as they passed. Little purple sparks arced across her hand.

"I knew you would help, Oa. I can tell you are honest. When you crashed into our door, Susan gave her happy growl. It's the same one she gave me when I first met her," Kai explained as she walked toward the far edge of the room.

"Did she tackle you when she first met you, too?" Oa asked, amused as Susan whizzed by looping around them in excitement.

"Nah, she took me and flew me far away," Kai said, fondly remembering her first encounter with Susan. The two Awoken reached the edge of the cavern, stopping in front of several metal cabinets lined across the wall. Kai opened one of the cabinets and pulled out a thick belt composed of cinder-black strips of metal linked together by a shimmering mesh. The belt carried twin holsters made of a thick black material. A purple bandolier hung under each holster. Kai strapped the belt around her waist, over her jumpsuit. Then she buckled her jacket up, covering her soul ember. Oa thought of the cavity in his chest where the mystical stone should be.

Kai pulled open several drawers, from which she grabbed three fist-sized cylindrical objects. She set them on an empty shelf. Various symbols and hazard warnings were crudely painted on the canisters. She pulled out a box of glowing blue blocks from another drawer. Oa noticed that the pieces where transparent and could easily fit in an Awoken's palm. The glow came from blue energy swirling inside. Kai removed the bricks from the box one at a time, sliding them into her left bandolier. Then after some hunting, she found more of the strange rectangular bars. These were black instead of transparent, and Oa could not tell what was inside. Kai slotted them into her right bandolier.

"What's all that?" Oa asked, feeling left out in all the preparation.

"Ammo for my guns and a few embersplitters, just in case the Legion is unlucky enough to spot us," Kai replied cockily. She grabbed the three embersplitters from the shelf and slipped them into the pockets of her baggy jumpsuit.

Kai snatched two pistols from another shelf in the cabinet and placed them in the holsters on her hips. They were the same dull, gray color as her jacket.

"Are those boltspitters?" Oa asked, thinking he recognized the firearm.

"Gross, no! I made these myself. I never named 'em, but they're much more elegant than a boltspitter," Kai replied proudly.

"We should start now. I want to spend one last cycle wind-hopping through these canyons before we make the steal. I probably won't come back here once we leave in the ARI," Kai explained as she slapped the clasp on her belt. Immediately, the mesh between the metal tightened, cinching the belt around her waist to support the added weight of the gear.

"I understand. I'll be right back. I just want to go make sure Ohm is still alright," Oa said, intrigued yet slightly puzzled. He had no idea what Kai meant by wind-hopping.

"Don't take too long," Kai called while opening another cabinet. She grabbed several compact tools and tossed them onto a nearby table.

Oa was already running back up the tunnel to the chamber he had left Ohm in. He knelt down next to his friend. Nothing had changed. Ohm still lay motionless. The blue light behind his mask flickered.

"Fred, are you sure Ohm is fine?" Oa asked worriedly.

"I am sure, Oa. I cannot predict when Ohm will reawaken. I frequently attempt to create an algorithm that mimics Ohm's sleep patterns, but I still have not succeeded," Fred replied apologetically.

"That's alright, Fred. I need you to give Ohm a message for me when he wakes up," Oa said hurriedly.

"I would be happy to relay your message," Fred replied.

"Tell Ohm he is currently in a cave not far from Bolleworth. Tell him that I met an Awoken named Kai, and this is her home. We are going to steal something called a fusion drive from a nearby Legion outpost; it's for her ship. We should be back in a cycle or two," Oa instructed Fred.

"I will relay the message. Be careful using Seeker, Oa. My programming is not fully functional without Ohm. His sleep stopped us just short of a resolution to the data we gathered on you. Our findings were beginning to point toward several dangerous conclusions. We cannot complete the analysis until Ohm wakes up. If you are going off alone, be cautious. Take this tracker so Ohm can locate you when he wakes," Fred advised. A tiny disk slid out of a slot in the pack. Oa grabbed it and placed it in his satchel. The disk began to blink red.

"I'll be careful. Thanks, Fred," Oa said. He stood up and raced back to the hangar. He arrived back at the ARI's chamber to find Kai and Susan waiting for him. The varl was still roughly Kai's size. Oa figured it must be her preferred volume.

"Ready to go?" Kai asked.

"Yeah, I guess," Oa replied, slightly nervous. He had been unsettled by Fred's ominous and annoyingly vague warning.

Kai sensed the hint of worry in Oa's voice so she slapped him on the back reassuringly. "Don't worry, Oa. I have done this type of thing a bunch. They won't even know what hit 'em." She turned and picked up an oddly scrunched pack from the table she was standing in front of.

Oa noticed that she was already wearing a similar pack. It was made of the same shimmering mesh that held her belt together. The top section of the pack was enclosed in a matte-gray shell, just behind the shoulders. A mesh sack hung beneath the shell. Oa could see the shapes of various tools and supplies through the taut material. The pack had two straps that ran over the shoulders and buckled together in a cross over the chest.

Kai turned back around and handed the pack to Oa. "Put this on. You will probably want to put that bag of yours in here as well so you don't lose it. We are going to start that lesson in flying."

Excited, Oa took of his satchel and placed it into the mesh pouch hanging beneath the hard shell portion of the pack. He pulled the cover of the pouch down and buckled it to the bottom of the pack. He then slipped the harnesses over his shoulders and buckled the straps together across his chest. The pack fit loosely. He shrugged his shoulders awkwardly, feeling the baggy pack slide around.

"Hit the button on your right," Kai instructed. Oa looked over and saw a small button on the strap running over his right shoulder. He pressed it; and the mesh of the pack tightened suddenly, conforming to his body. Oa jumped up once, trying to shift the pack. The pack did not slide at all; it fit securely against his back.

"What are these for?" Oa asked.

"Gliders for wind hopping," Kai explained. She stepped away from Oa and slapped a second button on her left shoulder. Immediately, the shell covering the back of her shoulders cracked open, and a blur of dark gray fabric leaped up into the air. The thin material sprung into a wide chevron-shaped wing an arm's length above her head. Two loops of the thin material dangled down from the wing just over Kai's shoulders.

"This is air-skin material. It's very light and compact, stretched over a micro-skeleton of memory alloys. Never forgets the shape it was crafted in, and it's tough enough to withstand all my crashes," Kai explained as she slapped the button on her left shoulder again. With a whoosh of air, the whole assembly folded back down into the pack. The hard shell closed again with an audible click.

"I can't wait to try this," Oa said, growing excited.

"It's a lot of fun," Kai admitted, walking toward the back of the ARI. "Alright, let's get going before all the good currents run off." Oa and Susan followed close on her heels as she circumnavigated the large ship. Back behind the engines three tunnels split off from the chamber headed toward unknown destinations.

After a moment of consideration, Kai grabbed a scrap of metal from the floor and threw it down the middle tunnel. The metal chunk clattered down the corridor and echoed back out to the trio. Susan barked happily, sparking with a bright purple light as she flew down the tunnel after the scrap. Kai started jogging after the rambunctious lightning varl and Oa followed. They had not gotten far into the tunnel when Susan came back with the scrap in her mouth. She followed by Kai's side, dropping the scrap once she realized Kai was not likely to throw it again. This tunnel was the longest of the three Oa had been through during his stay in Kai's hideout. There was no need for light, as Susan gave off a comforting glow that guided them through the darkness.

The corridor sloped downward, and Oa began to wonder where he was in relation to the bottom of the canyon. They rounded a corner, and the path abruptly ended. Before he could ask about the dead end, Kai walked over to a hand-sized device resting on the floor. She pushed one of the buttons on the square gadget, and a portion of the wall disappeared, revealing a hidden exit out onto the floor of a ravine. The terrain was unfamiliar to Oa, but he realized he had seen so many glimmering rock faces, that he doubted he would recognize this one even if he had walked past it before.

"That device is quite useful. Is that what disguised the other door?" Oa asked

"Of course. I invented this as well. It's a camo-buffer. It projects an image and a force-field simultaneously. So far, neither the Legion nor the Howlers have caught on to the trick. I have gone unnoticed for many cycles now," Kai said, proud of her work.

As they strode out into the canyon, Oa turned around to look for the exit. The device must have reactivated because there was no sign of the opening as far as he could tell. Kai motioned to the immense stone walls surrounding them.

"The Legion outpost is up on a nearby plateau. They should be looking toward Bolleworth still, so we will make sure to come in from the opposite direction. We will take the long way around—partly to be safe, but mostly because I want to get a good long glide in," Kai explained as she looked around the rocky ground for a good spot to start.

There were several deep rifts in the cracked stone. Kai walked up to each of them, putting her hand over the edge for a moment before moving to the next one. When she had concluded her investigation of the fissures she returned to one of them, motioning for Oa to join her.

"This crack has the best updraft. We will launch from here. I will go first to show you what to do, then you will try. Once you can handle being airborne, we will head out," Kai said with anticipation in her voice for the coming flight.

"I'll be sure to learn quickly so we can get up there," Oa replied, gazing out of the deep canyon toward the distant sky.

Kai took a few steps back from the fissure. Then, she sprinted forward, slapping the button on her left shoulder strap. The shell on her back snapped open, releasing the large wing. The bunched-up ball of memory alloy and air-skin snapped out into its chevron shape as Kai jumped out over the crevice. Immediately the wind caught the wing, sending Kai sailing upwards toward the rock face. She grabbed the loops of air-skin dangling above her shoulders. Using them as handles, she hauled her body weight hard to the left. The wing's left edge dipped down and Kai turned just before hitting rock. She made a lazy half circle out of the updraft, gliding back down to land next to Oa. She slapped he left shoulder again, and the wing retracted into the shelled pack.

"Okay, so the handles control your direction left and right. Pulling them back will speed you up while pulling forward will slow your speed. Don't worry about messing up. If you do, just collapse the wing; and Susan will rescue you. She is great at catching me after stupid crashes," Kai said, as she playfully shoved Oa toward the rift.

"I got this," Oa said, bolstering his own confidence.

"Don't worry; you'll be fine," Kai called as Oa took off running toward the edge of the cleft. He mimicked Kai's launch as best as he could, slapping his wing-launch button just before he reached the edge. He leaped out over the gap. Instead of falling, Oa felt himself jerk up into the air as the wind whipped up from beneath him. The force of the current took the young Awoken by surprise, and he fumbled to find the control handles. His hands found the holds, and he grasped them tightly in relief. Oa shifted his body weight to the left as Kai had done. He looked up just in time to smack face-first into the rock wall. Oa was stunned briefly, but he managed to remember to collapse the wing. It crumpled down into his pack as he fell back off the rock. Before he had time to worry about his descent, he felt himself lifted up by strong, crackling paws of energy and dense cloud. Susan snatched him out of the air and floated him down to the ground next to Kai.

Kai laughed, "Nice! A 'wall face' on your first try. I pioneered that move, you know," she teased, patting Susan on the head.

Oa gasped as he recovered from the rush of his first attempt. "I did not expect the launch to be so fast."

"Yeah, it comes up quick. You gotta be ready to maneuver immediately," Kai instructed. "Give it another go."

Oa nodded and ran at the crevice a second time. As soon as the wing deployed, he grabbed the control handles. When the wind caught him, he was ready. He yanked the controls forward to slow his ascent. He pulled down hard with his left arm, managing to turn the glider away from the rock. Oa was elated that he had not repeated his embarrassing first flight. He glided out of the current in a wobbly half circle. He tried to land smoothly next to where Kai was standing, but he overshot his target. As he landed, Oa tripped over a pile of stone, spilling forward onto his face. Kai jogged over and helped him up.

"That was fun!" Oa exclaimed, hardly caring about his fumbled landing.

"I'm glad you liked it. You did great," Kai encouraged.

"I think I got the hang of it," Oa replied, knowing Kai was eager to be in the sky.

"Okay!" Kai said happily. "I'm going to take us in a wide arc out of these canyons and up into the ridges behind them. When we launch, keep turning back into this current so you can spiral up and gain altitude."

Kai walked over to the launching point. "I might throw in some tricky maneuvers." She glanced impishly over her shoulder. "If you can't keep up, Susan will carry you the rest of the way. Just follow me and have fun."

Kai ran forward and vaulted out over the breach. Her glider deployed, and the current sent her sailing upward. Oa immediately sprinted after her, enjoying the rush of the launch. He jumped out into thin air and felt the sudden jolt as the wing above his head caught wind. He quickly latched onto the glider's control tillers and turned hard, keeping himself in the current as he corkscrewed through the air in Kai's wake.

As they sailed upwards, Oa was amazed at how deep the ravine was. The stone seemed to rise forever. *It must be thousands of body lengths high*, he thought to himself in awe. They finally came out of the gorge. The rock wall ended, flattening out into a plateau. Their altitude revealed other connected cracks in the landscape. Around them, stone spires and sharp ridges of rock rose to even greater heights.

"Canyons within a canyon. This place is huge," Oa muttered to himself.

Kai straightened her flight path and flew out of the current to glide between several spires. Oa waited until he had reached a similar height before following. He wove through the towers of stone as gracefully as he could manage. In front of him, Kai caught another updraft, and she shot up over a sharp ridge of rock. Oa aimed for the same spot. He caught the current and hauled back on the control handles, angling the glider into the wind. He shot up after Kai and cleared the jagged edge of rock. Oa glanced briefly behind himself to see Susan winding through the air lazily as she followed them.

Far off on the horizon, the peak pulsed forth the dawning of a new cycle. A refreshingly cool green light filled the sky as they rose up above the landscape. Kai gradually led them up into higher airstreams. Oa reveled in the serene flight. There were no sounds or distractions, only the wind. He gazed down to see a shimmering blue-green sea of light and realized that the sky was reflecting off the numerous glowing strands of silver that ran through the stone below. Oa lost himself in the beauty as they sailed higher and higher. Far below, the stone landscape rose into ridges and small mountain ranges, forming roots that trailed off toward the great peak on the horizon. Behind them, Oa could see the valley where Bolleworth lay. It was tiny. The great gashes in the stone desert continued from the basin and led out to the edge. The land below seemed so peaceful. The chaos of his early cycles and the Void seemed a distant memory.

Oa let the currents carry him far away from his worries and questions. He laughed as Susan hurtled over him, speeding up to overtake Kai. Ahead, Oa saw Kai reach down and pet Susan as she passed. Susan wheeled through the sky then looped back toward Oa. The lightning varl danced playfully between the pair of Awoken as they soared over the land in quiet bliss.

They traveled in a wide, meandering arc through the sky. Eventually Kai dropped out of the high airstreams, beginning a slow descent. They glided down toward the mountainous ridges that overlooked the distant city of Bolleworth. Oa watched as Kai flew in low, straight toward a thin shallow groove atop a sharp ridge. Oa wondered what she was going to do. His question was quickly answered as Kai swooped down to the rock. As she passed a body length or so above the ridge, she retracted her glider, dropping the remaining distance to the ground. Her precision was perfect as she landed on a narrow strip of stone, no wider than her shoulders. Kai sprinted the short length of the flat top then dove off the left side, redeploying her glider. It was a smoothly executed maneuver. Oa reasoned that she must have practiced the trick on numerous occasions. He stared ahead, nervous but determined to mimic Kai's daring feat.

Oa lined himself up with the slim runway. He came in straight but retracted his glider too soon. He landed where the stone was too narrow to stand on. His foot slipped on the keen edge; and he lost his balance, falling off the ridge. Before he could panic, Susan slipped under him. He found himself now riding on the lightning varl's back. She had enlarged to about three times his size. Oa was slightly embarrassed. After a moment, he disregarded his blunder, choosing instead to admire Kai's finesse and skill as they followed her down into the canyons again.

Kai led them to a broad tipped steeple. She circled above the rock then spiraled down onto the top of the tower. Susan floated in lightly, allowing Oa to jump off her back. Kai retracted her glider and sat down on the smooth stone, facing the distant valley that Bolleworth lay in. Oa sat down next to her. The light of the sky had faded off toward the edge. The cycle was nearly over.

"I was glad to see you try my little stunt," Kai said with a chuckle.

"Yeah, I didn't quite get it," Oa replied.

"That's okay; I am just glad you came along. When I built that spare glider, I always hoped someone would use it to go flying with me," Kai admitted.

"It was a lot of fun; thanks for lending me your gear," Oa said warmly.

"I hope this makes us buddies," Kai said turning to look at Oa. "I have never had anyone besides Susan. I mean, Cale and Jess are there somewhere in my head; but sometimes I don't know how real that is. Things are all muddled from before I met Susan."

"We are definitely friends. And don't worry; I'm sure you will figure it all out when we find them," Oa said encouragingly. He took note of Kai's mental struggle. Perhaps Ohm would know something about it.

"Great! Trust me, I won't let the Legion catch up to you and your friend," Kai said happily. She turned back toward Bolleworth and pointed to a plateau below them where two canyons merged together. "The Legion outpost is … right there. Susan will fly us down so we can get that fusion drive and then we'll clear out before the Legion knows what hit 'em."

"Let's do it," Oa agreed, determined.

With a nod, Kai plunged off the spire, gliding down to the plateau below. Susan allowed Oa to climb up onto her back, and they floated off the spire after Kai. As they neared the fringe of the canyon-top below, Oa spotted four matte black vessels lined in a row. They landed a fair distance back from the ships, where the landscape was littered with boulders that provided excellent cover. Susan dropped back down to the Awoken's size. The group snuck through the rock until they were right on top of the Legion outpost.

The trio peeked around a wide stone slab. Directly in front of them, the four vessels rested in a clearing. Beyond the ships, the canyon-top tapered to a cliff. Numerous boulders littered the edge of the crag. The vessels were shaped like round-nosed projectiles. They had been lined up side by side in a row that led away from Oa and Kai, toward Bolleworth and the cliff. Next to the row of Legion fighters, several strange pyramid structures had been erected. Their dark metal frames held up shimmering panels. Through one of the openings, Oa could faintly make out the oily blackness of the Void. Just beyond the structures, several Legion soldiers stood quietly overlooking the distant city.

Kai pointed to the pyramids. "Those are the portals they come through. That's how they get so far inland so quickly. We need to stay away from those," she warned softly.

Oa nodded in understanding.

"Okay, let's go. You keep watch while I retrieve the fusion drive," Kai reminded him in a whisper.

They dropped low to the ground and scampered from the cover of the concealing boulder out to the farthest Legion vessel. Susan followed along quietly. The Legion fighter was made up of a spherical cockpit with three wings folded back behind it. Behind the cockpit; in the tunnel that the collapsed ailerons created, Oa could see an engine. He motioned to Kai, and she followed his gaze. She nodded and slowly crept inside. Susan floated close behind. Kai took off her pack and began to inspect the engine. Oa remained outside of the wings' cover. He peered around the craft looking for any Legion soldiers. He counted ten out in front of the portals. They were standing like silent sentinels gazing out over Bolleworth. Oa watched a bit longer then ducked inside the wings.

"Did you find it yet?" he whispered to Kai. Susan took up most of the tunnel space as she floated behind Kai, providing ample light for her task.

"No! I can't locate it. I'm not even sure anymore if these machines run on fusion drives," Kai whispered back, frustrated.

Oa grew worried so he crawled back outside to check on the Legion soldiers. *Good, they are still just standing there,* he thought to himself. He paused, looking closer. Then fear suddenly gripped him. There were only eight Legion soldiers. Where had the other two gone?

Oa ducked back behind the wing. He peeked out and glanced down the row of Legion fighters. Then he saw them, walking with eerily calm steps toward him from behind the ship at the far end of the row. Oa scurried back out of sight.

"We have to go now!" he shouted at Kai "They spotted us."

***

Ohm awoke suddenly. Consciousness flooded back to him. The calculations he and Fred had been running completed, resulting in a dire conclusion. Ohm lunged to his feet, looking around urgently. He quickly took stock of his surroundings. The chamber he was in was cluttered with various engineering notes; but more importantly, no one else was in it.

"Fred, where is Oa?" Ohm asked, moving about the room.

"He left through the far tunnel, with an Awoken named Kai. They were headed to a nearby Legion outpost to procure a fusion drive. I sent him off with one of my beacons," Fred explained.

"I hope they aren't getting themselves into too much trouble. We must catch up to them," Ohm said, as he ran into the tunnel with exigent purpose. "How long was I out?"

"Roughly 4902 weebles," Fred replied.

"Not too bad. We have been through worse," Ohm admitted optimistically.

He ran out of the tunnel into a cavernous hangar. Ohm skidded to a halt as his gaze fell upon the ship. After a stunned pause, he ran up to the vessel. He reached up and brushed his hand lovingly across the worn hull. Ohm stopped as he caught sight of the glyphs that spelled the word ARI.

"Another sign of fate, eh Fred?" Ohm whispered softly.

"It is an uncanny coincidence," Fred replied.

"It's been completely restored. Fred, find me an exit. We have to go get Oa," Ohm commanded. He looked around the room to give Fred a chance to scan the walls.

"The wall over there is metal, not stone. Notice the lack of mineral veins. It appears to be a gate. The panel to its right should contain the controls," Fred replied almost instantly.

Ohm sprinted over to the panel and mashed buttons at random until he heard the loud creaking of the door as the wall began to part. He ran back to the ARI, bounding up the ramp and through the front door with speed that implied familiarity.

"This is probably what they are trying to get a fusion drive for," Ohm said shaking his head and chuckling at the humor of the situation. He sat down in the power hub and leaned back in his command chair. The hub fit him perfectly. Fred whirred and clicked as he connected the ARI to Ohm.

"I would have remembered to tell Oa, but your condition grossly hindered my programming," Fred accused.

Ohm sighed. "I know. I am sorry, Fred. At least you had the foresight to send him with your beacon. We still have time. Patch me into all the ship's major functions," he commanded.

The vessel hummed to life, and the roar of the engines filled the cavern. The heavy gates groaned to a halt as they fully opened, revealing a gap in the rock that led to the outside world.

"It feels good to be home," Ohm said. The engines roared louder, lifting the ship off the ground. Air rushed through the hangar, buffeting cabinet doors and scattering tools and equipment across the floor. With a thought, Ohm retracted the landing pads back into the ship, and sent the ARI rocketing through the open doors and up towards the sky.

***

Kai dropped her tools, cursing as she bolted out to the edge of the Legion fighter's wings, leaving her pack behind. She flinched as deadly bolts of nihilistol fire filled the air, deadening all sound as they whizzed by. Kai fished one of the embersplitters out of her pocket and tossed it back toward her tools. She dove away from the ship, grabbing Oa's hand and pulling him along. Susan wrapped herself around the pair. Behind them, the Legion vessel exploded in a ball of light.

"We have to get out of here! Throw me your glider!" Kai shouted. Oa pressed the button on his right shoulder and the mesh of his pack went limp. He slid the sack from his back, grabbed his satchel from inside. He tossed the bag to Kai. She sat up and raised the pack, facing it toward their enemies. She slapped the wing deployment button. Sound died again as the Legion soldiers let loose another volley of Void bullets. The glider burst open in front of the trio like a shield, catching the Legion fire. The air-skin fabric dissolved away, protecting them from the deadly blasts.

"Susan, get us behind those boulders!" Kai yelled, as she tossed a second embersplitter at the Legion soldiers.

Susan uncurled from around them and snatched the two Awoken up in her paws. Her size in no way hindered her strength as she dragged them across the ground, racing toward the boulders that dotted the edge of the rim. Behind them, the embersplitter exploded, providing a momentary distraction. They slid to a halt behind a medium-sized slab of stone. Oa and Kai got up into a crouch to peek over the top of the rock. Oa slid the satchel's strap over his head, returning it to his side. He grabbed Seeker from inside the bag.

The ten Legion soldiers spread out and formed a line across the narrow plateau. They walked forward, trapping Oa, Kai, and Susan. There was nowhere to go but the edge of the cliff. The trio retreated back, crouching to stay below the cover of the boulders; and Susan wound through the stone, laying low to the ground. The Legion weapons obliterated the rocks behind them.

Ducking behind a thick slab, Kai turned to Oa. "We have to fight or they're going to drive us off the cliff! Susan will be an easy target if she has to carry both of us out of here." The bold Awoken jumped out from behind cover, hauling her left pistol out of its holster. She fired ten shots back at the Legion warriors, Oa peeked out from behind the stone, watching as eight of the projectiles struck true, leaving tiny blinking receivers on the Legion soldier's chests. Kai had barely finished firing before her right hand had whipped out the other pistol. Her arm swung in an arc as she pulled the trigger. Lightning exploded from the gun, arcing through the air and seeking out each of the previously fired receivers. The blast plowed into eight of the Legion soldiers, overwhelming their physical bodies with energy. They shattered, dissolving into Void dust.

Susan's ears flattened back, and her body sparked up angrily. She struck, hurdling over the boulders onto one of the remaining Legion soldiers. The varl swelled to a fighting size as she opened her jaws and roared. Purple lightning poured from her mouth shattering the Void warrior beneath her. Oa stretched out his hand and with a thought, sent Seeker plowing through the remaining Legion soldier who had turned to fire at Susan.

"Back, Susan!" Kai shouted as more Legion began to pour from the Void portals. They sprinted out to surround the Awoken. Oa whipped Seeker through several of the soldiers, knocking them off their feet.

Kai fired her pistols in rapid succession, obliterating six more of the Legion. Her efforts were merely a dent in the Legion's growing ranks as they continued to rush out of the Void portals. One of the warriors leaped over the boulder the Awoken were behind. The demon descended down upon them with a raised fist, its red eye flashed evilly in the dim light of the dying cycle. Susan snarled and reared up at the enemy. Placing her powerful frame in the path of the Legion soldier, her lightning fangs tore the monster apart before it could land a blow on Oa or Kai.

Oa stepped back, but halted as he felt his foot slide off the edge behind him. There was nowhere left to run. The Legion had backed them up against the edge of the rim.

"Well, it was nice meeting you, Oa," Kai quipped as they stood their ground, facing annihilation from the Legion horde. Oa readied himself for whatever flimsy escape plan he knew his mind was about to concoct.

Suddenly, thunder filled the air; and the face of the ARI rose up behind them. A powerful beam of light shot from the front of the craft, illuminating the plateau. The only thing the Legion soldiers could see were the silhouettes of the trio standing on the cliff's edge.

"It's the ARI," Kai cheered. "But how?"

"Ohm must be flying!" Oa exclaimed as he grabbed Kai in his arms. With a thought, he sent Seeker flying into the ship through the open ramp. As soon as Seeker latched onto something solid, he pulled them up into the ARI. Susan gave one last roar at the Legion before she turned and followed Oa. The ramp closed behind them with a hiss. Outside, the ARI's floodlight grew to an impossible brilliance, driving the Legion to their knees. Suddenly, the light popped and blinked out in a barely audible explosion. The triumphant vessel turned and blasted off. Powerful engines propelled the ship far away from the outpost.

The Legion slowly returned to their feet and stared at the ARI as it faded away into the horizon. From one of the Void portals, the shrouded form of Eol emerged. He walked to the edge of the cliff, gazing at the spot on the horizon where the ARI had fled. Eol and his Legion remained eerily still, with a quiet patience that foreshadowed the inevitability of the hunt.

EPISODE 06

LIGHT CHASERS

Oa and Kai flew through the open ramp and crashed into the support beam that Seeker had attached to. Susan's enlarged frame barreled into the pair, further squashing them into the metal pillar. Oa heard the ramp hiss shut behind them. He thought about letting go of Seeker but quickly changed his mind as the ARI accelerated to a ludicrous speed. He held onto Kai and Seeker as the acceleration of the ship attempted to peel them from the sturdy support and fling them to the back of the vessel. Overhead, the air howled as it whipped over the open ceiling. Oa was glad to be rescued, but he wished the escape was a little less wild. He wanted to regain his bearings and get inside. Before long, the ARI settled into a steady cruising speed. Oa and Kai were finally able to unglue themselves from the support beam. They toppled over, their internal sensors scrambled from the acceleration. Susan bounced around the deck excitedly as Oa and Kai stumbled shakily to their feet.

"That better have been necessary, Ohm," Oa grumbled looking about for the entrance to the ship's interior.

Next to him, Kai pulled her pistols out, inspecting them for damage. She sighted down the barrels, glancing at a gauge at the back of the guns. She squeezed hard on the weapons grip. A depleted ammo block dropped out of the butt of each gun and hit the deck with a hollow ring. Oa noticed the transparent cartridge was no longer filled with blue energy. Kai kicked the empty clip off the edge of the deck. She reloaded her guns with ammo from their respective bandoliers before sliding the weapons back into their holsters.

Oa spotted the door. He walked over and slapped the access panel next to the entrance. The portal slid open. He stood to the side, politely allowing Kai to enter ahead of him. He looked back to see if Susan would follow, but the varl was busy peering over the deck's railing at the land speeding by below.

"Susan, come inside and meet Ohm," Oa called, daring to make a suggestion. The beast's gentle nature with him had lessened his fear of the lightning varl.

Susan turned her head, sparky tongue lolling out of her smiling face. She looked at Oa for a moment then jumped through the air and floated to him, lowering her head. She barged into him playfully. Oa laughed, marveling at how quickly Susan transitioned from deadly force to goofy antics. She growled happily, compacting down to her normal size. Then she whirled around, and flew into the ship. Oa followed, stepping through the entrance. The door slid shut behind him.

Oa found himself in the power-hub chamber again. The room was lit by a ring of bright orange panels in the center of the roof. The light drifted down through floating motes of dust that had become unsettled during the speedy getaway. The panels covering the interior of the ARI were as worn as the exterior. Splotches of scoring and discoloration scarred the alloys, betraying the vessels old age. Light glinted off exposed rivets and bolts in the walls. Several light panels separated from the main ring-formation, leading off down a corridor to another part of the ship that Oa had not yet seen. He turned to peer out the forward view port of the chamber. The sky ahead was dim, and several weak flares of light wound above the speeding craft. A new cycle would begin soon. He turned back to the center of the room where Kai stood in front of the power drive facing Ohm. Susan sat regally in the air by Kai's side, her tail coiled tightly beneath her. Oa stepped up next to the pair.

"Well I never would've thought of that," Kai said, arms crossed as she stared at Ohm sitting in the power hub, his head bowed. Ohm did not appear conscious of the statement and gave no response.

The ship began to slow before coming to an abrupt stop. Oa checked his balance, not wanting to fall over and look foolish. As soon as the ARI halted, Ohm came alive. His head slowly lifted, and he took notice of Oa and Kai standing in front of him. Motors whirred and clicked as Fred disengaged from the power hub. Ohm jumped up and stood in between Oa and Kai, facing the power hub. He pulled them in close, draping his arms around their shoulders.

"Fantastic! I have not done that in a long time," Ohm said, turning to Oa then Kai. "Oa, I am so very glad to see you're not dead. I have important findings to tell you about. Please introduce me to your new friend. I am more than grateful that she repaired my old ship."

"What do you mean *your ship*?" Kai said, arms still crossed. "I am the one who—"

"Fred, look!" Ohm exclaimed, interrupting Kai. He hopped over the power hub to embrace Susan. The varl had floated unnoticed to the other side of the room, where she goofily hung upside down in the air. "A lighting varl. I have not seen one of these noble sky-wads in heaps of weebles," Ohm said, hugging the billowing creature tight. Susan growled happily, wriggling her body right-side up so she could lick the old Awoken's face. Her tongue sent purple sparks flying. Ohm turned away from Susan's affections so he could face Kai.

"Do not fret; the ARI is yours now," Ohm said courteously. "You put it back together so it belongs to you. I am just one of the previous owners."

"In that case, my name is Kai; and that cloud bomb you're holding is called Susan," Kai said in an accepting tone, though she was still slightly wary of Ohm.

"Oa brought you in asleep; and now that you're awake, I want to know who you are," Kai demanded in a gruff tone. She draped her arm over Oa's shoulder. Ohm turned and let go of Susan. She floated up and began to circle lazily overhead.

Oa tried to answer on Ohm's behalf. "Don't worry Kai. Ohm has been around for a long time; he knows a lot. Despite his appearances, he has been—"

"It's alright, Oa. I can speak on my own condition," Ohm interrupted. "Even though you already know it, my name is Ohm. I am infected with the Void, but I have no addictions to it. My actions will prove you can trust me."

"Ohm ..." Kai paused, mulling over the name. "Ohm. Ohm! I remember that name now! And the blue ocular plate. You're the Traveler, the instructor from the academy that Jess and Cale always droned on about," she said, excited at the sudden reclaimed memory.

"I did dabble in teaching for a while," Ohm admitted reflectively. "I definitely recall Jess and Cale, very creative. They did not have any straightforward or sensible programming, but together they were geniuses. They had several noteworthy achievements." He was filled with pride as he remembered his favorite students.

"That's them," Kai said happily. "They were the first Awoken I ever met. They taught me ... about building things? I think they had already graduated from the academy when I— No, that's not quite right. It was all back in ..." Kai's words trailed off as she struggled to complete her recollections.

Ohm studied Kai closely as she tried to piece together her memories. "You met them in Istaar?" he offered up gently.

"Of course, it's Istaar. Why couldn't I remember that?" Kai muttered angrily to herself as she tapped the side of her head.

"But you knew them, too, Ohm. Back in Istaar. They loved Istaar. Istaar is where we used to live. They must still be there. If I could just remember how to get there," Kai said, purposefully overusing the name of the city in an attempt to affix it to her memory.

Ohm watched Kai carefully. Oa noticed the previous excitement of seeing Susan drain from the old Awoken as it was replaced by somber thoughtfulness. "They are most definitely still in Istaar. Is that where you are trying to go with the ARI?" he asked softly.

"Yeah, it is," Kai responded. She paused a moment to glance down at her boots; then she looked up at Ohm. "I'm going to trust you, Ohm. I know Cale and Jess respected you. I don't care if you sleep—what matters is that you're a vital part of this ship. You can fly the ARI with that fusion drive of a backpack." Her faceplate glowed brighter as she realized her goals were finally achievable.

"Please call me Fred," the pack chimed in.

"Oops, my error, Fred; I forgot," Kai apologized hurriedly. "I'm just so happy that the ARI works. Now we can go find Cale and Jess. Ohm, do you remember where Istaar is?" she asked hopefully.

"I do, and I will help you find the city. But we are going to need a new light. Istaar is dark and I seemed to have burned out the ARI's current flood lamp. We will need to catch ourselves another photorb," Ohm explained calmly, refusing to get caught up in the excitement oozing from Kai.

"Okay, but, before we go get one of those photorb things, I need to go do some final adjustments to the engine. It sounds alright but I heard a few odd noises when you pushed the poor thing into overdrive back there," Kai complained, concerned about her ship.

Kai strode out to the open deck. Susan followed her into the chamber at the rear of the vessel, driven by curiosity. The hatch to the engineering room closed behind the pair as Kai set to work perfecting her masterpiece.

Oa remained where he was, facing Ohm. He had questions for his mentor. Once Kai was gone the Traveler spoke up.

"So, Fred and I discovered—"

"That can wait," Oa said, cutting his friend off. "Things got a bit scary back in those canyons. You picked a wonderful time to drop. The Legion nearly had us." He folded his arms across his chest.

"Yeah," Ohm said sheepishly. "My apologies regarding that whole incident. I was meaning to tell you about the arm and stuff." The ancient Awoken reached up and adjusted the hood on his head in the awkward silence that followed.

"Well, things worked out," Oa said, breaking the silence. "Anyhow, Fred wouldn't tell me about it, and Kai doesn't seem to need answers, but I want to know how it happened. Were you addicted to Void immersion or something? Do you still do it?"

Ohm stopped fiddling with his hood and began to idly tap the microbur canister attached to his mask. "Honestly, I don't remember how I became infected. I just woke up from my first sleep all besmirched, and Fred is unable to tell me what happened." He shrugged his bandaged arm. "I can surmise with some certainty that one whopper of a beating occurred."

Oa sensed his friend's honesty. He sighed and leaned back against the chamber wall. "There is a lot of selective memory going on around here. Am I the only one with a working brain?" he huffed in exasperation. Then he chuckled slightly at the absurdity of the situation.

"Well, I don't know what Kai's excuse is, but I have been living with this crazy headache for close to a bajillion weebles," Ohm said defensively as he pointed to his mask.

Fred pounced on the opportunity to correct Ohm. "The actual number is 5,289—"

"I don't want to know the number, Fred!" Ohm said, interrupting the pack.

Ohm walked up to Oa and tapped the top of the shorter Awoken's head. "You still have a lot to learn. You never considered the idea that not all Sleepers are voluntary addicts. Some might just be infected."

"Alright, alright. I didn't think of that. I believe you," Oa said, annoyed as he swatted Ohm's hand away. "So will that infection get worse?"

"The infection has not spread from my right side. Other than the inconvenient sleep, it doesn't seem to affect me. I cover it up, though, because I despise the sight of it," Ohm said, anger bleeding through his voice as he tried to brush the wrinkles out of the patched cloth that covered his right leg.

Oa nodded sympathetically. He decided not to push the topic any further. "So what did Fred discover about my powers?" he asked expectantly. "It might help explain why I couldn't heal your Void infection. It thwarted my abilities somehow. A similar thing happened during my first cycle," he said, remembering Buri.

"Ah, yes, our discovery. That is much more important than my deformities. You really derailed the conversation, Oa," Ohm grumbled. He stood silently for a moment, choosing the best way to disclose his findings. "Fred and I were able to analyze Seeker's inner workings when you used it in Bolleworth. It appears that Seeker runs off an unknown form of Void technology. Simply put, Seeker creates out of nothing. That sounds impossible, but we watched it happen." He walked over to the viewport and gazed out at the dim sky. "I believe that Eol will hunt you using Seeker as a beacon. The Void is Eol's home. He dwells within his own emptiness. He will never allow you to fix the infection he has spread. That is why his will defied your power. You must not create with Seeker anymore. Your gift is a thief to Eol. He knows when you try to steal from him. I hate telling you to suppress your potential, but you need to be patient until we can figure out a way to outwit Eol."

In his mind Oa, called out to Seeker. The silver sphere obediently rose out of its satchel to hover above his hand. He looked at it for a moment, and his shoulders drooped slightly in disappointment. "I really dislike Eol, but there is nothing we can do about him right now. We need to stay out of his sight and head toward the Enlightened." The young Awoken looked up hopefully. "Can I still use Seeker to swing around?"

"I believe so, that feature does not stimulate the Void core within Seeker so Eol should have no awareness of it," Ohm reassured. "Your mental link to Seeker is outside of his realm. That device is quite the dichotomy. Our data indicates that Seeker links you to the universal programming as well as the Void, but that should be impossible. Perhaps Fred and I are getting daft in our age." He turned from the viewport to face Oa. "Your new friend is quite amazing. Only Jess and Cale could have taught her so well. I am sure you have noticed, though, that Kai's mind is not whole. She is missing pieces, or she is refusing to accept them. Istaar was destroyed in the great cataclysm that reduced this world to its current state. I was away from the academy at the time. Once I heard it had been obliterated along with the rest of the city, I decided it was time to retire. Fred and I have been wandering ever since."

Oa thought for a moment before responding, "I promised Kai that we would assist her in return for a ride. We need to go to Istaar and help her piece her memory back together."

"I concur. Cale and Jess were my greatest students, but a rift opened between us when they pursued research with a government I was not particularly fond of. I need to know what happened as much as Kai does," Ohm agreed.

"Maybe we will find clues about Eol there; he might have had something to do with it," Oa suggested. Ohm nodded, deep in thought.

"I'm going to go see if Kai needs any help," Oa said as he walked over to the door. He was knocked back as Kai and Susan rushed back in to the chamber.

"Oops! Sorry, Oa," Kai said quickly, brushing imaginary dust off of Oa's tunic. "The ship is ready Ohm, so you sit back down and power the ARI while Oa and I go to the front and fly our way to some photorbs," she commanded, eager with anticipation.

Ohm snapped stiffly to mock attention, then nodded and sat down into the power hub. Fred whirred and clicked as the pack reconnected to the ARI. Oa shook his head at Ohm's quirkiness then followed Kai through the corridor at the other end of the chamber. Orange light panels led them in a short arc around a corner into a cockpit. The ceiling dipped down, curving into a wide window panel that wrapped around the front end of the room.

"Welcome to the bridge!" Kai said proudly, motioning to two comfy looking seats in front of them.

She grabbed the chair on the right and spun it toward her. Kai sat down then whirled back to face the complex flight console in front of her. Susan came floating in. She brushed past Oa, winding her way into a small alcove behind the bridge. Oa realized that the hallway they had come through curved around the antechamber Susan had floated into. The walls, floor, and ceiling of the room were dotted with minuscule metallic nubs spaced out in a hexagonal pattern. He looked closer. Each nub was composed of an array of shiny rings stacked on a tiny pole.

"Oa, pull the lever on the side there," Kai said, pointing to a blinking green switch next to the alcove entrance. Oa pulled the lever down into *on* position. It stopped blinking and remained lit. The room sparked and crackled as arcs of violet hued energy bounced around, shooting randomly between the nubs on the walls.

"I built it for Susan so she can rest better," Kai explained as Oa sat down in the pilot's chair next to her. "It reminds her of the sky knots she would nest in if she wasn't following me around. Lighting varls enjoy the energy dense spots in the sky. It took a lot of work, but I turned that wasted storage space into a storm simulator and tuned it to Susan's frequency. I was barely able to power it with the generator back at my cave, but she liked it so much I didn't care if it made the lights go out." Her face plate glowed at the happy memory.

"It was actually a hat closet," Ohm interrupted. His voice seemed to come out of nowhere, startling Oa and Kai.

"Ohm, I thought you were in the power hub," Oa said, spinning his chair around to see if Ohm had walked into the bridge.

"I'm still in the hub with Fred. Kai, you may not have realized the full functionality of the ARI when you rebuilt it. The seats contain cerebral audio feeds. If you're sitting in one of the piloting seats, we can hear each other's words no matter how noisy things get. So we don't have to shout down the halls at each other," Ohm explained.

"The accurate relaying of information can be vital while piloting this vessel during dangerous situations," Fred added curtly.

"I love my ship!" Kai said enthusiastically. "So where do we go to find a photorb, Ohm? Also, what is that?" Oa leaned back in his chair, bored at the thought of another one of his mentor's informative lectures.

"You must have found the ARI's flood lamp intact, then, to not notice its custom inner workings," Ohm reasoned before continuing to answer Kai's question. "The flood lamp is not lit by heated loops of alloy like other lamps from this craft's era. A living luminous creature powers the ARI's flood lamp. Fred and I named it a photorb."

"We have to stop asking questions he can drone on about," Oa whispered humorously over to Kai.

"I heard that!" Ohm snapped. "Pay attention! Photorbs zip about, racing through the energy of the lightning forests. Most photorbs are too fast to catch; but when they get old, they grow weary of their pace. They become slow enough that we can see them. Photorbs can't stop moving until they're dead; but if you catch one, you can give it a peaceful way to rest its remaining weebles, comfortably fed by the ARI. Photorbs are incredibly radiant. They last a long time, even though they are relatively near death by the time they can be caught."

"Oa's right. That's definitely the long answer. All I learned was that we need to go to a lightning forest," Kai teased, flicking switches and adjusting knobs on the control board in front of her. "Oa, you'll be having your second lesson in flight while Ohm and I navigate us to a nearby forest," she said warmly.

"I thought you would want to fly the ARI first," Oa said, surprised at the gesture.

"Don't worry about it. There will be plenty of time for me to fly later. Besides, I've never piloted this exact model before, so you're the test dummy," Kai admitted cheerily.

"Thanks … I will try not to crash us," Oa replied. *I hope I do better at this than the glider*, he thought to himself.

"Kai, if you will monitor the readings on the scanners for lightning forest energy signatures, I will pinpoint which branch has the highest concentration of photorb wakes. Don't worry, Oa. You probably have the programming to fly. You will do great," Ohm instructed encouragingly, knowing that Oa and Kai were slightly nervous about piloting the newly refurbished vessel.

Oa looked at the controls in front of him. To his left was a lever with a crosspiece handle on the top. On his right was a dome-shaped controller with a slot made for a hand to fit into.

"Activating restraint harnesses," Fred informed the crew. Harnesses sprung out from the chairs snapping together across the crew's waists and chests.

"Place your right hand into the navigation dome and grip the handle inside. It rotates in all directions, and the ARI will mimic the movements your hand makes. To adjust the power of the engines, push that lever forward with your left hand. It's sensitive so you might want to start out slow," Kai instructed Oa.

Her last words were strained by the force of acceleration as Oa thrust the speed adjustor forward. He slid his hand into the navigation dome and gripped the handle inside, rotating it down and to the right. The engines roared to life; and the ship arced down in a spiral, following his guidance. He let out a whoop as the ground seemed to rush up toward them. Just as they were about to hit the dirt, Oa halted their spin, leveling the craft out upside down as he raced across the surface of the world. He hovered close to the ground, weaving through the jagged terrain.

"Flying is way better than walking, Ohm," Oa joked.

"This is amazing," Kai agreed.

"I find they both have their rewards. Just don't crash my ship. Kai probably can't rebuild it again," Ohm countered, bating Kai.

"Don't tempt me old one. I will crash us just to prove I can rebuild MY ship," Kai retorted. Ohm laughed.

Oa dipped the controls down as they went over a cliff enjoying the sudden drop. A solid looking wall of rock was ahead so he flipped the ARI right-side up and sent it rocketing back toward the sky before they crashed into the stone. They sailed upwards, drawing closer and closer to the sky. The beautiful dark clouds glowed with a bright golden hue. The light filled the cockpit as an especially grand coil of energy burned overhead. Oa leveled the ship off, flying directly beneath the clouds. He pushed the speed adjustor even further, taking care to dodge through arcing energy beams that flared out from under the clouds. The young Awoken was elated at how natural flying felt. He charted a course straight toward the peak on the horizon.

"Swing around to the right a little. I see a lightning forest up ahead on my scopes," Kai instructed.

Oa brought the ARI into a hard turn rolling the ship end-over-end a few times for added fun. "Is this good?" he asked.

"Just get us there in one piece," Kai said, thoroughly enjoying herself.

Oa dropped down out of the edges of the clouds and pulled the speed adjustor back slightly; casually winding the ARI back and forth as he followed the glorious vein of light in the sky.

"There it is," Kai said, pointing to a glowing spot on the horizon. The land below was flat and desolate. Not a gust of wind stirred the dust on the smoothly-cut rock floor. Oa raced over the dry and desolate wasteland toward the deep green light Kai was pointing at. It appeared to rise up from the ground to meet the sky. Oa watched in wonder as they neared the pillar of light. Gradually, the blurry image sharpened into a green energy stream that rose up from a great fissure in the rock. The trunk split into numerous branches of lightning that danced and jigged as they tangled with the gold tinged veins in the sky. The sight was beautiful. Oa reached over and slowed the ship as they neared the forest.

"Do you see this, Ohm?" Oa asked in awe.

"I do. No matter how many times I have seen one, they never cease to amaze me. Head into the thick of the branches, up close to where they meet the sky. You have quick reflexes, but take care not to run into a branch. They tend to move about a bit," Ohm replied, respect for the fierce natural beauty of the forest filling his voice.

The ARI cruised up into the forest. Gold and green light danced about in the cockpit and played across the metal paneling.

"Bring us further in toward the center," Ohm commanded.

Oa weaved in and out of the branches gracefully, guiding them deeper into the forest.

"Bring us to a stop in the clearing ahead, Oa," Ohm instructed.

Oa reached over and pulled the speed adjustor back, reducing the engine power to a crawl. They quietly glided into a clearing in the center of the forest where Oa brought the ARI to a halt. Around them, beams of energy crackled with life. Pinpricks of light drifted together, swirling around the branches and chasing each other through the forest.

"The ship is immobile. Releasing restraint harnesses," Fred informed the crew. The harnesses retracted from around Oa and Kai to return into the seats.

"Come on, Oa. Let's go take a look," Kai said, jumping out of her seat. She ran out of the cockpit, flipping off the power switch to Susan's storm simulator as she passed. Susan immediately perked up and flew out of the room in pursuit of Kai. Oa was not far behind the pair as they ran through the empty power hub chamber and out onto the open deck of the ARI. Ohm was already outside, leaning with his hand on the railing as he gazed out into the forest of light. He turned his head slightly as the excited trio came up beside him.

"You can see a herd of photorbs there," Ohm said, pointing with his bandaged stump to a nearby branch of pulsing green energy. Numerous little balls of light flitted playfully about the branch. "I will go and wrangle one. Susan should come with me. It's time she followed in her parents' wake and caught the ARI its next beacon," the Traveler said, his voice mysteriously reminiscent as he leaned down to pat Susan on the head. She bobbed lightly in the air, tongue lolling out happily.

"Susan, please follow Ohm now and go get us a big, bright light," Kai encouraged the varl. Susan barked an affirmative. Her body exploded in purple light and she threw her paws up, soaring over the edge of the deck railing. She plunged off the ship and sped up toward the stream of photorbs. The varl's body fluctuated in size as she tried to decide what form would be best to take for the hunt.

Kai's curiosity was piqued by Ohm's words. "Did you know Susan's parents?" she asked.

"I have been around for a long time. I know everyone," Ohm replied vaguely. He took a step back then vaulted forward over the railing. He dropped a bit before Fred activated the aqua jet, sending them rocketing after Susan.

"It would be more efficient to warn me of your sudden urges to leap from high places, Ohm. Then I could time the aqua jet better," Fred informed Ohm as they rose up toward the deep green tendril of energy.

"My spontaneity keeps your programming sharp," Ohm retorted.

"That sounds like an excuse to remain reckless," Fred replied evenly.

"Stay focused, Fred. This is no time for you to make valid points. We clearly need to teach Susan how to catch a photorb," Ohm said, amused at the sight of the varl attempting to hunt one of the stray photorbs. She reeled through the air chasing after the speedy ball of light.

Oa and Kai stood on the ARI's open deck, leaning against the railing. They stared out at the beautiful streams of green energy flowing upwards. They watched as Ohm flew over to Susan. The duo floated in midair together, plotting. Ohm leaned in close to Susan, imparting his plan to her. The photorbs continued to dance around the branch in ignorant bliss.

Ohm made the first move as he slowly advanced towards the living cloud of light while Susan stalked down a branch to where it met with several others. Her body shrunk down to half it's normal size as she crouched low in the energy. Her own smoky purple aura interlaced with the deep greens of the forest. Ohm slowly jetted up to the pack of photorbs which were now spinning around a single spot. He drew ever closer until all at once the photorbs took off, shooting straight up the branch. Oa heard the Traveler shout, "Now Fred!" Then the aqua jet shot out a geyser of water, sending him rocketing up after the creatures. Ohm was slowly gaining on the photorbs. He stretched out his hand to snatch one from the tail of the pack, but the balls of light rapidly shifted tactics and began to corkscrew around the branch.

Ohm did not follow the evasive path. Instead, he let the aqua jet cut out. He sailed upwards, slowing down but still keeping pace with the photorb cloud as they began to corkscrew tighter and tighter, decreasing their movement up the branch with each rotation. Impulsively, the swarm changed directions and shot straight down; but Ohm was ready. Almost out of momentum, he flipped over and Fred reactivated the aqua jet, throwing them down after the photorbs. This time Ohm did not try to close the gap as he chased the cloud down the branch to where Susan had crouched in the energy waiting.

"Where is she?" Kai asked, scanning the branch.

Oa peered into the area directly ahead of the speeding cloud of photorbs. "Right there," he said, pointing as Susan charged out of the energy. Ablaze with excitement, she rolled through the cloud, jaws snapping and tail whipping about. The photorbs dispersed chaotically for a moment before reassembling at another spot on the branch to continue their dance. Ohm caught up to Susan, and the two of them returned to the ARI. The lightning varl lightly pawed through the air, pleased with herself. Oa could see a bright light shining out from between her clenched jaws.

Ohm sped in, ceasing the aqua jet before he was over the deck so he didn't splash water everywhere. He sailed over the railing. As he hit the deck, Ohm tucked into a roll. He sprang to his feet as Kai and Oa turned around to look at him.

"She learns quickly. I never thought hunting photorbs would be so instinctive for her," Ohm praised, as Susan sauntered onto the deck, clearly gloating. She reared up to her normal girth, placing her big paws on Kai's shoulders, her bushy tail waving out behind her and brushing all over Ohm's face.

"Champions clearly have the right to gloat," Oa joked as Ohm sputtered, brushing the undulating sparky tail out of the way.

"At least we have a photorb now. Put that in the flood lamp, and we can fly into whatever storm is waiting for us at Istaar," Ohm said, chuckling.

"Hooray! Susan, you are the best varl there ever was!" Kai said, hugging her purple friend.

"Would you like Fred and I to fly out to the flood lamp and replace the photorb?" Ohm asked.

"No thanks, Susan and I can figure it out. The access hatch to the floodlight is inside the ARI. I rebuilt it that way so I didn't have to fix things from the outside. I don't have a talking water jet to fly around with, and Susan gets too bored to hold me steady while I work," Kai explained, lightly jabbing Susan with her elbow.

"I am a fusion pack. The idea that I am a mere water jet is a gross misconception," Fred scoffed, clearly offended.

"Oops, sorry again, Fred. You just seem to be best at flying Ohm around," Kai apologized as she turned away and hurried into the engineering room. Susan trailed behind, head held high.

"Of all the Awoken I have met, there is a high probability that she is not my favorite," Fred pouted.

"I prefer to think of you as a complex fusion device, too," Ohm consoled his talking backpack.

"So do you remember how to get to Istaar?" Oa asked, leaning over the railing to look down on the land far below the lightning forest.

"Yes. Fred and I have explored this world extensively. Fred keeps track of every location since he has the better memory," Ohm said, walking over to stand next to Oa. "The peak is to our front, so Istaar is that way." He pointed to the horizon on their right.

They heard a crash followed by Susan's thunderous roar. Then they heard several more crashes coming from the engineering room behind them. They turned to look as the door opened up.

"This won't take long if Susan doesn't let the photorb go again to play with it," Kai said, sounding flustered as she stumbled out, tools in hand.

Susan floated out, growling with the little light ball trapped in her mouth.

"Would you both mind cleaning up the mess back there while I fix the floodlight?" Kai asked, still ruffled as she stumbled into the power hub chamber. Susan followed, and the entrance closed behind them.

"Sure, no problem," Oa called after Kai as the door was closing.

The pair walked over to the engine chamber door, not knowing what to expect. Oa hit the panel on the side, and the portal slid open. Oa had never seen the engineering room before; but as he stared into the mess, he could see why it had put Kai in a bad mood. The room was rectangular in shape and cozy in size. It was lit by more orange lighting in the roof. Soft blue beams flickered around the chamber, originating from the wall opposite the door. Oa looked at the far wall; the lower half was filled with dials, knobs, and levers. The upper half of the wall was cut open to reveal the, slowly spinning rotor of the ship's engine. The soft blue light of the engine leaked out into the room. The walls to either side of the door were lined with hatches and shelves. Tools and other supplies from the shelves were strewn about. Several hatches had been knocked open, their contents spilling out on the floor.

Ohm waded into the mess. He began to pick up instruments and set them back into their places. Oa did not know where anything went so he just started to pick up things. "Where do these go, Ohm?" he asked, trying to make himself useful.

"Probably over there," Ohm responded pointing to an open hatch across the room. Between the two of them, the mess was cleaned up quickly. Oa closed the last open storage hatch and turned back to look at the whole place. It was immaculate.

Ohm had several objects in his arms, some bundles of fabric, and a coil of thick metal fibers.

"What's all that for?" Oa asked.

"I'm going to make myself a sling to lay in when my infection puts me to sleep," Ohm said, hitting the exit panel. The door opened, and he walked back out onto the deck. Oa followed and watched as Ohm began to tie the metal fibers between the two metal support struts on the deck.

"Alright, I am going to go check on Kai and Susan," Oa said as he walked over to the front door and opened it. He walked inside the power hub chamber and the door slid shut behind him. He looked down to see Kai torso-deep in a maintenance shaft beneath the forward viewport. Susan had crammed herself in next to Kai.

"Susan shrink down!" Kai exclaimed with humored frustration. The varl seemed to disappear as she contracted down so small that Oa could not spot her. After a few moments, Kai pulled herself back out of the hatch, tools in hand. "Hey Oa! I just got finished replacing the light. Here is the old photorb." She held up a gleaming black chunk of rock. "This must be the burned-out one. I am going to keep it cuz it looks pretty." She put the stone in her pocket and stood up. "Wait, where did the old cloud-bomb go?" A minuscule Susan popped up next to Kai's shoulder. The tiny varl let out what she intended to be a mighty roar, but it came out as an adorable squeal. Both Oa and Kai burst into laughter. The lightning varl ballooned out, filling the chamber and squishing the two Awoken up against the wall. Her face was pressed up against Oa and Kai. She panted happily, as if sharing in the joke. "Very funny! Let us down," Kai complained through muffled mirth. Susan reduced to her normal size, bouncing around the room with excitement.

Kai quickly recovered from the varl's antics. "We're finally ready to go!" She rushed to the door, opened it, and poked her head out. "Let's move! The ship is ready." After a moment, Ohm walked in. "Wait, can you go put these back?" She grabbed the tools off the floor and handed them to him. The old Awoken gave an overly dramatic sigh, but nodded and left. Kai walked back over to the maintenance shaft and closed the access panel. She looked up at Oa. "If you don't mind, I'm going to fly the ARI to Istaar."

"Of course, Ohm and I will navigate for you," Oa replied. He knew finding Istaar would be an important accomplishment for Kai.

Ohm walked back into the chamber. He sat down in the power hub, and Fred immediately reconnected with the ARI. Fred finished synchronizing with the vessel, and the lights in the room brightened slightly as the ARI returned to full power. Oa could hear the engine gearing up. Anticipating the coming journey, Susan floated down the corridor to her storm simulator.

"Your engine room is clean. I apologize if not everything is in its proper place," Ohm said.

"Don't worry about it. Thanks for helping me with that," Kai replied. She stood up and walked with Oa to the bridge. Oa took a seat in the copilot's chair. Kai turned Susan's storm simulator on and eased herself into the pilot's chair next to Oa.

"Ohm says Istaar is that way," Oa told Kai, pointing to the spot on the horizon Ohm had showed him earlier.

"Initiating engine burn," Kai informed the crew.

"Activating restraint harnesses," Fred replied. The harnesses on the seats snapped into place. Kai placed her hand into the navigation dome then used her other hand to push the speed adjustor forward. The ARI glided out of the forest. Kai's movements were a bit hesitant at first. A few of the energy branches nearly grazed the ship, but Kai quickly figured out the controls. By the time they exited the forest, she was flying the ARI with ease. Pushing the speed adjustor to three quarters power, Kai sent them zipping toward the spot Oa had pointed to. She kept them flying steady and straight, not feeling comfortable enough to attempt the aerial acrobatics Oa had experimented with earlier.

Oa looked over at Kai. Her leg was bouncing slightly as her heel nervously tapped the floor. Whatever was waiting for them at Istaar, Oa knew it would force Kai to confront the fate of her friends, ill or fair. He looked ahead toward a growing dark spot on the horizon. Istaar laid there, the focal point of the world's current disarray. The young Awoken hoped the city held some answers for them all.

EPISODE 07

REFLECTIONS OF THE PAST

The ARI tore through the air, racing headlong into the dim shadows that surrounded Istaar. An oppressive fog swelled out to engulf them, growing heavier as the ship waded further into the frigid embrace. Oa and Kai stared out of the cockpit window to see that the golden glow of the sky had receded. The rivers of light evaded the desolate region, forsaking Istaar to its despair. A pall of gloom stretched from the barren rock below to the darkened clouds above, swallowing the city in eternal darkness and obscuring it from any passerby's.

Oa had dimmed the lighting in the cockpit to enjoy the sky; but as they entered the outskirts of the city, he reconsidered the decision. He reached up and twisted a glowing orange knob on a panel above his head. The cockpit brightened considerably. The added light was a small comfort to the crew in the growing dusk. Next to Oa, Kai steadily guided the ARI's flight toward her lost home.

"Are you sure we are heading the right way?" Kai asked for the fourth time since they left the lightning forest.

"We are still heading in the correct direction," Fred informed her. Oa had been watching Kai periodically throughout the flight. They had been traveling for most of a cycle. She had relaxed at first, but then her nervous leg twitch started again once they passed into the shadow of the darkened sky.

Oa sensed that her repeated question contained a hidden plea to alter their course and go somewhere else; somewhere that would not force her to accept the events long absent from her mind. *Perhaps she just refuses to remember*, Oa thought to himself. He spun his chair around to see what Susan was doing. Behind the two pilot seats, Susan napped inside her storm simulator, the soft crackles of energy providing a constant ambient noise that grew comforting in the stillness.

"Oa, activate the flood lamp," Ohm commanded calmly, breaking through the young Awoken's silent ruminations. Oa turned back around and began to scan over the numerous controls in front of him. Kai glanced over and pointed at a switch that sat next to a raised circular glowing panel.

"That switch there turns the lamp on. Use the sensor pad next to it to point the beam," Kai instructed curtly. She returned her attention to piloting the ship. Oa sensed a slight strain in Kai's voice. She wasn't her normal cheery self.

Oa flipped the switch on and a bright yellow dot appeared on the glowing white panel next to the switch. Outside the ARI, the flood lamp activated. The iris in the lamp opened releasing the concentrated power of the photorb within. The beam cut through the fog in front of the vessel. Oa placed his finger onto the control pad, and the yellow dot tracked his movements as he traced a path across the pad. The flood lamp obeyed his guiding motions, scanning the space in front of the ARI. The beam was so powerful that the mist fled from its touch, regrouping just outside the periphery of the glow. Oa continued to pan the light back and forth, scanning the area in front of the ship.

Kai reduced the ARI's speed as they hesitantly crept through the darkness. "It's so thick! We are going to hit something," she said, nervously shifting in her seat.

"We should be above any structures. Oa, focus the lamp beneath us and look for some buildings," Ohm replied, his voice calm.

Oa moved his finger to the bottom of the control pad, adjusting the flood lamp so that it pointed down from its mount at a sharp angle. He slid his finger back and forth, cutting wide swaths through the haze as he searched for any signs of the city. For a long time, nothing happened. He considered asking Fred how many weebles had passed when suddenly, he noticed a hesitant metallic gleam through the fumes.

"There!" Oa exclaimed, pointing toward the faint sheen. Kai responded quickly. She brought the ARI around and pointed it at the spot that Oa was illuminating with the floodlight.

"It's definitely the top of a building. Nice work, Oa. We're in the city!" Kai said with a mixture of thrill and apprehension. She eased the ship down and sailed alongside the superstructure. As they passed by, Oa illuminated the architecture, revealing a large metal tower. Its surface glinted eerily in the light and appeared to be undamaged. There were no signs of aging. Immaculate window panes reflected the disk shaped vessel as it slowly passed by. The fog oozed back into place behind the ship, reclaiming the tower in its jealous grasp.

Kai increased the ARI's speed slightly. Then she leaned her left hand forward in the control dome, swooping down into the city. All around them, abandoned spires of the once great metropolis seemed to rise up out of the mist, watching over their journey like silent sentinels from the past. Oa aimed the flood lamp at several of the towers they passed. Each one appeared untouched. The alloys were untarnished and not a single window was cracked or shattered. He illuminated a bridge stretching between two of the buildings. Oddly, not all of the fog dispersed. Several patches of the murky shadow remained, lingering in the light. Oa did not have time to point out the shadows, as Kai drifted under the crossway. She turned the ship to the left passing between another two towers. The pristine stillness was eerie, as Oa had expected to see desolate ruins, not a completely intact city.

"I didn't know finding my old place would be so easy. I only see like … seven buildings, maybe? Four hundred at most," Kai joked, attempting to lighten the foreboding mood that had settled amidst the crew of the ARI. Oa was glad her jovial side couldn't be contained by the gloom outside for long.

"Fred has begun collecting data on the shroud surrounding the city, and he believes the ARI's scanners can pinpoint its source. We will start our search there" Ohm said. His voice had grown colder to match the mist hovering outside the hull. "It seems the focal point spreads out in a nature very akin to that of an explosion."

"Explosion? Everything is undamaged, Ohm. What are you talking about?" Oa asked, confused.

"I don't understand yet either, Oa. There was only one weapon that could have done something like this. We need to find the center of the blast. The view screen in front of you will direct us to the focal point. Fred has input the parameters for the scan," Ohm replied somberly.

Kai looked over at Oa. He shrugged, not knowing what weapon Ohm was talking about. Then he remembered Ohm's revelation about Cale and Jess. *Could their research be involved somehow?* he thought. This was not the aftermath of catastrophe Oa had imagined when Ohm told him Istaar had been destroyed.

"Alright, but remember we are still going to find Kai's friends, Ohm. That was part of the deal. Kai, I think we should come back around that tower and head the other way because these buildings are getting shorter. We don't want to go too far from the center of the city," Oa said.

After a moment, Ohm responded. "I have a hunch that both Cale and Jess will be at the source of this shroud."

All this must be related to the research he was referring to, Oa thought to himself. He looked over at Kai. Her heel was bouncing nervously again. He turned to the view screen on the console in front of him. The ARI was depicted as a little blue dot at the center of the screen. The cityscape was depicted by grey outlines. Around the ARI, numerous pulsing red lines permeated the city. The lines jaggedly traced the explosion's signature that Fred had taught the ship to read. Oa realized that the lines flowed together, all heading toward a singular point of origin. He followed the trail, guiding Kai through the city toward the epicenter of the blast. Suddenly, their destination appeared on the screen, a chaotic jumble of red so thick it looked solid. From within the node, every trace of the mysterious explosion emitted out to the ends of the city.

"We are approaching the source of whatever Fred is tracking. It's coming from within a squat, round structure just past those three towers," Oa said, pointing ahead.

Kai banked the ARI to the left, arcing around the farthest spire Oa had pointed to. She pulled back on the speed adjustor, bringing her ship to a halt. As they hovered in midair, Oa pointed the flood lamp at three towers curved in a half circle. Each structure had a giant metal glyph on it. From left to right, the glyphs read 'UNI'. He tilted the beam down below the superstructures to where a squat round building stood on a single metal pillar rising out of the ground. The upper architecture consisted of a broad flat disk with six pods hanging from its edges. The pods appeared to be a mishmash of cubes, collaged together. The rooftop was marked with yellow guides that Oa assumed indicated landing zones. He aimed the lamp at the center of the guides.

"We should land there, Kai. This has to be the where Fred's scans are leading us to," Oa said, looking over at Kai. She sat motionless, staring at the building.

"Kai," Ohm's voice cut through the silence.

Kai jumped slightly. "Sorry Ohm. I just remembered this place ... I think."

Oa could see that the eeriness of the city was getting to Kai so he reached over and put a hand on her shoulder. "Nothing seems to be damaged here. Maybe whatever caused this mist only concealed Istaar and did no harm. Awoken might still be here somewhere. Cale and Jess could still be alright," he insisted reassuringly. *Ohm might be mistaken. Something is definitely wrong here, but Awoken could still be alive. I don't see a reason for them to be dead,* he reasoned to himself.

The landing pads extended from the bottom of the ARI, and Kai set the ship down within the perimeter of the guides. It settled with a slight bump. The safety restraints retracted off of the crew, and Oa reached forward to shut off the floodlight. Immediately, darkness surged back around the hull. Oa got up out of the chair and walked back to turn off Susan's storm simulator.

"Come on, Susan; it's time to help Kai find her friends," Oa said, waking up the varl. Susan uncurled out into the cockpit and filled the space as she stretched out lazily. She reared her head up and yawned. Her whole body lit up with new energy. Oa shoved the giant creature down the hallway, snickering. "There's no time for all that. We have to be quick." He looked back to see Kai slowly getting out of her pilot's seat; he waited for her to catch up. "It's going to be alright, Kai. You have Ohm and I to watch your back, no matter what we find in there." Kai nodded silently and they followed Susan down the corridor.

They arrived in the power-hub chamber to find Susan already floating eagerly by the exit. As Ohm stood up out of his mechanical throne, Fred disconnected from the ship. The lights overhead dimmed slightly as the ARI entered into a dormant state, in order to conserve the power it had stored up during the flight.

Ohm leaned forward slightly and rolled his shoulders as if to adjust the weight of Fred on his back. "We are going to need some way of navigating through the mist outside."

Oa called Seeker from its satchel. The little orb leaped to his hand. "That's easy. I will just make Seeker glow really bright."

Ohm shot a look at him. "You can try, but if Fred says it is drawing power from the Void then you must stop."

Kai looked back and forth at both of them. "I don't get it. What's the worst that little ball can do?"

"Ohm and Fred believe that some of Seeker's abilities can be traced by the Legion. But we're in this thick haze, and we need a light. I think we will be fine," Oa explained optimistically. He levitated the silver orb in his palm. *Seeker knows how to glow, I have seen it when I heal.* He willed the strange device to become luminous. The orb responded slowly, growing brighter as he focused. The light cast the group's shadow up against the chamber walls. Seeker's blaze filled the room, until even the shadows where lit.

"A happy medium between complete darkness and blinding light will suffice," Fred remarked dryly.

"I can dim it, of course," Oa laughed. With a thought, he diminished Seeker's light, reducing it to a comfortable glow.

"That's gonna work fine," Kai said. She clapped Oa on the back then turned toward the exit. "Well, all my preparation and work rebuilding the ARI has led me here. I have two new friends supporting me and the greatest varl ever. I'm ready." She walked over to the door, opened it, and walked out. Susan followed, floating just behind her.

Oa looked at Ohm. "Is there a chance her friends are alright?"

"With those two, anything is possible," Ohm replied warmly.

They walked out to the open deck and joined Susan and Kai on the ARI's exit ramp. Kai reached over and pulled a heavy lever on the hull. With a whirr of turning gears, the deck lowered them down. They stepped off the ramp, looking around in silence at the rooftop they had landed on. The access ramp folded up behind them with a heavy thump. Seeker illuminated a decent portion of the landing zone around them but not enough to see the edges of the structure. The fog isolated them in a cocoon of light.

"Well, we sure got off to a roaring start; but what now?" Ohm asked. "Fred can't get us any closer to the source because he claims to be too accurate." He reached back and patted the pack condescendingly.

"The source of the explosion is everywhere around us. According to my readings, once the explosion was initiated, each point of space in the vicinity of this building simultaneously became the source of the blast. It is unlikely that I would guess the exact point that started the chain of events," Fred countered defensively.

"A lightning varl can find the source," Kai replied quietly as she stroked Susan's head. "Thank you for leading us here Fred. I would never have found this place without your theory. Cale and Jess seem to be involved in this. I want to know what part they played."

"You're welcome," Fred replied as warmly as his monotone voice would allow.

Kai reached down and grabbed a tiny chunk of metal from a pocket in her baggy jumpsuit. She held it up to Susan. The object was a small cube carved with intricate symbols too minuscule for Oa to read from where he stood. "This used to be Cale's. He carved it for Jess. She gave it to me just before—before ..." Kai let her words trail off as she struggled to remember.

Kai shook her head once in agitation, as if she were trying to rattle the memories loose. She gave up and continued to speak, ignoring the gaps in her story. "Susan can track anything," Kai explained as Susan took the cube in her paws. Power swelled from deep within her chest and pulsed once, coursing down to her two paws. There was a loud crack and a flash of light. Susan dropped the little cube to the ground then gracefully glided across the surface of the roof, pressing her paws to the ground at regular intervals. Her pads filled with energy, which sizzled and cracked in the air.

At first, nothing happened. Susan thoroughly investigated around the immediate vicinity of the group. Suddenly, her search yielded success. As her paw lightly tapped the ground for the umpteenth time, a coil of purple energy sprang out, arcing along the ground away from of the group. The sparks died out after a short distance. Susan floated in the direction the energy had gone. She pressed her paw to the ground lightly and several more tendrils of violet lightning darted out, leading toward the edge of the roof. The ARI's crew followed silently as the varl moved away from the ship. Seeker floated above Oa's outstretched hand, providing a soft warm glow that parted the mist ahead of the their steps.

They had not been walking long, when they came upon a round white depression in the seamless reflective gray material that made up the top of the architecture. At the center of the sunken platform sat a head sized black dome. Susan stopped next to the black dome. She turned back to the group and let out a growl, power rumbled in her throat.

Oa looked to the boundary of Seeker's light, but he still could not tell how close to the edge they were. *We should be directly over one of the hanging structures by now*, he guessed. Kai stepped down onto the white platform. Immediately, the black dome lit up, projecting rays of green light up onto her. Oa was startled and staggered back slightly. Ohm seemed unfazed by the event. The emerald beams traced Kai's outline, mapping her body completely.

"It's just a lock. Hopefully Kai is one of the keys," Ohm explained quietly to Oa. The dome gave an affirmative beep. The rays blinked yellow and disappeared. The platform rotated slightly. A sequence of faint thuds reverberated through the ground as bolts drew back, unlocking the door. Oa heard a slight hiss as air long trapped within the dwelling escaped. The platform began to lower down into the floor with Kai standing resolutely at its center.

"Better get on now unless you want to jump," she called. Ohm quickly stepped onto the descending platform. Oa followed, hopping down. Susan shrunk back to her normal size to fit with the group on the elevator. She nuzzled Kai's hand with the tip of her snout, looking for attention. Kai reached up and lightly stroked the lightning varl's head between her pointy ears. The creature curled up in contented bliss. Oa looked around, curious to see what they were headed into. There was nothing to see as the platform continued to drop down the shaft. As they descended, the walls lit up in a cool white glow. Above them, a secondary door slid shut closing them off from the outside world. The loss of a clear exit worried Oa, but he didn't voice his concern.

The platform dropped out of the shaft, lowering into the center of a dark room. Seeker's light did not reveal anything, causing Oa to wonder just how spacious the place was. He noted that the mist was also with them inside the dwelling. The gloom stalked around the edges of Seeker's light, concealing the full extent of the room. The elevator softly landed in the center of an open plaza. A soft white glow spread from where the group stood, gradually flowing through every surface of the chamber. The fog melted away to reveal numerous flights of stairs that branched out from the plaza. Some steps climbed upwards and others descended below. The glow spread across the steps, reaching various antechambers that populated the interior of the structure's shell. The rooms were various shapes and sizes, and some protruded further into the main chamber than others. Eventually, every surface was lit: walls, floors, and ceilings. Not a trace of the mist could be found. Oa slipped Seeker back into the satchel at his side. He decided that the complex hive of odd rooms and stairs must be one of the strange hanging pods they had seen from the ARI.

"Omni-glow alloy? I haven't seen this in a long time," Ohm said softly. Kneeling down, he brushed his bandaged stump over the luminous floor. Oa noticed that Ohm's hand strayed to the strand around his neck again. Ohm stood up quickly. "Lead on, Susan," he said. His voice seemed to warm with the light of the room.

Susan uncurled and renewed her hunt, tracking the purple sparks as they bounced from her paws. She led them across the plaza to a set of stairs. These stairs led straight up to a completely enclosed room that hung from the ceiling. Susan floated upwards, tapping several of the steps to make sure she was still hot on the trail. She was followed by Ohm, Oa, and then Kai. At the top of the stairs was a short landing which led to the only entrance into the tear-drop shaped chamber. Susan and Ohm walked through the door without pause. As he reached the top, Oa turned and looked back. Kai was a few steps behind, her head hung down.

"I don't want to go in there," Kai said quietly.

Oa could hear the fear and hesitation in her voice. Questions nagged at him. Where had the Awoken of Istaar disappeared to? Who was responsible? Instinct told Oa that answers lay in the room ahead. Despite his burning curiosity, he still felt uneasy about the nature of the answers, for Kai's sake.

"A part of me doesn't want to know either, Kai. I want Cale and Jess to be alright. I don't want to see your hopes dashed. Ohm says I have the ability to believe things will turn out alright no matter what happens. I think you are similar. No matter what we find in there, it's going to be okay," Oa said comfortingly. He paused and waited while Kai considered his words.

"We will see about that, Oa," Kai said wryly. She looked up at the entrance, her visual receptors bright and ready. "I have to know either way. I dragged all of us here, after all." She walked up the stairs and brushed past Oa into the room. He turned and walked in behind her. He looked over her shoulder at the chamber's interior.

Ohm stood to the side of the door. His blue ocular plate was dim, and his hand clenched his ruined arm tightly. Susan floated next to him, her head held up nobly, her task complete. The lit room was a workshop similar to Kai's. The shelves were clean and all the tools had been put back into the storage hatches that lined the walls. There was no more work to be done, the tools were no longer needed. Only two things remained in the vacant room. The first was a metal birth cell resting in the direct center of the chamber. It did not glow as the other surfaces in the room did. The cell was scorched black, and the hatch laid open. Oa observed that the cell was much bulkier than his own. Extra sheets of alloy had been grafted onto it like armor. The second thing in the room was far stranger. The sight disturbed Oa. On the ground, next to the birth cell, a cloud of haze refused to disperse with the light. At first glance, it seemed merely to be an amorphous cloud of fog. As Oa looked closer, he realized with horror that it had a shape. The shape of two figures. *Cale and Jess*, he thought to himself with grim certainty. The figures where kneeling on the floor facing each other, arms clasped around each other in a final embrace. Kai walked over to the mist. She dropped down to her knees next to the apparition. Ohm stood in silence, his head bowed. Oa walked over and stood next to Kai, looking down at the strange figures in the mist.

"Where did they go?" Kai asked. The sight of her lost friends released the holds on her mind. Memories poured forth as she reached out to try and touch the spectral images. "There was so much confusion. They told me we would see each other again after it was all over. I waited in my birth cell until it was safe to come out but there was no one. Just this ..." she trailed off, motioning to the fleeting echo of her former friends: her family. "There wasn't even a soul ember left to hold." Her voice broke slightly.

Susan rested her head on Kai's shoulder, sharing in her friend's grief for a moment. Then she glided over to the far wall. Susan pawed at the omni-glow alloy as she traced another trail. She uttered a thunderous roar and lightning leaped from her mouth, tearing open a gash in the wall. Startled, the Awoken looked over at the varl. Susan had burned away a fake wall revealing a concealed cubby. Inside the slot sat another black dome, similar to the lock at the entrance. It activated automatically, casting light out into the room. This time instead of scanning the group for a key, the light formed two outlines.

Oa recognized the shapes as Awoken. The taller one began to speak. His was a bold and educated voice, though it was tainted with worry and urgency.

"We don't have much time left, but if you have found this, Kai, then you are safe. That is all that matters to us at this point. You need to know what happened and how sorry we are. This new job was so alluring, a chance to study and create technology reverse-engineered from the remains of the Destroyer. That is what we were told. We jumped at the chance to work on something we thought was only legend."

"It was as if we were living in one of the overused and long-worded stories Instructor Ohm used to tell us at the academy," the second figure added in a kind and spirited female voice. Ohm gave a derisive cough at the statement.

"Our curiosity was naïve though, Kai. They only wanted us to weaponize our findings. We tried to get out of the project; but they threatened us, saying they would use you if we left, so we built the weapon. We tried to convince them it was dangerous, but we knew they meant to use it no matter what we said. We can't let them win. We have to destroy it before they have a chance to use it on a large scale. We engineered a remote containment field to hold the blast. We had to sneak over to the lab to place the field projector, but we will be right here next to you when we detonate it. There is a chance the fission will tear through our containment field; this whole place would be caught in the center of it …" the voice paused, "well, we just hope we are there to greet you when you step out of your reinforced birth cell. We redesigned it to withstand the Void itself.

You will be safe no matter what happens. If for some reason our efforts fail and we aren't there when you emerge, please know that you are the most special Awoken we have ever met. You're always so eager and ready to learn. We know you will do amazing things. Be safe, Kai," the figure said with a wave. *That must be Cale*, Oa decided.

"Hey, sorry about the stasis ring knockout," the second figure apologized sheepishly. "We knew you would pull some crazy stunt if we told you beforehand. You can be mad at us later. Don't worry, though; nothing is gonna happen. No problem has outsmarted us yet. Cale is just being a wimp," The female voice added with a lighthearted laugh. *Jess*, Oa thought to himself. He heard sadness hidden in her voice. Jess spoke again, her words sincere and warm, "We love you Kai; remember that." The image of the two Awoken froze for a moment, then the light flickered and died.

Kai got up and walked out of the room. Susan followed closely, sensing Kai's distress. Oa stayed, staring at the specters of Cale and Jess.

"Ember fission—a piece of the Destroyer's power. It annihilates only the Awoken. Cale and Jess were brilliant, but I didn't teach them enough. There was no way they could have known it would engulf the entire city. Their containment field was no match for the raw power of the ember fission bomb they must have made. The city will be forever covered in the shadow of that blast. These reflections of the Awoken are burned into place for the remainder of time," Ohm said sadly as he motioned toward the fallen figures.

"Kai refused to accept it," Oa said, kneeling next to Cale and Jess. His head bowed with crestfallen realization. "It must have driven her mad—finding this, only to then spend countless cycles wandering blindly through the fog as she tried to escape the city. Her dead friends were probably the only thing she was able to see in the darkness."

Oa and Ohm walked out to the landing at the top of the stairs. Down below, Kai sat on the edge of the plaza, looking around at what used to be her home. Susan rested next to Kai, tail curled around her comfortingly.

"She never could have made it out on her own. Susan must have found Kai and guided her out of the mist," Ohm reasoned.

"Susan flew her away from this," Oa said softly as he recalled Kai's tale of her first encounter with the lightning varl.

"Now that Kai has closure about the fate of her friends, she needs a new purpose," Ohm said. He turned and looked at Oa intently.

"I understand," Oa replied knowingly. He was about to walk down to Kai, but he turned back to Ohm. They needed to discuss the implications Istaar had on their ultimate goals before he could hope to comfort his friend with a clear mind.

"It seems like Eol was not involved in this. It was a weapon made from the Destroyer ..." Oa theorized, pausing in thought to contemplate any possible answers to the puzzle. "Now I know you say they're crazy, but the writings in Bolleworth did seem to link the Destroyer and Eol."

Ohm gazed around the spacious dwelling, then down at Kai again. She had not moved. "The original Destroyer is gone, but I am afraid you're onto something. The oracle's ravings may hold some truth. Fred has been analyzing this place since we arrived. Now before I continue, you should know that nothingness has always surrounded our world—but only recently has it come alive," Ohm explained. He grew somber as he unveiled his theory. "This mist is composed of an emptiness; blank spaces in existence. Hidden within, is a clue to the nature of Eol. Notice how this black fog moves, as if it has an instinctive consciousness of its own. This Void is not like the lifeless abyss of old. This is a Void like Eol, not the same but a close and primitive relative. If this prototype Void was birthed from ember-fission technology, Eol might have been created in a similar, more controlled circumstance."

"Eol was created," Oa asked baffled.

"I can not be sure yet," Ohm replied. He stopped looking down at Kai and glanced toward Oa. Their gazes locked. "I am uncertain how factual the stories of the Enlightened are, but one thing is certain—many Awoken have been making pilgrimages to the Enlightened City to start new lives. If knowledge of other ember-fission experiments still exists, it will be found there."

Oa nodded. The mystery of Eol was beginning to come together. He wanted to discuss the topic further, but he remembered Kai. Mysteries and plans could wait. His grieving friend was what mattered most. He turned from Ohm and walked down the stairs to the plaza. The young Awoken sat down next to Kai and Susan. His feet dangled off the edge of the deck. Down below, a web of catwalks connected the various chambers. The trio sat together for a long time. Oa did not want to speak. He knew nothing needed to be said yet, and so he just sat. It was a simple act, the best method he could think of to remind Kai that she was not alone. At first, Oa had to work to quiet his mind, to let go of his speculations regarding Eol and the Legion. Then he found himself trying to track the time, wishing he had a pack like Fred to count the weebles his mind was experiencing. Quickly, he let go of the notion, refocussing on Kai. He joined her vigil with both his body and mind, letting his thoughts clear until he sat in total serenity. Time passed unmeasured by the group as they rested in silence. Ohm watched from the doorway to the lab above. Eventually, instinct prompted Oa to place his hand on Kai's shoulder.

"You said I should hope even though I have always known deep down what happened. And for a moment, I did, Oa. I just don't know what purpose that hope serves if it's still crushed in the end," Kai admitted sadly.

"Want to see something weird?" Oa asked changing the subject. He had no answer for her. She didn't need one.

Kai turned. "I guess."

Oa pulled up the tunic draped over his shoulders. "Look, I don't have a soul ember. Bizarre, huh?"

Kai stared in puzzlement. "Yeah, that is pretty strange," she agreed, slightly more engaged.

"Ohm says I'm special or something. That I might be the first Awoken ever made, and that I've got a gift. I sometimes wonder what good gifts are if they can't be used fully or if they ultimately fail. I suppose in the end it could all lead nowhere. When I'm gone, that's it. I won't leave behind an ember," Oa admitted, drawing a parallel between his life and the life of Kai's friends. He turned and looked at her.

"While I am here, I want to make this place better, the way Cale and Jess did by saving you. I won't run from the Legion forever. I want to fight back, to resist Eol. He is hindering my gift, and he is hindering this whole world. I want to defeat him and help make things better to honor the memory of lost Awoken, like Cale and Jess," Oa said, pulling out the bag of soul embers from his satchel. He loosened the drawstring to show Kai its contents.

"I started by stealing these embers from Eol. We are taking them to the Enlightened City to see if the Awoken there will help us fight him. Rumors say they are great warriors," Oa explained. "So, do you still want to help us get there after all this?"

Kai stared down at the embers for a moment before she looked back up at Oa. Her visual receptors glowed warmly. "Of course I do; don't be stupid. I'm the one with the ship, right? How else are you guys gonna get there? Some dumb water jet?" she joked, shoving Oa lightly. Passion returned to her voice. "Count me in. You guys are my friends now. I want to help protect the Awoken, even if it means taking a bunch of shiny rocks to some random place we have only heard rumors of, so we can fight an unstoppable monster."

Oa chuckled. "Thanks, Kai. I'm so glad we met you." He hugged her gratefully.

Ohm jogged down the steps. He strode over to the elevator platform in the center of the plaza. "Actually, our ultimate mission can wait a bit longer. Let's go find another lightning forest. I have something to show you two. We are in much less of a rush to get to the city now that we have the ARI," he said warmly. As Ohm stood waiting, the rest of the crew got up and walked over to meet him on the center of the lift.

"I disagree, the constant advance of the Void requires us to expedite our journey to the Enlightened City," Fred said, expressing monotonous concern.

"That is pure, weapons-grade malarkey, Fred. It is because the universe is collapsing that we should spend some time showing our friends something fantastic," Ohm teased, turning Fred's cherished word against him.

The platform began to rise back up into the ceiling, returning them to the world above. Kai looked over the edge. "Goodbye," Oa heard her whisper.

He moved to stand closer to her. "Don't worry, there is always still time for a happy ending," he said reassuringly.

"Ha! You and that hope stuff," Kai laughed, slowly shaking her head.

"It's why I keep him around. I discovered I am quite fond of his naive attitude. I certainly get none of Oa's cheer from Fred, the potentate of damp jackets," Ohm joked.

They rose up through the dwellings entry portal, back out into the darkness. Oa called Seeker to his hand and led the group home in silence.

Back aboard the ARI they all stood out on the open deck, basking in the soft orange glow of the ship's lighting. Behind them the ramp closed shut.

"Why are we going to another lightning forest?" Kai asked Ohm.

"To use that equipment there to make some atter," Ohm replied, pointing to the controls of the mechanical metal arm that rested in a folded position on the support struts above their heads.

"Of course, atter ..." Kai said. She paused to let her sarcasm sink in before asking, "What is atter?"

"You will find out when we get there," Ohm replied secretively.

"Fine," Kai huffed impatiently. "Oa, it's your turn to drive."

"Thanks! I do want to fly recklessly fast through this fog," Oa admitted enthusiastically.

Even with the boisterous statement, no one moved to go inside; they all stood in silence, held fast by the dismal aura of the city.

"Let's go already! I want to see what the big crane on the roof does," Kai said loudly, ruining the stillness.

All at once, everyone returned to themselves and hurried back to familiarity. Ohm and Fred regally sat down into the power hub, reconnecting to the ARI and bringing all the ship's systems online. Oa rushed past them to the cockpit and threw himself into the pilot's chair as Kai and Susan flooded in after him. Kai sat down in the copilot's chair. Susan floated between the pair, eager to be a part of the flight. Oa had them in the air before Fred could activate the restraint harnesses. The safety straps clipped into place as Fred rushed to catch up on his flight protocol check list.

"Which way do we go?" Oa asked.

"According to the our scanners, the closest lightning forest is directly behind us," Ohm informed him.

"Then let's get out of this city!" Kai said, eager to be far away from Istaar. She activated the flood lamp to light their way. Oa spun the ARI around then shoved the throttle, sending the ship hurtling though Istaar.

Oa corkscrewed past the towers and bridges as the thrill of flying rushed through the crew. Kai kept the flood lamp pointed dead ahead to reveal objects they were about to crash into. Oa let out a whoop as they cleared the edge of the metro. Fractions of a weeble later, they burst forth from the thick fog back into the world. Skylight returned, brightening the cockpit with glorious shades of rosy pink, revealing a new cycle. Oa had no idea how many cycles they had been gone. Straight ahead of them lay rolling dunes of fine gray sand.

"Lightning forest dead ahead," Kai called out. Far off in the distance, a brightly glowing maroon beam rose up to the sky out of the windswept dunes. The peak towered over the horizon behind the forest.

"This is one of my favorite places in the world," Ohm said.

"The energy flow is truly intricate and remarkable," Fred agreed.

Filled with eager anticipation, Oa edged the throttle to near maximum as he roared over the dunes. Down below, the reflective sand gleamed beautifully in the sky light. They sailed over valleys and ridges. Susan peered out of the window, her deep violet eyes ever watchful of the horizon. They sat in silence, gazing at the beauty before them. As they neared the column of fire, Oa realized that this forest was different. Instead of one stream of light splitting into many, the maroon forest was made up of numerous stems of lightning. The roots rose up from the ground, weaving in and out of each other to create a mighty pillar that seemed to hold up the sky.

"Anchor us just off the ground, as close as you can to the branch right there," Ohm instructed, pointing out a root rising out of the ridge closest to them. Kai quickly located the spot Ohm was referring to and pointed it out to Oa. He slowed the ARI and cruised casually over a shallow valley in the sand. The far end of the basin rose up into a smooth winding ridge. The root they were heading toward sizzled up out of the hilltop. The sand around the base of the stem pulsed a deep red as the energy of the forest flowed through it. Oa halted the ARI as close as he could to the crackling pillar. Fred shut of the engines and released the restraint harnesses. Oa spun his chair around and hopped out of the seat, exiting the bridge ahead of Kai and Susan.

Ohm was already out on the deck of the ship, standing next to the forward support strut. He was fiddling with the buttons and knobs on the control panel attached to the metal pillar. Oa noticed the sling Ohm had set up for himself.

"Hey, you finished it," he said pointing to the fabric stung up between the two support beams on the deck.

"With little time to spare—Fred says there is a high probability that I have a sleep approaching—but before that happens, I want to show you both how to make some atter," Ohm replied. He grabbed a tiny mechanical arm on the control panel that Oa noticed was a replica of the crane above the deck. Ohm unfolded the mini appendage, and immediately the crane over their heads began to unfold as well. The ancient machinery creaked and groaned; but it moved smoothly, mimicking the position of the miniaturette was Ohm adjusting. He rotated the crane to point toward the branch and extended the end. Overhead, the automated crane extended out toward the pulsing energy stream until its claw was just barely touching the stem. The whole contraption started to hum as the power of the forest began to flow through it.

"Now that I have made the connection, neither of you should mess with the positioning. I spent heaps of weebles perfecting the proper placement of an atter gatherer. You're both lucky I'm around. Otherwise you would have to mix with impure energy. The only things you are allowed to touch are the mixing controls," Ohm instructed them sternly.

Oa knocked his hand against the metal support strut he was leaning against, making a loud interrupting clang. "Ohm, what's atter?" he asked impatiently.

Kai was sitting with her back against the railing as she stroked Susan's head. She raised her hand. "I already asked that question and I'm still waiting in suspense for an answer."

"Ill-mannered class," Ohm muttered to himself shaking his head. "I was getting to that part. Mixing atter is the ancient art of harnessing the natural life energy of these forests and experiencing it directly. You trap the energy with the device above and adjust the frequencies you collect. Once your atter is complete, you absorb it; and the energy passes into your veins. The experience is quite unique. This skill has been lost to the rest of the world for a long time, but I built my own atter gatherer up on the roof so I would not forget about it," he said, reminiscing about his old hobby.

"Come on over here, and let me show you both how to make some. Then I'm going to collapse on this sling," he said waving Oa and Kai over to the control panel.

They walked over and looked at the console. Other than the miniature crane, there were not many other controls: six rotating knobs and a single button.

"These six frequency adjustors will allow you to distort and select the different types of energy being harvested. That big button activates the collection channels and will send the harvested energy over there," Ohm said, motioning to the other support strut on the deck. "When the process is done, just grab the little atter orb in your hand and apply some pressure to it. The energy will disperse into your body," he paused to make sure they understood. "Alright, I'm going to go lay down now." Ohm walked over to the sling he had strung up. Without hesitation the old Awoken collapsed back onto it.

"Can I try it first?" Oa asked Kai.

"Sure, why not? I'm in no rush. It looks like we have plenty of time to use it," Kai said, shrugging. They both peered around the beam to see that Ohm was already motionless in the sling, asleep. Oa followed Ohm's instructions, and began to fiddle with the frequency adjustors. There was a small screen on the control panel, and it displayed the different wave patterns being adjusted. Oa tried to adjust the waves so that they flowed in a coherent harmony with one another. He decided there was no way to know the quality of his efforts until he tried the atter out. He pressed the lone button and the hum of the crane became a loud whine for a moment as the accumulated energy drained down to the containment unit on the other support strut. Oa and Kai strode over to the other side of the deck. They looked into the solidly built canister bolted to the metal beam. A thick cable snaked out of the canister up to the crane. There was a single switch on the side of the canister. Oa flipped it, and the container popped open. Inside were several nodes similar to the ones in Susan's storm simulator, each of them faced in toward an amorphous blob of energy floating in the center of the cramped container.

Oa reached in and grabbed the bubble. When nothing happened, he pulled the blob out for further inspection. The partially transparent globule had a bright blue hue. The inside appeared to be flowing like liquid. He squeezed the bubble tightly, and it burst into a tight cloud of sparks and light that dissolved into his hand. He found that his mind did not have a word to describe the experience. He strained briefly, trying to think of the right word. Then suddenly, it came to him: taste! *I am tasting it*, Oa thought to himself. The sensation was so strange that he decided he needed to try it again once Kai had had a turn.

"Give it a try, Kai," Oa said excitedly. "It's the strangest feeling. I still don't really know how to describe it."

"Looks weird. Alright, I will give it a shot," Kai said. She rushed over to the control board and began randomly spinning the knobs. Oa flipped the switch back up, and the canister snapped shut. After a fraction of the time Oa had spent making his atter, Kai slapped the button, sending a new stream of energy down from the crane. She rushed back over to the canister. Oa opened it, revealing a muddy brown glob of energy. Kai grabbed it and pulled it out. She squeezed it like Oa had; and, as expected it burst into light and sparks but with the unexpected addition of some foul looking smoke.

"Bleah!" Kai exclaimed as she rolled around on the deck. "That's the most disgusting thing ever." Oa laughed, and Susan perked up from her spot by the railing. She surveyed the antics for a moment then, deeming them unworthy of her attention, the lightning varl laid her head back down, returning to the quiet serenity she had been enjoying.

Oa tried the machine again, this time his efforts produced a deep green atter. He gave the atter to Kai, who enjoyed it much more than her previous attempt. The two friends spent the majority of that cycle creating different types of atter. It was quickly discovered that Oa better understood how to use the equipment, although Kai had several successful attempts that did not leave them both rolling around the deck in disgust.

They were so involved in their newfound hobby that they did not notice the mutterings of Ohm in his sleep. "You're here ... glowing red, shrouded in shadow, but it saved you? ... No, I saved us … We are safe … Soon everyone will be as well." His words were anxious and erratic.

When Ohm finally woke up, neither Kai nor Oa noticed as he rolled off of the sling and walked over to the railing next to Susan. Ohm looked back at Oa and Kai who were engaged in their next great masterpiece at the control board.

"They are enjoying this so much. Let us give them one more gift of the past," Ohm suggested wistfully to Fred the pack.

He dropped off of the railing; and as always, Fred's sharp reflexes activated the aqua jet before they could fall far. The pair flew out to the middle of the valley hovering far above the sand.

"Fred, let's run a full-capacity fusion," Ohm called over the noise of the aqua jet.

"Understood. Activating full fusion now," Fred replied.

Fred lit up brightly, shining like a blue star over the valley of dust. Water thundered down from Fred's jet, increasing in volume exponentially. The liquid pooled below, spreading rapidly to fill the wide trough. Back on the ARI, Oa and Kai heard the roar and rushed to the railing to see what was going on. They stared in wonder at the brilliant blue light glowing from atop a column of water that coursed into the dunes. Before long, the whole valley was filled to its brim with crystal-clear liquid. The maroon light of the forest danced across the water's surface.

In the center of the lake, Fred ceased the full fusion. Ohm rocketed back to the ARI, deactivating the aqua jet just shy of the deck so as not to splash water everywhere. The momentum of Ohm's flight sent him sailing over the railing and onto the deck. As before, he rolled spryly to his feet, completing the well practiced maneuver.

"These dunes are the dust of everything beautiful the Great Planes used to hold, but they can still be a sight worth seeing," Ohm said, pleased with his work.

Oa and Kai nodded silently as they stared in wonder at the lake. After a moment of silence Oa turned and held out his hand. "Here, try this." He offered up the latest atter he and Kai had made.

Ohm took the atter from Oa and crushed it in his hand, absorbing the flavors of energy. His faceplates lit up in surprise. "Either you cheated somehow, or I must have been sleeping quite some time for you two to get this good." Despite the good natured jest, the old Awoken was quite proud of his pupil's efforts.

They all laughed as they climbed up to sit on the deck rail. Their legs dangled down, lightly swinging in the breeze. The group watched the glimmering water below as the wind painted strokes of foamy white crests across the lake

"This is one of those rivers from the stories Cale and Jess used to tell me, isn't it?" Kai asked.

"Sure, why not? It's our very own river," Ohm said amused at Kai's innocence.

Susan peered over the top of the railing. Upon seeing the lake, she soared out into the air. The lighting varl threw back her head and howled to the sky in primal joy. A violet bolt sprang from her mouth, striking upwards in a blinding flash that sent a ripple of her energy coursing through the sky. Susan sped across the water, her body ablaze with amethyst light as she danced about wildly. Her glow mingled with the mirrored image of the forest that flickered out across the waves. Reflections of the past, beauty that had long since faded, played out for the three friends as they sat on the deck of their ship.

EPISODE 08

A HAT FOR ALL OCCASIONS

The three friends sat on the deck's railing, watching Susan play as the lake drained away into the dry and parched dunes.

"That was spectacular. Too bad the water won't stay longer," Oa said, hopping back off of the railing he was perched on.

"Where did all that water go?" Kai asked, gazing longingly at the rapidly dwindling pool far below.

"It runs straight through these dunes. There is no life to hold it so the water just keeps flowing down through the cracked foundation and into the Void below. This world is too close to death to hold any new beauty for long," Ohm responded, a moody undertone creeping into his voice.

"That's a terrible way of looking at things, Ohm. Did Fred calculate that?" Oa asked jokingly as he leaned against the railing

"Actually, Fred and I did spend many weebles recording the decay we were witnessing; and our meticulously crafted projections confirmed its inevitability. We named it the Law of the Void, or Eol's Law as other Awoken now call it. All things unto disorder," Ohm replied evenly.

Oa stood silently, weighing his friend's words. Ohm did not offer any more explanation as he sat silently looking out at the forest. Oa knew he did not have the knowledge to debate

Ohm's theories or Fred's computing skills. He knew that his friend had reason to be disheartened; Ohm's research and warnings had been ignored by past Awoken. *Deep down, he has lost the hope that things can change,* Oa realized. *That is why he comes to such dire conclusions.*

"If that Eol's Law stuff is true, then you did a ton of work for an incredibly useless discovery. Your time would have been better spent making that atter machine easier to operate," Kai teased, shattering the self-importance of Ohm's discovery. "Why didn't you add an alternate setting fo—" she was interrupted as Susan came hurtling back from the dry lake bed, bowling Kai backwards off her perch on the railing. She landed on the deck with a thud.

Kai laughed. "Hold off on the speedy landings, Susan! I am happy to see you, too." She hugged the giant lightning storm of a friend. Susan licked Kai's face then floated over toward Oa in pursuit of more attention.

Oa decided to drop the topic of Eol's Law. He snatched the ornate bag of soul embers from the satchel at his side. "So what is our next move? Are we ready to fly to the Enlightened City?" he asked. Susan had reached him; and she nudged his hand until he patted her head, ruffling her thick, puffy ears.

Ohm swung his legs back over the railing and hopped down. He walked over to Oa and grabbed the bag. He tossed it in the air. "Not quite yet, there are still some interesting places to visit. Places that have Awoken. Awoken who possess information. We need information," Ohm outlined as he looked over at Oa.

Oa nodded remembering their discussion about the possible existence of more ember-fission labs and Eol's creation.

"Information about what?" Kai asked.

Oa had not wanted to talk about the ember-fission bomb with Kai until he knew exactly what was going on. He didn't want to imply that her friends had a part in creating Eol and the Legion, but there was no avoiding the topic now.

"We think that the experiment Cale and Jess were working on might have something to do with Eol. Other labs with the same research might have existed," he summarized.

Kai's face plate dimmed slightly. "I see …" she paused then perked up. "I guess I'm stuck with you losers, so let's go get whatever information we need to stop the Legion." She reached out and petted Susan's sparking tail as it wound past her. Oa was glad that he met Kai. Even though she was saddened at the reminder of her dead friends, he knew she would fight to be a bigger legacy than any of the dangerous experiments Cale and Jess had been a part of.

"So where are we going?" Kai asked, moving past the topic. "I have only been to Istaar and Bolleworth; and other than that Enlightened place Oa mentioned, I don't know of any other cites."

"Well, seeing as you turned my old hat closet into a storm simulator for Susan, I think we should start at the Careening City of Artisans. I can begin rebuilding my collection there," Ohm said jovially as he tossed the bag of soul embers back to Oa.

"That's a weird name. Cities don't usually move, do they?" Oa asked, curious about the strange title.

"This is a flying city. It has a very literal name. The residents are not known for their nomenclature or their piloting abilities," Fred informed Oa dryly.

"Though they are fantastically artistic. It is a great place really," Ohm noted.

"Sounds mildly interesting, but I don't think it's going to be cooler than our river," Kai said dubiously as she headed back to the cockpit. Susan perked up at Kai's exit. She whizzed around in a tight circle and bolted after Kai. Oa heard Kai's exclamations of protest as the speeding lighting varl crashed into her somewhere inside the ARI. Oa took one last look at the maroon forest then he followed Ohm, who was also heading to the power hub. Back at the helm, Oa saw that Kai had already taken the pilot seat, so he plopped down into the copilot's chair. He looked at the scanner, but there wasn't anything helpful on the screen.

"How are we going to find this runaway city, Ohm?" he asked.

"I installed a transceiver on Fred a while back when ray-com was a big hit among the Awoken. Everyone used to broadcast all sorts of things through the air on rays of light. Most of that technology has died out and become obsolete, but an old acquaintance of mine lives in the Careening City. He never lost the habit of broadcasting the city's coordinates whenever it moves. According to his last transmission, the city is located at (64.34,-39.8); I will relay the coordinates to your screen. We don't have time for me to teach you the grid system that the maps run off of, so don't ask, Oa," Ohm explained, pretending that he didn't want to teach the skill of map reading.

Oa laughed. "That's fine, Ohm. Your lectures are a bit lengthy. We should get going, since the world is ending and all." He watched the coordinates pop up as a red dot on the screen in front of him. They needed to get beyond the forest and head off to the left side of the great peak on the horizon.

"Kai, let's swing around this forest and head toward the mountain. I will correct our vector as we get clos—" Oa's directions where cut off by Ohm's harsh command.

"Don't move the ship. Fred, shut down all power, even the hover-anchor. Legion vessels have been detected."

Kai flipped switches all across the control board, and the lights in the cockpit went dark. The engines halted completely. Lifeless, the ARI plummeted from its shallow hover above the dunes.

"I'm glad I didn't repaint this thing," Kai muttered as they dropped. The distance was far enough for the old metal structure to strike the ground heavily. Sand sprayed in all directions from the impact. Inside the bridge, Oa and Kai were flung from their seats. Susan's cushioning tail enlarged and coiled around them both, holding them back before they could smash through the cockpit's forward window pane. Through the hallway, they could hear Ohm crash into the front of the power-hub chamber. The ARI slid forward down the steep dune for a short distance before it halted at a skewed angle, the front of the ship partway buried in the dune. Susan's tail unwound, dumping Oa and Kai back into their seats. The lightning varl whooshed back up the hallway to the power-hub chamber, returning moments later with a slightly battered-looking Ohm in her paws.

"I'm fine Susan, you can let go of me," Ohm said. Susan set the old Awoken down, and he propped himself up in the doorway. "I think we cut the primary power in time. The Legion should fly by overhead and think we are just ruins of some old junker," he assured the crew.

Ohm carefully edged himself down to where Oa and Kai sat. They all peered up out of the forward window. Overhead, squadrons of Legion fighters glided toward the mountain. Oa tracked their vector carefully, noting that the fighters would end up on the opposite side of the mountain they had planned on going to.

"That's a lot of ships. More than I have ever seen," Kai said in awe.

"The Legion is Eol's will or the Void manifested in physical form, depending on who you ask. Their strength grows as the Great Planes fade away. Few are left who care to oppose them," Ohm said quietly.

"Susan can take 'em," Kai scoffed. Behind them Susan growled in agreement.

"What about the Enlightened?" Oa asked.

"They may try, but who knows how true the rumors are? Perhaps it's all fiction to keep the Sleepers and Marauders from venturing too far inland," Ohm replied, shrugging.

They watched the remainder of the Legion fighters pass overhead. Kai spoke up, her voice serious and concerned. "Let's get back in the air. We should warn the Careening City of Artisans, if it's still around. That army is going to be trouble for whatever gets in its way."

"I agree," Ohm said, bounding back up the hallway past Susan. He reattached to the power hub, and Fred reactivated the ARI. The metal groaned slightly as the ship pulled up out of the dune. The fine sand cascaded off the hull as the ARI returned to a hover above the dunes. The engines burned hot and ready. Kai glanced at the navigation chart in front of Oa before sitting back into the pilot's chair. Fred activated the crew's restraint harnesses as Kai navigated around the maroon lightning forest.

Oa looked at the beautiful pillar of nature spanning the distance between the Great Planes. He wondered if he would see such beauty again. Kai aimed the ARI along the navigation vectors that Oa gave her, then she pushed the throttle to near full speed. They flew fast and low, reaching the end of the dunes quickly. The ground became rocky and desolate. Gradually, the terrain became more treacherous and erratic. Sharp spears of stone and jagged mounds of rubble made the landscape chaotic. Kai dodged through the rock formations, causing a few moments of terror for the rest of the crew. Oa continued to inspect the screen, trying to gauge the distance they had left to travel. Eventually, he understood the readings well enough to guess that they were drawing near their destination.

"Kai, slow down. Let's get some elevation and see if we can spot the city. It should be close now. Look for a giant hole in the ground," Oa instructed.

Kai set the ARI on an ascending course. She pulled the throttle back to half speed. Out in front of them lay the rocky hills they had been flying through. Off in the distance, a ring of ridges appeared to slope down into a deep valley. As they flew closer, Oa realized the valley did not have a floor, the ground merely dropped off into a gaping, black abyss. Hovering over the center above the pit rested what appeared to be a metallic disc.

"Good, the city is still here," Ohm said in relief. He paused for a moment as if expecting the rest of the crew to appreciate the good fortune that had befallen them. "This may come as a shock to you both, but it is so much easier to find this place with the ARI. Fred and I used to trek halfway across the world to just barely miss the city as it skidded off to some other forsaken corner," he complained.

"Well, you shouldn't have crashed this ship," Kai retorted. "Now where do I land us?" she asked, looking at the mess of metal they were flying toward.

"Get in close, and you should see several landing structures scattered about," Ohm replied.

As they neared the Careening City of Artisans, Oa began to make sense of the strange place. The city was circular in shape; a sharp tower pointed toward the sky from its center. Some sort of broad energy collection plate sat atop the needle. Thick conduits ran down the spire, splitting off into three groups to run along sturdy metal rails. The rails connected from the central tower out to three clusters of engines that were built into the edge of the city at equal intervals. A collage of metal filled the space between the three spokes of the wheel-shaped city. Oa slowly realized that the mishmash was actually an intricate pattern of machine pieces grafted together in a complex and artistic architecture. The three engine clusters rotated downwards. The thrusters glowed white-hot as they fired down into the chasm to keep the city aloft in the air. As Kai slowed the ARI down to hover just outside the city, Oa was able to differentiate some of the puzzle pieces that made up the hodgepodge. He could make out dwellings, walkways, bridges, and platforms with other vehicles on them.

He pointed to an empty platform, saying, "Land there, Kai. That looks like it will fit us." Kai glanced at where Oa was pointing, then nodded in agreement. She flew in low and set the ARI down, landing with a slight bump.

Kai leaned back in her seat and looked over at Oa. "You and Ohm should go get that hat. I want to see this place too, but I need to make sure the ARI wasn't damaged in that fall we took back at the forest." Concern for the ship had curbed her curiosity about the exotic location. "Come back when you have the hat and the information we need. Then we can all go do some exploring together and Ohm can ramble about the architecture."

Oa nodded. "Alright, we will be back soon." He climbed out of the seat and walked back to the power hub chamber, where he met up with Ohm.

"You should enjoy this city more. It will be more active than the last two. Many Awoken who have an interest in leading a normal life end up here. Most decide to stay. It's one of the few communities left," Ohm explained, excited to show Oa around.

"As long as I meet a few Awoken, I will consider the trip a success." Oa ran out of the door and down the open ramp of the ship. "Not that you and Kai aren't good company," he called jovially over his shoulder.

Ohm caught up to Oa and they walked off of the platform together. They strode down a sloping walkway that connected the landing platform to the rest of the city. The lane they were on appeared to have been fashioned out of the cylindrical hull of some old aircraft. As they walked down the long alley, Oa began to notice that most of the surfaces in the city had been marked with colorful drawings and artwork that depicted strange scenes. Ohm noticed Oa's stares.

"This is all impressionistic, of course; but these scenes depict the world before the Great War and the cataclysm of Istaar that brought the Great Planes to their current state," he said, taking the liberty to supply some information.

"You should tell me about that war in detail sometime. In fact, you just need to tell me all the history you know at some point," Oa said throwing his hands in the air. "But for now I'll just learn from these walls. Look! That's a lightning forest: I like how the colors flow and swirl. It's a nice interpretation of one," he said, pointing happily to a drawing on the wall he recognized.

Up ahead, an Awoken was kneeling next to a wall, blasting its surface with a flaming torch. The Awoken sat back and adjusted some knobs on the tool. The flame shifted from pale green to a deep blue. The Awoken returned to the drawing, painting more strokes on the wall. The blaze from the tool left deep colored scorches on the metal. The color displayed on the metal appeared to match the color of the flame. Oa walked up and watched quietly so as not to disturb the artisan's work. He reached over and nudged Ohm, pointing to the wall. The image appeared to be a sea of translucent blue rock, smooth but jagged in spots, like sharp stone spires rising out of great rolling dunes.

"It's an ice storm, very fierce; but it would create the most interesting landscapes for those who could brave the weather long enough to enjoy the scenery afterwards," Ohm whispered to clarify the strange scene for Oa.

The Awoken in front of them turned around at Ohm's voice. "What a surprise! I didn't know I had admirers. You must be new. I have never seen either of you around before," she said cheerfully. Her giant apron was stained with numerous burns from her tool so it looked like a color bomb had gone off in front of her. The Awoken flipped up her goggles and held out her hand. "I am one of the artisans here; my name is Rida."

Ohm reached out and clasped her forearm, their arms linking in a gesture of greeting. "I am called Ohm, and this is Oa. We are visitors from the edge," he explained in a friendly tone.

"Ah yes, the Traveler. I have heard about you," Rida said nodding. She turned and then repeated the arm clasping gesture with Oa who followed Ohm's example even though the ritual seemed absurd.

"Did you decorate this whole corridor?" Oa asked in awe as he looked around.

"No, but I have contributed to this mural and others across the city. We artisans like to collaborate so this place is always a patchwork of creativity. You should walk a while and look at it. We always welcome visitors," Rida replied warmly.

"Actually, we are looking for Simon at the moment. He still lives here, right?" Ohm asked, hoping for some directions.

"Yes. Take this corridor. Turn left down at the end, then right, then make a second left. Go up one level and take the fifth corridor to your right. Follow that corridor down to the lowest level; Simons shop will be the third on the main strip," Rida replied quickly.

"You know this place very well," Oa said, impressed at Rida's keen memory of the city.

"Thank you. I do take pride in my knowledge of this city," Rida said with an audible haughty air. "Would you like me to write it down for you?" she asked, humored at the notion of the pair remembering her complex instructions.

"Not necessary. I pride myself on my ability to lug around a computing backpack, and Fred takes emotionless pride in his ability to remember and record everything. We won't keep you from your work any longer, Rida the Artisan," Ohm replied cordially.

Rida was taken aback slightly, but she laughed and knelt down to her art. She reactivated her color torch and immersed herself back into the masterpiece on the wall. Ohm started walking down the corridor. Oa watched Rida work for a while longer then ran after Ohm, overtaking his mentor at the first left turn. As they journeyed through the city, Fred would occasionally chime in to direct their movements. At one point, their path led them under one of the city's giant spokes. They walked across the rail, passing beneath the immense conduits that ran from the center of the city out to one of the engine clusters. Oa looked up and listened to the deep hum that the conduits made as they transferred vast amounts of energy to the engines.

"Hey, Ohm, does all this energy come from the disk at the top of the central tower?" Oa asked, knowing Ohm would relish the opportunity to explain the process.

"Correct. You clearly understand the technology of the Awoken now. That tower is a sky silo. It draws on the energy of the Great Plane above us and feeds it down to the engines. The machine is complex and requires a sizable crew of Awoken to maintain it—Awoken with Kai's skills; artisans of machinery," Ohm lectured as they walked under the conduits. Long, narrow portholes in the giant chords allowed bright white light to spill out into the hall, guiding their steps. They walked in silence through the rest of the corridor.

Oa was lost in the many images scrawled across the surfaces of the city, portraying strange things from a world he had never known. He remembered the image depicted back on the ceiling of Bolleworth. *The Awoken in both cities are consumed with the past*, he thought to himself. With so few Awoken left, he realized all they had were their memories. Even Oa's current purpose of battling Eol could be seen as an attempt to rescue the past. He pondered the memory-worshiping culture and the decaying world it seemed to encourage. He tried to decide if it was truly an inevitable progression as Ohm believed.

They came out from under the conduits to the other side of the city. Oa's thoughts were interrupted by the sight of numerous Awoken milling about. Some of them painted while others passed by, heading to other parts of the city with various errands and duties. Every Awoken Oa encountered would wave and call out a greeting. They treated the sight of another Awoken like a normal occurrence. Oa waved back to them and returned the greetings. He reveled in wonder at the experience of such a lively community. Fred guided them to their final turn and informed them that they had arrived at their destination. Oa reasoned that the platform they wound up on must have once been a vessel used for carrying cargo. The street was lined with shops with unique and creative signs hung out in front of each one. Oa instantly spotted Simon's shop because the sign had a likeness of Ohm's head wearing a hat.

"Ha! That's your face on a sign," Oa pointed, laughing.

"I am a good customer," Ohm conceded.

"So I'm guessing that Simon is also your informant here. He's the one who might know about the labs," Oa surmised.

"Yes," Ohm replied. "A lot of gossip and rumors go through Simon. He might know something of value."

They walked up to the shop. "Let's see if he still remembers me," Ohm said, opening the door.

Oa was about to follow Ohm when his visual receptors caught sight of a strange and more interesting sign down the lane. It was more of a statue than a sign, sitting atop an archway that led into a mysterious shop.

Oa tapped Ohm on the shoulder. "I'll meet you in a bit. I'm going to go look at another shop across the way."

Ohm half turned and replied. "That's fine; I might be a while. I wouldn't advise wandering far though. We are being hunted, you know."

"Got it. No wandering, lots of hats to see, so meet back in a while!" Oa said excitedly, backing out of the doorway. He ran down the lane, waving to the Awoken he passed by. When Oa reached the archway he stood beneath it and gazed up in wonder at the art above him. The statue, like the city, was composed of numerous chunks of alloy, each grafted together seamlessly. The differences in shade and color betrayed each piece's uniqueness.

The figure was the body of an Awoken. It knelt with head bowed, a single arm outstretched toward the sky. Hovering above the figure's open palm floated a small shiny object that glinted in the light as it spun. Oa instantly recognized that the object was the depiction of a soul ember. Oa looked at the figure's chest; the cavity was empty like his own. No inscription could be found on the strange sign, which further piqued Oa's interest in the shop.

Behind the archway, Oa could see that the curious boutique was cube-shaped with a domed roof. The structure lay grafted into a much bigger framework that housed two repurposing emporiums to either side of the modest outlet. He looked at the two signs to either side of him, reading aloud to himself: *Tunjee's Flying Lodges* and *Ripwark's Lodgeable Flyers*. Oa looked back and forth, and then again, trying to figure out the conflicting businesses. He gave up, shrugging to himself as he walked through the archway to the center shop. Oa pushed on the door, but it did not swing inward like the one at Simons shop had. Instead, the hatch lowered into the ground with a sharp clang. He walked through the entrance and the portal slammed shut behind him. He looked around, a multitude of various Awoken parts lay on shelves and tables that filled the shop. Several partially complete bodies of Awoken stood in rows along the wall. Oa tensed at the strangely disturbing sight. He cautiously walked toward one of the walls and picked an arm up off the shelf that held it. The arm shook slightly in his nervous hands, making a faint rattling noise.

"Do not be alarmed," a high-pitched male voice behind Oa instructed, resulting in the opposite effect as the startled Awoken dropped the arm he was holding with a loud and awkward clatter.

"Those are not from Awoken. I do not scavenge the dead," the voice continued. Oa spun around and looked at the diminutive Awoken behind him. He had been sitting in a chair along one of the walls the entire time, but Oa had not noticed him. He had blended in with all the other Awoken pieces scattered about.

"Well, where did you get these?" Oa asked as his courage returned, assisted by the fact that in front of him was the shortest Awoken he had ever seen. The little Awoken had a rotund body shape and an oversized coat that dragged across the floor behind him as he walked around on his stubby legs.

"I am Mordecai the Builder. I fashioned each and every piece in this room," Mordecai replied, walking over to Oa. He picked the arm up off the floor and placed it back on the shelf.

"For repairing damaged Awoken? You probably splice them on with microburs, huh?" Oa asked trying to figure out Mordecai's trade and purpose.

"You seem to know a little about Awoken medicine," Mordecai said, shuffling back over to another table with some parchments and twigs of black material. Mordecai found himself a blank parchment, then grabbed one of the slender sticks. He began to draw the image of a crude Awoken on the parchment, explaining as he drew.

"Everyone wakes up already assembled. We are all comprised of water and alloys bound together by a life force that flows through us. This energy comes from the soul ember, which some say came from the sky. It is the key to the whole contraption; the soul ember gives the alloys life," Mordecai explained. He tapped on the crystal he had drawn in the center of the Awoken to emphasize his point. "The Awoken's body is bonded to the soul ember. No one knows how this occurs. I have studied many cadavers. Their alloys are no different from the alloys we use to make our ships and cities, but each of us can sense and feel through the alloys that make up our bodies." Mordecai chucked an artificial hand from the table at Oa, striking him on the shoulder.

"Hey, you didn't have to do that. I know what senses are," Oa said, sightly annoyed.

Mordecai chuckled. "That was for dropping the arm earlier. Now do be careful with that hand," he said absentmindedly, forgetting he had just thrown it.

Oa picked the appendage up and looked at it. It was very similar to his hand. He placed the piece back on the table. "So can the soul ember flow its energy into a new body part?" he asked, thinking of Ohm's missing hand.

"You would think so, but it never does. Before the invention of microburs, Awoken who lost limbs would have them replaced; but they never were able to feel or move them. The soul ember is complex; and it does not accept the pieces it did not wake with. Once a soul ember has lost its body, it can never be re-awoken in that body or any other body for that matter," Mordecai replied, drawing another Awoken without a soul ember and scribbling a cross through the figure to visually prove his point.

"Well then what makes microburs so special? They produce alloys that didn't come bonded to the Awoken," Oa pointed out, growing increasingly interested with the topic Mordecai was discussing. The shopkeeper did not seem to be quite as selective in divulging information as Ohm was.

Mordecai started rapidly tapping the parchment with the marker, producing many tiny black dots. "Microburs are tiny fusion devices, like little builders. The high energy of fusion bonds each new piece of alloy to the existing energy field of the soul ember, extending it gradually. It is not a perfect match, but it is almost like new. The area feels numb but can still be functional," he explained.

"But that's not good enough for you is it?" Oa asked, observing as Mordecai picked up the hand and began to gaze at it intensely.

"No it is not, young sir. Microburs only work to fix simple wounds. You can never recreate a whole body with them. I want to bring back the ones I love. I have devoted the majority of my life to building these parts. One day my work will be worthy enough to reawaken embers and turn back the tide of decay in this world," Mordecai said, sighing. He set the fake hand back down and patted a tough-looking box strapped to his waist. Oa assumed it contained soul embers.

"That's a noble goal. Just don't go too far in your quest. I have seen the obsession to reunite oneself with the past destroy Awoken out near the edge," Oa cautioned, remembering the Howlers of Bolleworth. He was still impressed with Mordecai's work.

"Never!" Mordecai said in disgust. "I had a former friend try and force me to cross that line. He had a treasured soul ember he wanted to revive. He experimented with the cadavers of Awoken, trying to acquire them closer to the point of life. Things went too far when he brought me a near-death Awoken and tried to make me switch out the embers before mending the wound. He was obsessed and mad with grief. He is the reason I never want to study another cadaver." The memory angered the old builder and he thumped his fist on the table.

"I see," Oa nodded somberly. He picked up a piece of gear off a nearby shelf. It seemed to be a bulky monocle. "What is this?" he asked, changing the subject.

"My working monocle. I invented it to allow me to see through things. It helps when I am tinkering inside all this machinery," Mordecai replied with fondness as he described his favorite tool. "That monocle is the closest I have ever come to improving on the Creator's work. Awoken are programmed to near perfection when they awake, but they cannot see through solid objects. See! The Creator did not think of everything, young sir. An independent thinker, that is what I am." Mordecai tapped the side of his head knowingly.

Oa laughed and replied, "I am glad I met you. My name is Oa. You sound a lot like my friend, the way you talk. Ohm always goes on about stuff like the Creator and program—"

"What name did you say your friend had?" Mordecai demanded, raising his hand to cut Oa off.

"Ohm, his name is Ohm," Oa replied, taken aback by the sudden question.

"Get out. Get out! No friend of Ohm is a friend of mine. He is the one who tried to defile my noble goals. Leave my shop," Mordecai shrieked, shoving Oa toward the door.

"I don't understand; wait a weeble! At least take this back. I don't want to take your best invention," Oa stammered, the monocle still in his hand.

"I have more. Just get out!" Mordecai snapped, pushing Oa through the open door. It slammed closed as soon as Oa was through.

He looked down at the monocle in his hand and placed the tool in his satchel next to Seeker. *So Ohm was the Awoken Mordecai spoke of,* Oa thought to himself. Mordecai's words had revealed that despite Ohm willingness to lecture on random topics, he kept much hidden. Oa knew he would have to confront Ohm about it. Oa trusted his friend, but he needed to know what happened. Why had Ohm gone so far to revive a soul ember, and how had he been infected by the Void?

"Oa! I see our timing is perfect; that's the Creator's programming for you," Ohm joked. His voice carried from down the lane as he stepped out of Simon's shop.

He would come out saying that exact phrase, Oa thought to himself, amused by the coincidence.

"I see you found your hat," Oa said as he ran over to greet his friend. "You look ridiculous." He laughed after a brief attempt to control his mirth.

"I think it's quite dashing, and so would Fred if he could comprehend style," Ohm replied evenly as he adjusted the nonsense resting on his head. His hood was pulled back to make room for the cone-shaped hat resting on his head. A narrow, round brim ran around the bottom of the cap.

Oa laughed again. "I must not be able to comprehend style either," he admitted.

"Apparently not," Ohm agreed. "So, what did you explore?"

"Er, I just went over to *Tunjee's Flying Lodges,* but they didn't have anything close to the caliber of the ARI," Oa said casually, concealing his visit with Mordecai for the time being.

He expected there would be an opportunity later to discuss Ohm's past.

"Too true. Nothing can outperform the ARI. Let us head up to the top of this market and take a look. We should be able to see most of the city from there," Ohm said cheerfully, putting his arm around Oa's shoulder.

They walked up over to a nearby flight of stairs at the outer edge of the market plaza. They ascended through several levels of the city until they reached a long ramp that led up to a balcony. There were no shops or stands, just a railing that ran around the edge. Oa leaned out over the edge and looked straight down into the bottomless pit below.

"So how was Simon?" Oa asked. "Did he know anything?"

"He was still the same. Not much changes for this city other than the location," Ohm said lightheartedly. "And no. He hasn't heard of any other labs, which was disappointing. We should go get Kai now and show her ar—"

Ohm was interrupted as two figures pounced on him from behind, shoving him up against the railing. The force of the impact sent his newly acquired hat spinning off his head down into the chasm below. To his right, Ohm briefly glimpsed Oa struggle with a third attacker before his pupil tumbled backward over the railing with a yell. Ohm's hand shot over the railing after his friend. Fractions of a weeble later, Seeker slammed into Ohm's hand, sticking with an unseen force. He immediately felt Oa's weight on his arm as the young Awoken pulled himself back up.

Ohm refocused his full attention on wrestling off his attackers. He threw his right shoulder up and caught one attacker in the neck, sending her tumbling backwards. Ohm threw his elbow back and caught the second attacker in the midriff, causing the foe to lose his grip. Ohm spun around and shoved the second attacker back with his bandaged stump. Ohm's left arm still hung over the railing, trapping him in one spot as he held onto Seeker. He recognized the three Awoken immediately: the Marauders he and Oa had stolen from. As they rushed at him, Ohm leaned back against the railing and picked both of his feet up. He kicked Jad hard in the chest, sending the Marauder flying backwards to land square on his rear. Ohm leaned forward again and planted his feet on the deck. Fighting the weight on his arm, he pulled forward and swung his handless arm up like a club. The blow knocked Kiri back.

Bota was much faster than his comrades, and he dodged the strikes, charging into Ohm. "Where are our embers, thief?!" He growled.

"You idiots just shoved Oa and the embers into the Void," Ohm shot back. He head-butted Bota, sending blue sparks flying from the slits in his mask and cracking the goggles Bota wore.

"Then I will take this one at least," Bota grunted, grabbing hold of the chain around Ohm's neck. The soul ember Ohm treasured had slipped out in the fight, and the dangling object had caught the Marauder's attention.

"No!" Ohm roared, but it was too late. Bota merely had to step back and yank on the chain for it to break free of Ohm's neck. He was pinned up against the railing, clinging to Seeker as Oa pulled himself to safety.

Bota backed up, still clutching the chain as Oa came sailing over the railing. He retrieved Seeker from Ohm's hand as he passed, landing spryly on his feet. Oa saw the soul ember dangling from the chain in Bota's hands, and suddenly he understood the mystery behind the chain around Ohm's neck. Seeker bolted from his hand, flying straight at Bota. It stopped abruptly, lightly clinking against the soul ember. After latching onto the stone, Oa yanked Seeker back into his hand. He tossed the ember over to Ohm while Bota stared down in shock at the worthless chain he was still grasping.

"We really need to talk about that ember Ohm, but right now I want to know how these scavengers caught up to us," Oa demanded, surprised at his own awesome moves and smooth demeanor.

Bota pulled out his boltspitter, aiming it at Oa.

There goes the bravado, Oa thought to himself as he took a nervous step back.

"We hunted everywhere looking for the cripple with the Ice blade. Every rumor we heard said he was an ancient wanderer and that the one constant in his travels was a hat shop in this city," Bota said pointing at Ohm.

"Seriously, Ohm?! Your reputation is hats?" Oa said, turning to his mentor who had recovered from the scuffle and was gently placing the ember into a pouch strapped to his waist.

"When you have been around as long as me, building a fearsome notoriety gets boring. I decided to go for something less dramatic," Ohm replied, ignoring the trio in front of them.

"Shut up and give us the embers back!" Bota shouted.

"Not going to happen," Oa said backing up toward the railing. "I took them so you would stop serving Eol and find something better to do with your lives. If you want to give Eol the embers so much, why don't you consider giving him your own?"

"Eol can have those embers over our lifeless corpses!" Kiri snarled her face lighting up in anger.

"Wait, I don't understand. What are the embers for?" Oa asked in confusion. Fear and regret crept into his mind. Had he made a mistake?

"We tried to make you a part of our crew. We concealed you because Bota and I saw something special in you. So Eol killed the rest of our crew, our family," Jad clarified as he stepped forward.

"After you fell, we fought Eol to try and rescue our comrades," Bota added, his voice growing hoarse.

"You resisted? So you weren't going to trade me in, Bota?" Oa questioned, accusingly.

Bota just looked down in silence. Kiri and Jad looked over at their leader in confusion, keeping their questions to themselves in front of the outsiders.

"What makes them more worthy than the embers you fed to Eol in the past?" Oa asked, keeping his tone hard.

Jad stopped looking to his leader for an explanation and turned to Oa. "We just chose to protect the ones we loved. The

Sleepers would have torn us apart if they could have had just one more immersion. Our hands may be stained with ember dust, but our last fight was against Eol to rescue the souls of our crew. That bag is all we have left of our family," Jad explained.

Oa felt sorry for them. With deepening regret, he realized he had misjudged the situation, and made a mistake. He looked over his shoulder at Ohm, who merely shrugged. Oa turned back to Jad.

"I know you protected me, and I'm sorry I stole the soul embers from you. I was only trying to free you from Eol's grip and protect the embers. We were taking them to the Enlightened City where they would be safe," Oa explained, revealing his plan to the Marauders.

"You really think Eol won't find you there, too? Just give us back our crew and run for as long as you can until Eol leaves you nothing to run to," Bota scoffed.

"You're wrong! You gave up and betrayed your comrades as soon as you decided to bow to Eol. You all accepted his lie that someone had to die; no wonder you couldn't keep your friends safe," Oa shot back in anger. He grabbed the ember bag from his satchel and threw it towards the Marauders. "Here have this back."

Bota snarled in grief and rage, he was done tolerating Oa's self righteous attitude. The Lieutenant raised his weapon, pointing it at Oa's head. Kiri and Jad both stepped forward and quickly pulled his arm down. They stood huddled in silence around the remnants of their crew, grieved by the truth in Oa's words.

"Hey, I don't mean to cut all this ember-wrenching drama short, but the city is about to be swarming with Legion soldiers," Ohm interjected with grim humor as he stared down at the danger below. Oa turned and peered over the railing. Numerous Legion vessels were swarming up out of the abyss.

Jad snatched the bag off the deck as his comrades rushed to the railing. Bota leaned out further to look at the lower levels of the city.

"They already have Void portals planted!" he yelled, spinning around in time to see two Legion soldiers step up onto the far side of the platform. The red eye gleamed evilly from beneath their brimmed caps. Bota rapidly fired his boltspitter, shredding the ghastly demons into a cloud of black dust.

The group raced over to the platform entrance, gazing down the long ramp toward the city below. There was chaos everywhere as the Legion began to storm the city. Some Awoken had weapons and were fighting back, but they were quickly silenced. Each time the dark soldier loosed a volley, lives ended. All across the city, death reigned supreme.

Legion soldiers marched up toward the ramp that led to the platform Oa and Ohm were on.

"It appears we are trapped," Jad said somberly.

"I'll hold them back," Bota said grimly. He twirled the boltspitter in his hand deftly.

Jad turned to Oa and grabbed him by the shoulders. "We will cover your retreat, Oa. I hope you have better luck than us.

You had better protect our crew. Eol's Law seems inevitable, so please prove it wrong. Help us believe," Jad said earnestly. He placed the bag of soul embers in Oa's satchel. Bota looked over for a moment. Behind his goggles, ocular plates flickered in anger, but calmed as the Lieutenant understood and accepted Jad's decision.

"Might as well live it up while we can. If we are going to die, I am going to go out making music, no more fighting for me," Kiri said, pulling out one of the strange instruments from her pack she sat down and began to play.

"You're all fortunate that I'm a good enough shot to multitask," Bota said firing several bolts down the ramp. Each blast ripped a Legion soldier apart as more of the red-eyed monsters swarmed up the ramp. Bota pulled down the cloth that covered the lower half of his face, revealing a cone-shaped depression. It began to vibrate, filling the air with the deep, thrumming melody of his voice.

"Get out of here!" Jad shouted over the music. He sat down next to Kiri and pulled out his own instrument joining in the song. The three Marauders played together for the last time. Their melodies rose to the sky as the Legion's weapons tried to drown out the beauty of their harmony. Bota stood defiantly at the top of the ramp firing as fast as he could, determined to atone for the lives his crew had taken. Through ferocity of action he would prove that within him resided a spirit of resistance, and a remnant of hope for the way things could be. Overhead, the lights in the sky faded as another cycle followed the Marauder's final verse into oblivion.

Oa did not want to leave, but before he could linger, Ohm grabbed him around the waist. The pair aqua jetted off of the platform, dropping backwards into the city. The sky above was filled with Legion fighters, their three wings extended out around glowing red cockpits. Void weapons fired from the edges of the wings, tearing through the city.

Ohm landed on a narrow bridge outside the market. The Legion soldiers appeared to be concentrated within the area. Awoken rushed by them, trying to escape the carnage. Ohm and Oa ran with the fleeing Awoken into another open plaza. Ohm tackled Oa to the floor as the shots of Legion nihilistols silenced the air, killing several Awoken the friends had been running with. They jumped up and fled down a side passage, taking a short flight of steps up a level to lose their pursuers. They reached another bridge, and Oa was relieved to see the giant energy cables on the other side. Once they crossed under, they would be back at the ARI in no time. He rushed out onto the walkway; Ohm sprinted after him.

"Oa look ou—" Ohm's yell was cut off by a deafening emptiness followed by a concussive explosion from a strafing run of one of the Legion fighters. The blast tore the walkway in two, throwing Oa out into empty space as Ohm fell down through several levels into a cavernous statue gallery below. Oa instinctively sent Seeker whizzing out to latch onto the other side of the bridge. He pulled himself up and quickly scanned below.

"Ohm!" Oa shouted, trying to find his friend; but it was no use. He could not see Ohm anywhere in the chaos. He turned and sprinted under the energy conduits. He knew he had to get back to the ARI and make sure Kai was okay. Together they could find Ohm. Oa ran through back alleyways to avoid Legion troops. He let his sense of direction and keen memory guide him back to the ARI.

As he ran over a high-arching bridge, Oa spotted the beloved vessel. Some structure had been blown away, leaving a gap between the bridge he was on and the landing platform. Through the smoke, he could see Kai and Susan fending off Legion soldiers at the entrance of the platform. He launched Seeker toward the ramp that the Legion where swarming up. Oa flew in fast, swinging himself into three Legion troops at the top of the slope. The minions tumbled off of the walkway, plummeting back to their home below. Oa skidded across the ramp and off the side, catching himself with Seeker. He hauled himself back up to the deck, Seeker in hand, and ducked as Kai shouted from behind a barricade.

"Get down, Oa!" She called as she fired her second pistol, sending chords of angry blue lightning coursing into eight Legion soldiers that she had previously hit with her tracer pistol. Oa crawled up the ramp next to Kai on the landing platform.

"I lost Ohm. We have to get to the ARI and go find him!" he shouted.

Kai nodded and turned to Susan who lay crouched behind the barricade, panting from a previous attack on the enemy. "Can you buy us some time to get the ARI in the air?" she asked.

Susan roared in affirmative, swelling in size. Her body blazed with radiance as she charged forward, bolting down the ramp. Lightning extended from her paws; and she swatted the first Legion soldier with the deadly claws of light, flinging it off the ramp in pieces. Arcs of energy crackled out of Susan's tail as she spun around and whipped it through four more Legion soldiers, shredding them instantly. Bounding through the air, Susan pounced on another Void warrior. Emitting a harsh growl, she snapped at its head. Lightning poured from her jaws and tore the monster apart.

Oa and Kai ran to the ARI. They sprinted up the ramp and through the ship to reach the bridge. Oa dropped into the pilot's seat. He looked over at Kai, his face lighting up in alarm.

"I forgot! We don't have Fred. How will we fly with no power?" he asked.

"It appears that Fred has been storing backup energy in the ARI for an emergency; I found the reserve coils during my inspection. We should have enough until the next cycle starts," Kai responded.

She reached under the console and flipped an important looking switch. The ship came to life. Oa immediately lifted the ARI up above the platform, angling down so they could see Susan below. Kai pulled down a contraption on the wall next to her; it flipped out, revealing a visor and two handles. She put her face in the visor and gripped the handles, squeezing a pair of triggers. Two keen blue bolts tore through the ramp, taking the Legion with it.

Susan looked up from below. When she saw the ARI in the air she raced upwards, zipping through the open deck and into the power-hub chamber. The varl returned to her normal size as she floated into the cockpit to join Oa and Kai.

"Thank you Susan! You're purple and fierce as always," Kai said with a pride as she fired the ship's weapons again, taking out another chunk of the city and several Legion with it.

"We don't have much time, Oa. Use those piloting skills and get us to where you lost Ohm so we can scan for Fred; this ship needs its power source back," Kai commanded.

Oa nodded and tilted the ARI so it was pointing straight down. He slammed the throttle forward and sent them spinning down through the hole that Kai had made with her potent weapons.

***

Ohm picked himself up off of the ground. He was dazed and his vision was bleary from the blast and subsequent fall he had suffered. He instinctively reached for the spot on his hip where he had hidden the soul ember. When Ohm didn't feel the ember, he panicked and lost focus on his efforts to maintain his balance. He stumbled and keeled over onto his face. The old Awoken glanced up and saw a pair of imposing black boots standing several paces in front of him.

"The Destroyer lost something, but the piece has been found," Eol said. His whisper filled the air with menacing calm.

Ohm lifted his head. His blue ocular plate burned brightly. "Don't get too attached to that title. I wiped away all traces of the Destroyer; and I will do the same to you, Eol," he replied coldly as he pushed himself to his feet.

Eol merely chuckled, as if he had a joke he desperately wanted to share. Ohm stood facing the shrouded figure. The demon stood a head taller than Ohm, his face concealed, save for the two red eyes that shone out of the darkness. As wind blew through the city, it pulled at the numerous ends of the winding sheets that wrapped him, opening them enough to reveal two black metallic hands. His boots made a dull ring on the deck as the fiend took several calm steps toward Ohm. Eol held out his closed fist, slowly opening it to reveal a familiar gleaming crystal. The dead eyes of the lightning varl pelt atop Eol's head glared down at Ohm, daring him to take back his beloved treasure.

Ohm reached out toward the ember, but Eol's fingers began to curl around it. "Please don't hurt her," Ohm pleaded, his resilient defiance melting away at the sight of the soul ember in Eol's palm.

"She has a name, Ohm," Eol said. His voice was keen, piercing through Ohm despite the chaos all around them. "Ari," the demon hissed. The name echoed through the air, haunting and bitter.

"Don't hurt Ari," Ohm pleaded one last time. He stepped toward Eol, his hand still stretched out in desperate longing. His tired soul dreaded what he knew would come next.

"There it is!" Eol snarled with satisfaction. He tossed the small stone in the air; it glimmered in the light one last time before the monster caught it. Eol tightened his grip and crushed the soul ember. With a loud crack, frantic light exploded out of his hand. Ari's essence tried to escape Eol's cruel grasp, only to be pulled back into the Void of his closed fist. He sighed a pleasure-filled rasp of death before opening his claw to reveal the emptiness that remained.

Ohm stared for a moment then dropped to his knees. His head hung forward limply, shadowed beneath the hood he wore. He spoke no words as Eol softly laughed in elation. Ohm was still as he let the grief find its way to the corner of his mind where he never dared to tread. He extended his arms out to either side of him. From within the veins of his body, water surged forth, spiraling in streams around him. To Ohm's left, the disk of a shield formed, to block a world that continually sought to break his will. To his right, he cast the sharpest of blades, with which to exact his vengeance. His icy will drained all energy and life from the liquid's existence, hardening it down to the solid cold he felt inside. Ohm lowered the ice weapons to his sides.

"The Destroyer always reveals itself. My nature cannot be denied," Eol laughed, taunting Ohm with the fire of his words.

"You're mistaken. We define our own nature, and yours is to be destroyed," Ohm said with deadly calm as he rose to his feet. He strode across the gallery to meet Eol.

Around them, statues of immeasurable value crumbled as Awoken melted away under the blaze of the Legion storm. Ohm's gaze never wandered as he focused on his enemy. Eol's stance widened, readying him for battle. He reached and pulled the Void staff from his back, leveling the weapon at Ohm. The monster seemed to flicker in several places at once, becoming a blur as he rushed toward Ohm. Ohm finished his stride, dropping low into a lunge. He brought up his shield to block the attack with speed that matched Eol's. The demon's staff drove into the center of Ohm's shield but the Traveler's icy will held, as did the shield.

Eol's eyes blazed fiery red as he drove himself forward. Ohm did not falter, but his feet slid back across the deck. His right arm was stretched behind him, holding the blade ready. He tilted his shield slightly, letting Eol's staff slip to the side, which sent Eol careening off to his left. Ohm sprang after Eol, spinning through the air. His ice blade struck faster than any other Awoken could move. Ohm sliced at the monster that had taken Ari from him, but Eol had regained his balance and was prepared for the attack. The demon spun his staff up, deflecting Ohm's sword. Eol continued the staff's twirl, slicing viciously at the old Awoken with the other end. Ohm's instinct spotted the attack and instantly calculated the best evasive maneuver. He dropped out of his leap and tucked into a roll, sliding a micro-bur's width under the deadly stroke of the Void staff. He hopped to his feet outside of Eol's reach. Ohm spun around and raised the shield up in front of him. He faced his opponent with his sword drawn high, pointing toward Eol with lethal intent.

"You are not ready to remember, are you, Ohm?" Eol questioned, the Void staff held casually at his side. "Ask yourself, *how do I know her name?*" He extended his other hand toward Ohm.

"What, h-how?" Ohm stammered as he stiffened, realizing with horror that he hadn't been surprised at Eol's knowledge of

Ari's soul ember. "You shouldn't know. You can't! Why wasn't I surprise—? AUGGGHHH!" Ohm's protests were cut short as he cried out in pain. The blue light flashed behind his mask.

"Get out of my head!" Ohm screamed as he dropped to his knees. The ice weapons crumbled away as he clutched the side of his skull with his one good hand.

Eol shouldered his weapon and backed away from the fallen Traveler. Legion soldiers swarmed around their leader and rushed at Ohm, seeking to end his existence.

"Maintain a defensive position. I am flying us out of danger; the ARI is nearby," Fred commanded. The trusty pack reformed the ice shield on Ohm's left arm and activated the aqua jets to send them flying backwards out of the burning gallery. The Legion fired after Ohm, but the shots glanced off of the barrier that Fred had raised to protect them.

The pair dropped down between platforms and walkways toward the ARI as it flew beneath the city. In the cockpit, Oa and Kai were scanning the mayhem above looking for Ohm.

"There he is!" Kai yelled when she saw the familiar streak of the aqua jet as it lowered their wounded friend down.

"I'll get under him," Oa said, piloting the ARI so that Ohm would drop onto the open deck.

"We are on board," Fred's voice came through the control board a moment later.

Kai looked around for a way to reply. She took an educated guess and held down a button. "Okay, we are going to get out of here. How bad is Ohm hurt?"

"By my readings he is physically unharmed, though his mind seems to be in shambles," Fred replied.

"I'm alright now. I'll be in the power hub in a moment so we can leave," Ohm said. His tired voice rattled over the receiver.

Oa flew to the far edge of the floating metro. He lifted the ARI up and spun the ship around to look back at the Careening City of Artisans. The far side of the city was nearly consumed in flames and smoke as the Legion did their work. Despite the danger, Oa did not want to leave.

"We should go back and save the others. Kai, take the pilot's seat. I will go out and reel in as many Awoken as I can with Seeker," he said. His voice was set in determination despite the fear he felt inside.

Kai nodded in agreement. She could sense Oa was nervous, so she reached over and slapped him on the chest. Her reply was both encouraging and confident. "Don't worry, we are going to be fine. I can dodge these guys forever. Let's go be heroes!"

EPISODE 09

HEART OF RESISTANCE

"I take it we aren't leaving yet?" Ohm asked. His voice was weary and disoriented.

"Affirmative, buddy. We are going back just long enough to rescue some of the Awoken," Oa replied reassuringly as he climbed out of the pilot's seat.

"Somehow I'm not surprised. Alright, we must be swift. I'll take over copiloting duties. Kai, if my memory is correct, the ARI has a wind wing. We'll need it to make a quick escape," Ohm commanded, regaining his faculties with each word he spoke.

"If you mean the thrusters that used to be in the ARI's folded wing thingy ... I'll explain later, but we can't use that," Kai called back, edging past Oa to get in the pilot seat.

Oa was halfway down the corridor to the power hub chamber when Kai yelled out, "Oa, wait! Get back up here. Whose are those, Ohm?"

Oa rushed back up into the cockpit. Susan had eagerly commandeered the copilot's half of the helm. The lightning varl floated above the seat. Her paws sparked against the control panel as she watched events unfolding through the forward viewport. Susan's tail draped around the chair, claiming the right side of the bridge. Oa stood behind Kai and gazed out over the city. From the direction of the mountain, orange blurs streaked across the sky, diving down onto the city. Blazing white light shot from the orange vessels, cutting into the swarm of Legion fighters.

"Those are the colors of the Enlightened. The efforts of our search have paid off," Ohm congratulated the crew.

"I have not recorded any specific time spent searching for the Enlightened. We are far from the mountain," Fred said, deflating Ohm's statement.

"Then call it fate, my friend. That and hats have always led us where we needed to go," Ohm replied cheerfully.

Oa tuned out the duo as their sidebar conversation continued. "The smoke from the city is too thick. Kai, can you see what's happening?" he asked, leaning forward as he tried to peer through the chaos below.

"Not yet," Kai said. She paused, then an idea struck her. "Change of plans, Oa. We've got allies now, we can fight. Get me close enough, and I will pound those Void scum with the ARI's cannon. The targeting goggles will see right through that smoke." There was fire in her voice.

Ohm and Fred's conversation ended abruptly. "The ARI doesn't have any weapons," Ohm said, puzzled.

"It does now. Sorry Ohm, but I had to alter some things on this ship. It's got to be original. I couldn't just rehash the previous builder's model," Kai's replied curtly. She was proud of her work.

"You sound like Cale and Jess," Ohm said, reminiscing.

"I better sound like them. I had to learn all their crazy engineering techniques," Kai grumbled, hopping over to the copilot chair. She shooed Susan off the seat. The lighting varl relocated behind Kai, resting her pointed snout on top of the Awoken's head. "That works, I guess," Kai said in amusement as she pulled down the targeting controls from the wall.

Oa took control of the helm and looked out over the wreckage. Flaming pieces broke off and fell from the city, tumbling down into the abyss. The metro's thrusters belched soot and a dark smoke. Oa was daunted by the task of flying into the war zone.

"Can you get us close?" Kai asked.

Oa considered a possible strategy, then he remembered the strange tool in his bag. "I got a monocle back in the city. It should be able to see through the smoke," he explained as he grabbed Mordecai's monocle from his satchel.

"I'd like to take a look at that when we get out of this mess," Ohm said, "till then, I will manage our power systems and defenses. Now, let's go help save the city." His zeal was infectious, and it bolstered the crew's spirits.

Oa took notice of his mentor's sudden interest in the monocle, but it was not a good time to bring up Mordecai. Oa placed the device on his head. It covered his left visual receptor. He peered through the lenses, amazed by the clarity and enhancements the device gave his sight. He looked toward the city, and the lenses automatically whirred and clicked to adjust their focus. His gaze raced forward through the fog of war, picking out every little detail.

***

A nearby blast rattled Abur in his flight harness as he raced his Z-7 Torch through the desolation of the city. The other two Z-7's that made up his squadron kept pace with him and flanked his ship, one on either side. The two Torches matched Abur's every move as he dove down into the chaos, plummeting through the black flames of the Void. The squadron of Torches burst out from underneath the carnage for a brief respite from the fighting. Abur looped back up, piercing through the lattice structure of the city. His squadron reentered the battle behind an echelon of 6 Legion Tridents.

"Execute a full burn and flank left. Engage when the Tridents try to break," Abur commanded.

His squadron dropped back then sped off in a wide arc to his left. Abur lined his sights on the rightmost Trident fighter. He paused briefly, then fired. The two potent cannons above him shot forth white rays of light. The weapons struck true, shattering the Legion Trident. The rest of the Legion squadron spun off to the left, only to fall into Abur's trap. The other two Z-7 Torches ripped through the foes, tearing them apart with deadly accuracy that had been honed by countless cycles of combat. Abur banked to the right as his wing mates fell back into formation. He adjusted the channel on his ray-com transmitter.

"Torch 7, this is Torch 1. You're now in command of the aerial attack. I'm landing Torches 1 through 3 to hunt down the infantry portal," he reported.

"Copy that, Torch 1. May our fallen protect you," Torch 7 affirmed.

"May they protect us all," Abur replied, switching off the channel.

Abur looked down into the burning cityscape below. The targeting system in his helmet narrowed in on a structure that appeared to be the focal point of the Legion horde. *That must be where the infantry portal is*, Abur reasoned. He maneuvered his fighter in a tight arc around the suspected portal location.

Abut spotted the closest landing platform. It was missing a connecting walkway, but the support struts looked intact. He slowed his speed and dropped his Z-7 onto the platform, landing the ship deftly. He pushed the release lever, and the font of the cockpit cracked open in front of him with a hiss. Beside him, the other two Torches swiftly landed on the platform, each of the front hatches popping open. His warriors, Trae and Kendry, stepped out. They were the strongest of the Enlightened, undefeated in combat. This trio was the best defense the Great Planes had against the Legion. They stood together for a moment as Abur scanned for the structure that he believed housed the Legion portal.

The Enlightened warriors were identically clad. They wore helmets that masked their faceplates. A short cloak was draped over each of their shoulders. Underneath the cloak, they wore full-body flight-suits. These suits were built for combat and made of a heavy brown fabric. Horizontal grey bars of woven metal ran in columns down the sides of the suit's body, arms, and legs.

The heroes stood completely still as Abur plotted their strategy. He mentally mapped their path to the target building. When the Enlightened leader was ready, he stepped forward to the edge of the platform. Below them, a walkway circled around a bulky building. It led to a lane crowded with Legion soldiers and continued up to the portal's suspected location. Abur and his two warriors took several steps back. Then in unison, they ran forward, leaping out over the gap. They sailed through the air, striking the deck of the walkway below with a singular ring from their metal feet. They rolled into fighting stances as the Legion spotted them.

Abur glanced down at the bars he wore: twenty-two in number, each containing a sacred soul ember woven into the metallic mesh. The sight brought him comfort. The trio spoke together in unison, "Our past is set in these stones. Upon such a foundation we will not be moved."

Abur raised his arms up. His palms faced toward the Legion as the crimson-eyed demons raised their nihilistols. They fired at the Enlightened warriors. A shimmering white bubble formed from Abur's hands, encasing his warriors in a dome of light. The Void bullets struck the field and dissipated.

"May the Fallen grant us speed," Abur shouted, keeping his arms raised as he rushed toward his enemies. To either side of him, Trae and Kendry's bodies had become enveloped in the shimmering white light of their own ember armor. The warriors plowed into the Legion at full speed. Since Abur's shield only blocked the Void bullets, Legion soldiers passed through unharmed until they were met with the attacks of Kendry and Trae. Abur's comrades were whirlwinds of kicks and punches as they fought toward their goal. Ember energy swirled around Trae and Kendry's bodies, concentrating around their fists, knees, and elbows before each flurry they launched. Every strike tore through another Legion soldier, returning it to the Void.

The Legion fought back, attempting to overwhelm the Enlightened warriors with sheer numbers. They lashed out with their gloved fists, unable to use their nihilistols in such close combat. The Enlightened warriors were too filled with purpose to notice the occasional blow that landed upon them, as they battled through the Legion. The three heroes never stopped pressing their attack. Void troops shattered all around them, even as more rushed in to stop the trio.

Abur could see their goal, a less than noticeable domed structure at the end of the lane. It was built out of an old transport vessel, and inside lay the Legion's portal. The battle reached a crux, and the Enlightened warriors could hardly move as they were surrounded by such a vast horde. For every Void spawn that Trae and Kendry crushed, several more had taken its place. Abur was growing fatigued from holding back the numerous nihilistol blasts that poured down on them from the structures on either side of the lane.

"This is Torch 1 requesting aerial support on coordinates (49.3.4)," Abur yelled into the ray-com transmitter in his helmet.

"Copy that, Torch 1. Hold position. Torches 30 through 40 are on their way," Torch 7 replied.

Abur grunted in effort, driven to his knees under the strain of keeping the ember-energy shield up. Trae and Kendry dropped to their knees in a similar pose. Holding their arms out, they added their own concentration to the shield. The barrier increased in tenacity. The Legion beat down on it, no longer able to penetrate the shield with their physical attacks.

"We must hold," Abur said. His voice was strained. Trae and Kendry just nodded silently.

Suddenly, blue bolts of light cut through the air, striking into the midst of the Legion horde. The deck shook as each blast rattled the supports that held the entire lane together. Numerous Legion soldiers were blown away by the attack. Abur looked up through the ember shield. He saw an odd disk-shaped vessel, silhouetted in the smoke and flames.

***

"Clear the lane, Kai," Ohm commanded. "Apparently, I'm in communication with the acting commander. He says the fighters will keep the Legion off our backs while we help those three below take out Legion's portal."

"Is he talking about the Void structures we saw on the ridge above Bolleworth?" Oa asked Kai as he moved the ARI to provide her with a clear line of fire down the lane. Legion soldiers were running back from across the city to try and stop the Enlightened warriors below.

"Yeah, Void portals. Some Legion scouts must have snuck in and set them up," Kai responded as she opened fire on the avenue below, blasting the Legion away as they came pouring into the lane from the surrounding city.

Oa watched the three warriors rise up. They sprinted toward the building at the end of the street, making short work of the remaining Legion troops in their path. They battled their way into the structure. Not long after, the Legion below halted. They flickered slightly before dissipating into the wind, leaving the city ruined but safe once more. In the air above, the Enlightened Torches made short work of the remaining Legion Tridents.

"It seems the official commander is one of the warriors we just aided. He is requesting assistance returning to his ship," Ohm said, relaying the message he had just heard over his ray-com to the rest of the crew. "Can you set us down on the lane, Oa?"

"Yes, I can. I see a good spot," Oa replied as he dropped the ARI down, swinging around to face the heroic trio as they exited the building at the top of the sloping avenue.

"Lowering the entry ramp and disengaging restraint harnesses," Fred informed them. Oa stood up and threw Mordecai's monocle back into his satchel. He grabbed the bag of soul embers and ran out, eager to meet the Enlightened warriors.

Ohm and Fred were already waiting on the open deck when Oa came racing out. Kai arrived just behind him. They were in time to watch the three Enlightened Warriors stride up the ramp.

"Wow! That was awesome! You guys really showed those Legion," Oa exclaimed.

"It was the will of your predecessors, young Awoken, though we arrived too late. This city has already seen much loss," Abur said, halting in front of Oa.

"How do you know I am young?" Oa asked out of curiosity. "I could be a bajillion cycles old."

"No one who has lived long in this world would still have such a bright ember," Abur said laying a hand on Oa's shoulder. "I can sense its presence—a new ember, with a fire stronger than any other I have known … but it's a mystery. How could your ember feel so strong when your creation number must be so high?" He grew increasingly puzzled as he spoke.

Kai laughed nervously, pulling Oa back out of Abur's reach. She put her arm across his shoulder. "Would you get a load of these guys, Ohm? Sensing Embers? Ha!" Kai mocked as she looked briefly at Oa. She knew discretion was best; things would only get complicated if the newcomers discovered that the young Awoken had no soul ember. Oa nodded back at Kai in understanding. He knew that he should keep the number he had found on his birth cell to himself. Ohm stepped up, taking charge of the situation.

"Pardon my friend's ignorance to your ways. I, myself, was unaware the Enlightened could harness ember energy. I have only heard rumors of your order. We're grateful you rescued the remains of this city. How did you arrive so soon?" Ohm asked, diplomatically steering the conversation to safer territory.

"No offense is taken. I'm called Abur. I brought the Sky Sentinels here to evacuate the Awoken of this city to the mountain. The Legion is advancing in a large-scale assault. They have constructed a new vessel that can drag in the Void behind it. They intend to take the Great Planes. They are closing in on us faster than ever before, and this city will be consumed in roughly two cycles. Our timing was merely good fortune," Abur informed them, in a rich and authoritative voice.

"We would be glad to give you a ride out of here commander. We desire to reach the Enlightened City to preserve these soul embers we rescued," Ohm explained humbly.

Oa passed the bag forward. Ohm took it and held the treasure out to Abur.

"Then consider your mission a success! We are grateful for your assistance. The Sky Sentinels could use the help of Awoken such as yourselves to stop this new threat. Your warship is powerful indeed," Abur said, congratulating the crew of the ARI.

"Yeah, it appears it is," Ohm said wryly, glancing back at Kai.

She simply shrugged and replied, "Hey, don't give me that look. I just rebuilt what you wrecked."

Ohm chuckled. He stepped back next to his friends and threw his arms wide. "This ship is the ARI, and we are its crew. I'm Ohm, that's Kai, and the young fellow you met is Oa. He shall decide whether or not we take part in this fight."

"The Traveler," Abur said, recognizing Ohm's name. He paused before speaking to Oa. "There is no shame in seeking the sanctuary of our city. The battle will be fierce."

Oa stepped forward, looking back at Ohm and Kai. They nodded at him encouragingly so he turned to face Abur. "I believe our purpose is more than just delivering these embers to you. We will help you fight the Legion," he said, determined. His voice betrayed the microscopic seed of fear he felt inside at joining such brave heroes in a fight even they were wary of.

"We will not forget this noble act, Oa. You will be among the ranks of …" Abur's voice trailed off in dumbstruck awe as he stared over Oa's shoulder. "Impossible, it's a lightning varl."

The Enlightened warriors spun around from their posts guarding the ships entrance to stare as Susan floated out of the power hub. She glided up next to Kai and nuzzled her shoulder. Kai reached over and hugged the billowing cloud beast.

"Yup, this is Susan, the last of the lightning varls. She will also be fighting with us," Kai said happily.

"We cannot lose now. The sky itself is with us," Abur said, still in awe of Susan.

"Haha! He called you the sky," Kai laughed, patting Susan on the head. The varl growled softly, amused as well.

"May we take you to your fighters now?" Ohm asked.

"Yes of course we must return to the Stormfell. From there we can coordinate the evacuation. You can berth your vessel in the Stormfell's hangar for the duration of the journey," Abur offered. "After we deliver the refugees to the mountain, we will rendezvous with our sister ship, the Windhammer. Together we will proceed to meet the main Legion force in combat."

"Understood. Once you are back in your fighters, we will follow you up to your command station," Ohm replied, motioning for Oa and Kai to follow him back into the ARI.

The three warriors sat on the open deck in a circle. They meditated silently while the crew of the ARI flew them the short distance back to their Z-7s. Once the Enlightened had returned to their fighters, they guided the ARI up through the pollution of war to a massive orange and white vessel hovering above the city—the Stormfell.

"So would you say the Enlightened live up to the rumors, Ohm?" Oa asked in awe.

"Surprisingly, yes, for the most part. There must be a whole civilization living on the mountain if they could make all this. I have never even seen this class of aircraft before," Ohm replied, equally impressed.

"Sheesh. You'd think they would've shown up sooner. They're pretty late to the party that the world's been having with the Legion. That's okay, though. It's not like a giant warship would have helped much," Kai complained sarcastically.

"Well, I'm sure that flying fortress wasn't built in one cycle; and it probably takes an army of Awoken to operate. They came when they could," Ohm replied, amused by Kai's protest.

Oa piloted the ARI toward the biggest ship he had ever seen. In size, it was second only to the Careening City of Artisans below, which after some debate, the crew agreed should not be considered an aircraft. The Stormfell was an impressive sight to behold, shaped like a sickle. A humongous thruster sat at the back, like a handle. From the thruster, the bow curved around in a broad arc to a lesser jet cluster that helped to stabilize the unusually shaped vessel. The forward hull narrowed into an edge, like a blade. Numerous heavy cannons protruded from the forward bow of the ship. The light of the dawning cycle glinted off of thousands of viewports set into the hull.

Oa was curious about what was going on inside, so he put on the monocle Mordecai had given him. His sight pierced through the hull, revealing the inner workings of the Stormfell. There were several spacious bays around the thruster's engine where Awoken worked hard to maintain the machinery. Power generated from the multiple rotors, ran in intricate conduits through the ship to the cannons on the forward hull. Awoken were tuning the cannons and loading them with ammunition for the impending fight. Oa could make out storerooms for raw goods, living quarters for the crew, and several cavernous construction halls where essential vehicles were being built or repaired.

Behind the forward bow, the Stormfell had an open and exposed hangar. Torches returning from their fight landed inside to be recharged and refitted for future combat. Cargo vessels flew from one section of the floating harbor to another, ferrying supplies and workers. Refugee ships were being guided into empty safe zones set aside for them. Oa marveled at the order he saw. He took the monocle off and followed the three Torches as they circumnavigated the heavily armed forward hull. They looped back around to approach the open hangar that made up the rear of the vessel. The squadron headed for a section of the metal bay close to the engine.

"This is a nice ship, but I'm not keen on the color," Kai complained, clearly feeling outdone by the sheer size of the structure.

"It's big enough, but it's not the ARI," Ohm reassured her.

"Yeah they probably can't maneuver this thing very well. It's also completely vulnerable from the back," Oa agreed, pointing out the flaws he noticed with the Stormfell.

The Enlightened crew on deck waved glowing red batons to guide the ARI into a landing zone. Oa landed next to Abur's fighters. The circular ship took up enough space to fit a whole squadron of Z-7s. The ARI's crew met out on the open roofed side of their vehicle. They watched Abur and his warriors depart, heading for the bridge of the Stormfell.

"We will return to join you once we have delivered the refugees to the mountain. Then we will prepare for the battle. Rest for now. Your assistance isn't needed in the evacuation," Abur called over his shoulder.

"Look at that. He's calling you useless, Ohm. He must know all you can do is spray water at incoming refugees," Kai joked.

"Don't you have something to fix?" Ohm retorted as he sat back in his sling on the deck.

"Like what?" Kai quipped.

"The wing on my ship!? It used to be the fastest chunk of alloy in the sky because of those wing thrusters," Ohm complained.

"Too bad. Now it's the most walloping ship!" Kai said, sitting down on the deck. She pounded the metal with her fist. "I rebuilt that wing into a weapon. It's basically a huge version of my pistols. I call it the Sky Blade." She folded her arms proudly.

"Sounds ridiculous," Ohm huffed as he laid back in the sling.

"You saw how well my cannon was working earlier. I installed it on the roof when I rebuilt this thing, but that's just dirt compared to the Sky Blade," Kai said, pointing up to the top of the ARI.

Oa leaned out over the railing on the deck, watching as Z-7s escorted in refugee transports from the city below. The hulls were scorched and smoking, but they contained grateful Awoken who were happy to be rescued from the danger of the Void.

"I'm sure it'll work great Kai. We'll need it to protect these Awoken," Oa said sincerely.

There was a long pause on the deck of the ARI as refugees continued to pour into the Stormfell. Ohm was the first to break the silence. "Hey, Oa. That monocle you were talking about; where did you get it?"

Oa turned from the controlled chaos of the hangar. "I'm glad you brought that up. I got it from Mordecai; he had some interesting things to say about you, Ohm. First you're a sleeper, and now it seems that you're a defiler of the dead? Whose ember do you wear around your neck?" he questioned, slightly angered.

Kai scooted across the deck to lean back against Susan who was coiled up near Oa. "That all sounds pretty weird. What's the deal with that, Ohm?"

The old Awoken stayed in his sling as he spoke. "It's probably for the best you saw Mordecai. I don't have the ember anymore. Eol destroyed it, but her name was Ari. This ship is actually named after her …" he paused, choosing his next words. "I know I have said it before, but let me reiterate. I am old, old enough to have seen the Great War. I knew the Destroyer." He sat up to stare at Oa.

Kai perked up in shock. "Holy flork! You're ancient!" she exclaimed.

Ohm continued, ignoring Kai's outburst. "I used to be a lot like you, Oa. I wanted purpose. I believed that I was created to make things better. So I put all my time and energy into studying nature and researching the Great Planes history. I observed, I theorized, and I learned. The world was heading toward disaster, so I looked for any way to bring balance between the Awoken and the Great Planes. I concluded that the Destroyer was the source of imbalance. After much searching, I found him high up in the mountain. I thought ending him would be the answer, but he had already been defeated by his own failures. Instead of fighting, I learned from the Destroyer and the ice varls he lived among. He revealed to me how the Awoken had erred and why he had exiled himself. I thought this knowledge was enough.

"I returned to the Awoken with my message, but I was a fool. They did not care and things only worsened. When the dust of war settled, I helped rebuild. I became a teacher, and I tried to affect change in the embers of new generations of Awoken that emerged from the ground. The cycles dragged on, and my efforts produced no results. I was a voice no one wanted to heed. Even my best students turned aside my advice in the end. A bitterness grew inside me.

"It all changed when I woke Ari. She was different. She had such a shining ember; it gave me hope and we became great friends. Then the regime of that time began hunting me down for my knowledge of the Destroyer. Ari and I evaded their evil plans ... I am sorry that your friends were not so lucky," Ohm nodded sympathetically toward Kai before continuing. "I sought out the Destroyer once more. I had to warn him, but the others had gotten to him first. They had stolen a piece of his power. He asked us to stop his legacy, but he died before telling us exactly how. The quest sent us down a trail of clues, left before time by a being known through legend as the Creator. Eventually, we discovered a cave at the core of the world ..." he stopped, pausing briefly as his hand drifted to the spot on his chest where Ari's ember used to rest.

"We found the source of the Destroyer's power, and we ended it together. But Ari died and I was damaged and infected with the Void," Ohm raised his wounded arm, visually reinforcing his story with the bandaged stump. "I still don't remember exactly how she died or how I was infected; but when I rose from my first sleep, the world had been torn apart in the aftermath of the blast at Istaar. I had failed. I longed for Ari and could not handle the decay of a world I had spent my whole life trying to help. So I tried to bring Ari back, to reignite her ember in a new body. I lost myself in the obsession to repair just one thing in this world. It took Mordecai exiling me from his shop to make me stop.

"Then Eol appeared. His Legion became just as dangerous as the Destroyer once was, and the Void began to devour the world. I took responsibility again. Fred and I journeyed far and wide, following leads Ari and I had found. Riddles and clues left in the stone. They spoke of another One. We hunted for countless cycles until Fred found the answer, a launch button ..." he paused, and pointed at Oa. "I watched from atop a barren ridge as you were born, launching from the mountain top ... ."

Ohm laid back into the sling, sighing, "That is my tale. I never got to be the hero I wanted to be—but perhaps you will succeed, Oa. Somehow, I believe you can change things."

Oa listened quietly to the whole narrative. Ohm was his friend and he felt that he now understood the old wanderer better. Oa accepted Ohm's mistakes. He too, understood what it felt like to be wrong. He had stolen something precious from the Marauders, and they had died to protect him and their friends' embers. Oa hoped Ohm was right about him. *I want to make things better*, he thought to himself. Oa turned and looked over at Ohm.

"Do you think that's why the Creator made me? To fix this world?" he asked.

"That goal is your own. You must fight to make it reality," Ohm barked. He sat up again, there was fury in his voice. "There is one thing I remember from that accursed cave. I spoke with the Creator. I learned that I was merely playing puppet to a fate planned out by that cruel and treacherous being. The Creator never made me to succeed in my purpose: I was tricked! I know Ari died because I failed to realize the nature of the game. My life, my hopes, and my dreams all worked into the machinations of this being. I refuse to let the same curse fall on you, Oa. I will not let you lose the hope that I lost long ago. Do not concern yourself with our maker, he is a god of failure. The paths he conceived to build, led to ruin. Together we can forge a trail out of the broken system he built and stop Eol. You will fix this world." The Traveler fell silent, his impassioned speech concluded. The blue light in his mask sparked slightly then fell dark.

"Perfect timing," Ohm sighed, laughing humorlessly. "A fitting reminder. Such a good joke." His shoulders slumped dejectedly as he reached back and popped a hatch open on Fred. Ohm grabbed out another canister of microburs. He quietly replaced the empty one in his mask.

"If it means anything, you are still the same old Ohm to me. A wandering nut with a lot of long stories. What matters is what's happening right now. You're not a failure, Ohm. You met Ari and then us, and together we have a pretty grand time. We'll all work together to make things better," Kai said. She stood up and put her hand on Ohm's shoulder.

"Yes, Kai, we will," Oa said, still slightly overwhelmed at what Ohm had told him. "We will begin here and now, by fighting the Legion. I woke up with a vision inside me. I'm scared of this conflict with Eol, but I know how things need to be. And Eol must be dealt with before we can head in the right direction." As Oa spoke, Seeker rose from his satchel and hovered above his hand, spinning slowly.

"All this encouragement and good will is ruining my mope. Just remember, you can't use Seeker until we understand Eol's relationship to it," Ohm said. He chucked the empty microbur canister at Seeker, and it pinged off the levitating metal orb.

"Yeah, yeah, I know," Oa said, laughing. He put Seeker back in his bag.

Kai walked over to the front of the deck, looking out of the hangar. "Ew gross. The sky matches the Stormfell," she groaned. "Also, we've moved. I don't see the city anymore."

"Yeah. Ships stopped landing about halfway through Ohm's big backstory," Oa said, picking the empty canister up off the deck of the ARI and flinging it back at Ohm. It bounced off his shoulder.

"Let us enjoy this peace while we can. Fighting is not all that pleasant of an activity," Ohm suggested.

"Yeah. I don't really want to think about it. Let's just do something else until we have to go," Oa said, scuffing his boot nervously on the deck.

Kai walked past Ohm, flipping him out of the sling. Flailing, he fell and landed on the deck with a thud. "Alright then! No more dismal talk. Let's go swap fun stories while we recalibrate the engines. I don't want us exploding out of the air from some mechanical problem," Kai said, stubbornly.

Ohm chuckled and picked himself up off the floor. He brushed himself off and followed Kai and Oa into the engine room. Susan floated above them, happily watching as they all sat around the machinery, running diagnostics and tinkering with the settings as Kai directed. They laughed and swapped stories of their favorite times. Some of the tales were recent while others recounted times long forgotten. Together, the friends enjoyed each other's company, working together in community. Their minds forgot the impending danger. Their time together seemed as if it would last forever, but it could not. Four knocks sounded on the door, slow and steady. Oa got up and opened the portal; outside stood three Enlightened soldiers.

"Abur? Is that you?" Oa asked.

"Yes, it is," Abur replied in his familiar noble voice.

"I'm sorry, but you all look alike," Oa apologized.

"The garb is an old tradition of the order. Your confusion is understandable. I have returned to inform you that the Legion has moved faster than we anticipated so we will not be able to deliver the refugees. Our timetable has been advanced, and we have already joined the Windhammer. Your vessel will fight alongside the Sky Sentinel squadron, protecting the Windhammer's back," Abur explained. "Do you still desire to help us?" he asked after a brief pause. Oa nodded in reply.

"Good, I will be in command of the Sky Sentinels. I shall relay orders via ray-com to you. Windhammer will spearhead the attack. Our goal is to protect her back until the Void command ship is destroyed. That should halt the Void's advance on this front," Abur explained.

"How many other fronts are there?" Ohm asked.

"One other. The remaining two Defender-class warships are being dispatched. They will do their duty, and we will do ours," Abur clarified curtly. The crew of the ARI nodded in understanding. Abur waited briefly for any more questions. There were none.

"May the fallen protect you. We go to battle," he said reverently. Abur spun on his heels and led his two warriors back to their squadron.

"Yeah, you too," Ohm replied with less conviction.

The three friends stood in a circle and took hold of each other's hands for a moment, finding courage in community. Then they walked out of the engine room and into front section of the ARI. Ohm took his seat at the power hub while Oa, Kai, and Susan went to the cockpit.

"I'll fly this time," Oa suggested.

"Yeah, there's no way you're gonna be the gunner. These are my weapons," Kai agreed lightheartedly.

"I patched us in to Fred's ray-com so we can all hear Abur's orders. I'll manage the ship's defenses. If Kai didn't replace it, there should still be a sealed tank beneath the power hub attached to a piping system that runs to the outer hull. Fred can fill the tank with water, and I can use that to ice over parts of the hull. I can shield us from most attacks, but I cannot protect us from too many at once," Ohm informed them, his voice transmitting over the ARI's unseen communication system.

"Yeah, I was wondering what in the name of sanity that storage tank and all those irrigation tubes were for. They took me forever to put back together," Kai complained.

"I am glad you did. We stand more of a chance now," Ohm replied.

The ARI's engines activated, rumbling deeply. The craft rose into a shallow hover as the Z-7 Torches of the Sky Sentinel squadrons accelerated out of the hangar. Oa waited for Abur's command before falling into formation at the rear of the procession. The ARI followed the Sky Sentinels out into open air as they rose toward the dawning glow of a new cycle. It was a red sky, as red as the eyes that lurked within Eol's shrouds. It was as if the demon himself were above them, watching with gleeful anticipation for the outcome of the brewing storm. The orange army of Torches coasted dangerously close to the churning clouds. The sparks and flares of lightning masked the Enlightened forces as they charged toward the inevitable fight. Abur organized his troops, ordering them into a wide chevron shaped attack formation. The ARI flew behind the spearhead of fighters. Abur had tasked them to deal with any Legion ships that got through his ranks. Far off in the distance, Oa could see that the Windhammer had nearly reached the Void.

"Full speed ahead. Our timing must be exact. We will initiate a counterstrike the instant our enemy attacks the Windhammer," Abur commanded.

A thousand thrusters burned hot and bright in front of Oa as they accelerated to overtake the warship. Below them, the Stormfell followed slowly, staying out of range to protect the safety of the refugees it carried.

As they neared the edge, Oa saw the Legion vessel protruding from the Void. It was a monstrous sight; cylindrical, hollow, and even bigger than the Stormfell. Three grizzly structures jutted out from the prow, like teeth. The vessel formed a gaping maw into the Void. At the end of each blade sat a mighty thruster. The jets were pointed back at the Void, hauling it forward, feeding the Great Planes to the darkness. The Legion was driving inward, and the Void was coming with them. From the core of the ship, a black swarm of Tridents spewed out. Their glowing red cockpits made for an eerie and intimidating sight.

"Slow to three-fifths speed and wait for my signal," Abur commanded calmly.

Up ahead, the Windhammer approached the Legion horde, yet the warship launched no fighters. For a moment, all was calm as the two forces approached each other. Then shockwaves thundered through the air as the Windhammer opened fire. Hundreds of cannons blasted, shooting out meteors of blazing white light. The Tridents broke formation, dispersing to avoid the volley. The missiles of light shattered the Legion formation, obliterating those too slow to maneuver away from the attack. Oa noticed that the missiles dissipated far short of hitting the Legion command ship.

"They aren't in range yet," Kai muttered, worried.

The Legion reformed their echelons. The deft fighters maneuvered around the dangerous but slow cannons. The swarm swooped over the forward bow of the Warship, seeking to attack it from the rear. Suddenly, Z-7's came zipping out of several of the forward cannons. Oa realized that the Windhammer's crew had constructed launch tubes to allow their fighters to exit the front of the aircraft. They had been disguised as cannons. The Torches flew in behind the Legion, blasting away at the Void dwellers.

The Trident swarm was caught off guard, but it banked a hard turn, coming about to make a strafing run on the exposed hangar bays of the Windhammer. They were met with a head-on attack, as the remainder of the warship's fighter complement poured out to engage them. Chaos ensued as the attack from both sides devolved the Legion's formations. Their numbers were too great to be overpowered for long. The Tridents quickly recovered, engaging in a fierce dogfight with the outnumbered forces of the Windhammer.

"All squadrons stay in formation. We will strike through the center of their ranks!" Abur commanded sharply. The Sky Sentinels hurtled down into the battle to aid their comrades.

Oa and Kai looked at each other as they flew toward the chaos. Kai put a hand on her friends shoulder.

"We got this," she said confidently.

"Yes, we do," Oa said. His nervousness hardened into courage as he pushed the throttle to full.

"Let's show them what the ARI can do," Ohm called from the power hub chamber.

"Activating the deck shield," Kai called as she pulled a lever on the console. The broad metal plates stacked at the back of the open deck slid around the railing, forming a metal shield to guard the vulnerable side of the ARI.

"Open Fire!" Abur yelled over the ray-com.

Kai dropped down her targeting controls and began to blast away at the nearest targets. Oa followed the Sky Sentinels, diving down through the maelstrom of combat. Black and white rays filled the air. Oa dodged through the chaos, his concentration pushed to its limit. Next to him, Kai rapidly unloaded the ARI's firepower into the Legion. The twin azure beams sliced through Tridents with each blast the cannons sounded. The ARI was rocked from explosions all around.

Ohm grunted as he strained to merge his senses with the ship. He felt an incoming missile heading toward the engine and knew Oa could not dodge it in time. With a thought, Ohm sent water to the hull, casting his ice over the threatened spot. The barrier took the full force of the blow. The reinforced structure shook violently but remained undamaged. Ohm immediately melted the ice and redirected it to the underbelly of the hull just in time to deflect another deadly missile. Oa rolled and spiraled the ARI through the sea of conflict. He kept his movements erratic to shake off any ambitious Tridents trying to get into position behind them.

Screams of doomed pilots came in over the open ray-com. The victorious surprise attack was not without losses.

"We must defend the Windhammer until she is in range to attack the Legion command vessel. Regroup now and prepare for another run," Abur called out as the Sky Sentinels passed through the thick of the battle. The fighters leveled out, speeding over the desolate ground as they reformed their lines.

"Reengage," Abur barked as soon as his forces were ready. They looped back up for another strafing run.

Oa flipped the ARI end-over-end in a barrel roll, then looped around and sent the ship back into the fray. Kai toggled to another weapon on her guidance goggles. A cannon from the belly of the ship began to fire, spitting out projectiles faster than Oa could keep track of. Kai's accuracy made sure most of them struck Tridents that had slipped through Abur's lines.

None of her shots hit the orange and white hulls of the Z-7 Torches.

"These are just the tracers. We will need to make another pass through when we reach the other side," Kai informed.

Oa looked over quickly, and nodded an affirmative. He noticed Susan floating protectively over Kai. The varl's two soft paws rested on either side of her friend.

"I hope you have enough of those, 'cuz the other side of this fight is a long way off," Oa said. His voice strained as he banked a hard left to avoid an exploding Torch.

"I built the cannon to hold five-thousand tracers. Let's just say I had a lot of time on my hands back in those caves. We have enough," Kai assured him.

"I'll say," Oa agreed.

"You should've gotten a hobby," Ohm teased, joining the banter.

"Yeah, because building the coolest gliders and exploring every rock of those canyons doesn't really count," Kai retorted.

"We're almost through the thick of it," Ohm called back, refocusing the crew on the battle.

The ARI rocketed out of the fighting just behind the Sky Sentinels. Abur commanded another strafing run, and the Torches prepared to make another pass. Oa took a little extra time looping around so he could rest his mind and reflexes.

"Activating the Sky Blade," Kai said, as she flipped another lever on the control panel. "I really hope this thing works," she muttered. Outside, the ARI's wing folded out to its full length.

Along the front blade of the wing, panels popped up slightly then slid back to reveal a crackling bank of blue energy.

"Take us in!" Kai yelled. The hum of the Sky Blade filled the cockpit, rising to a screeching drone. Oa pushed the throttle to full power, sending the ARI racing past the other Z-7s and back into the fight.

"Stay in formation," Abur barked.

"Nah, how about you clean up after us this time," Kai called back.

Just as they were about to reenter the fray, Kai pulled the trigger on her targeting controls. All along the front blade of the wing, blue lightning shot forth, seeking out the tracers Kai had fired previously. The ARI cut through the middle of the warfare like a blue sword of light, searing a grim swath of destruction through the Legion ranks. The ARI's blade was inescapable. Tridents exploded all around them. The crew cheered in unison as the Sky Blade ripped through their enemy, in a strafing run for the ages.

The Legion's numbers had been greatly reduced, and the tide of the battle was turned. It seemed as though the Enlightened would be victorious. The Sky Sentinels and the ARI pulled out of their dive and headed back up to finish the fight. Over the ray-com, Oa could hear the cheering of the other pilots.

"Crew of the ARI," Abur said, his stern voice breaking through the cheers. Oa cringed inwardly hoping they hadn't offended the hero too much.

"Your reckless actions have paid off. The Windhammer is nearly in range," Abur congratulated. "All squadrons, pick your targets and finish off the remainder of these Tr—"

Suddenly, explosions shook the ARI. Enlightened pilots called out in surprise as their Torches were attacked from behind. Oa heard their dying screams over the ray-com. The enemy had launched a surprise counterattack. Sections of the ground below crumbled away as Legion reinforcements poured from gaping wounds in the Great Plane. The Legion had drilled through the foundation of the edge lands and waited for the Windhammer to pass before springing their trap. The Sky Sentinels were forced to scramble and reengage, but they were overwhelmed as the sheer number of incoming Tridents blew past them to attack the exposed Windhammer.

Pandemonium ensued as the ARI was hit with the full weight of the Legion's assault. Ohm did his best to protect the ship and Oa flew with skill unmatched while Kai shattered copious amounts of Tridents with her deadly cannons. But the crew's efforts were not enough. The hull of the ARI was torn apart by missile after missile. All around them, the Enlightened forces were being annihilated. The Windhammer was in flames. Its cannons boomed out, desperately trying to hit the Legion flagship; but it was still out of range.

Oa instinctively dove down to avoid a head-on attack from an oncoming Trident. His evasion was too fast for Ohm to register, and it placed the ARI in the path of an exploding Z-7. The debris struck the unprotected hull. The cockpit window shattered as pieces of the wreckage crashed through it. Oa grunted as he pulled the ARI around and accelerated out of the fight.

"We took a bad hit Ohm. I can still move. Kai, is—" Oa looked over at Kai, his voice catching in horror. "Kai is hit! She has a piece of debris through her torso."

Oa set the ship on a straight course away from the fight. He shoved himself out of the pilot's seat and knelt next to Kai. Her head moved slowly as she recognized him.

"Oa, that was some great flying. T-too bad that stuff got in the way," Kai laughed, though her voice faltered with pain. Susan hovered next to her, sparking in agitation and worry.

"Ohm, I don't care what happens. I'm using Seeker to fix her," Oa yelled, his voice panicked.

"Oa, don't!" Ohm called back, but he was too late. Oa already had Seeker glowing above his hands as he frantically called upon the power he had been suppressing. He dove headlong into the universal programing, throwing his will toward Kai. Seeker blazed with light, unleashing the power of creation. Tendrils of life reached out toward Kai. The orbs power was too glorious and pure to go unchallenged, so the Legion answered.

A lone Trident left its bombing run. It turned away and raced after the ARI, moving faster than any Legion vessel should. The Trident leveled off directly over the ARI, and the front hatch popped open. A Legion soldier dropped down onto the ARI. The Void warrior swung through the smashed cockpit window, tackling Oa to the ground. Oa's concentration ruptured, and Seeker dropped to the floor, no longer glowing. Susan growled and grabbed the intruder in her paws. She crushed the enemy and threw it back out of the cockpit as the soldier crumbled into Void dust.

Immediately, several more Legion fighters peeled away from their attack to pursue the ARI. Ohm darted out of the power hub and raced to the cockpit, arriving in time to see Susan defend Oa. Oa reached for Seeker, but his focus was fractured; and the silver orb did not respond. He grabbed Seeker, trying to reenter his inner sight. He yelled in frustration. Ohm wrapped his arm around Oa and snatched Seeker from his hands.

"Oa, we have to go! They're coming for you!" Ohm yelled. Oa struggled, not wanting to leave his friend.

Kai raised her head, lifting her arm up feebly. She grasped Oa's hand and spoke softly. "I know you'll change things, Oa. Thanks for everything."

Oa continued to resist Ohm. "No, wait! I can fix this," he said frantically.

Kai turned her head towards Ohm. "Get him out of here!" she growled. The Traveler nodded silently in farewell. Oa fought as Ohm aqua jetted them out of the broken window and away from the ship. They fled as the Legion fighters hurtled toward the ARI.

Inside the cockpit, Kai moaned in pain. She strained in effort to pull the jagged piece of metal from her midriff but was unable to remove the shard.

"Susan, help me with this will ya?" she murmured. The lightning varl took the piece of debris in her paws and pulled it free. Kai cried out but stayed upright. She heaved herself over to the pilot's chair. Susan assisted her wounded companion, using her gentle paws to support Kai's crippled body. The varl floated next to Kai, nuzzling her snout against Kai's shoulder.

"Susan, you have to go … Please, I need you to protect Oa now," Kai said, her voice breaking.

Susan growled in understanding but refused to leave her partner's side. Kai reached forward, whimpering in agony as she strained to take control of her ship. She spun the ARI around and dropped underneath the oncoming enemy fighters. Kai sent the ARI on a course around the dying Windhammer and toward the massive Legion flagship.

"Let's see how good my work really was, eh, Susan?" Kai said, her voice still cheerful despite the fatigue each word exacted on her mangled body. She reached across the console, nearly collapsing before Susan caught her. The varl supported Kai as she reactivated the ARI's Sky Blade. The weapon hummed to life, and Susan nudged Kai back into the pilot's seat. Her head rolled back weakly as she fell into the chair.

"Susan, you need to go now," Kai said, her voice growing quiet. She reached up to pet Susan's big soft head as she had so many times before. Kai rubbed the spot between Susan's pointy ears. Her fingers gradually lost their feeling until all she could fight to hold onto was the moment. Kai's hand fell limply to her side, all of her strength gone.

Susan nestled herself around Kai, resting her snout against the Awoken's chest.

"You're m-my best friend S-susan …" Kai fought to get the words out. "Thank y-you … ." Her voice faded completely as life left her. Kai's head slumped forward to rest on Susan's brow. She was an empty shell, no longer the playmate Susan had loved so much. As if in response, the energy in the ARI's Sky Blade sputtered and died as well. Susan stayed holding her head against Kai's. The energy in her body dimmed and throbbed in grief. She would not leave her fallen comrade as the ARI made its dying flight toward the Legion flagship, pursued by the Trident fighters. A small, meaningless scrap of metal, fated to wreck itself upon the unstoppable force of the Void.

Susan started to growl, a noise that grew from a grief stricken whine to a roar. Her energy began to churn, as heartache and rage consumed the gentle creature. She held onto Kai for a moment longer before barreling through the cockpit's shattered window, out into open air. Susan's roar was unending. It resonated through the sky, haunting and powerful: a eulogy to the spunky Awoken she had rescued from the darkness of Istaar. Her eyes narrowed to slits as tears of purple lightning leaked out, crackling and sparking. The Legion fighters had overtaken the ARI; to their great misfortune, as the lightning varl let loose her fury. She swelled to the size of a Trident, and each swipe of her vengeful claws ripped a foe into oblivion. Susan's eyes seared as she wept bolts of violet light. Coils of electric fire spewed from her mouth, consuming the creatures of the Void.

Susan threw back her head and howled. Lightning charged up toward the stormy clouds above, and she raced to follow it. She struck the sky with a bang that echoed across the Great Planes. It sent a ripple of her energy spreading out to the ends of the world. Deep in the clouds, the streams began to converge, changing from crimson red to a hurricane of deep mauve. The intensity of the storm built to unmatchable brilliance. Then the wrath of the last child of the sky was unleashed upon the Legion. Susan hurtled down from the clouds completely ablaze with amethyst rays. Behind her, the energy veins of the sky came as well, heeding her call. Susan dove down through the battle, burning through the Legion swarm. She tore their army to dust.

The varl flew back to the ARI, enlarging to match its girth. She gripped the wounded ship in her strong paws, empowering it with the radiance of her ancestors. Susan pushed the ARI faster and faster toward the Legion vessel. She howled one final time and rested her head against the hull of Kai's prized creation. Her eyes closed in remembrance and longing. The silhouette of the ARI could still be seen at the tip of the blindingly violet lightning bolt as it plowed into the Legion command ship. All the power of the sky struck with the ARI in an explosion of color and light: a defiant cry. The Great Planes would not be snuffed from existence so easily.

Ohm hovered in the air, holding Oa as the two stared at the fading glow. The Legion vessel collapsed in upon itself, returning to the Void. All at once, the few remaining Tridents faded back out of existence. The veins in the sky returned, casting a pale blue light across the land. Over Fred's ray-com Oa could hear the remaining Sky Sentinels cheering, but it was a bitter victory. Down on the ground, the wreckage of the Windhammer smoldered as a constant reminder of the losses suffered that cycle. Oa and Ohm did not cheer or speak any words as they watched in stillness. Ohm merely turned from the sight and jetted back to the Stormfell.

EPISODE 10

OA'S RESOLVE

The Stormfell turned about slowly as it plotted a new course toward the Enlightened City. The vessel's thrusters thundered mightily, rotating the immense structure that hung high in the air. Sky light glinted off the orange and white hull, painting the craft in a shining portrait set against the ominous backdrop of the Void. The gleaming vessel hovered in place, posing victoriously. Then the engines roared louder, propelling the Stormfell from the desolation of war. Far below lay the scattered debris of fallen defenders, their smoking remains smoldered on the cracked rock of the vast stone desert.

From the edge of the Void, at the point where nothing met existence, a lone glowing figure sprinted through the sky after the Stormfell.

Back in the hangar of the warship, Oa and Ohm sat in a silent vigil across from each other on the metal deck. They had returned to the same space the ARI had occupied a cycle earlier. Now it lay empty, a constant reminder of the loss they had experienced. The aftermath of the battle occupied the Enlightened warriors' attention. No one took notice of the pair, and none of the other Awoken refugees or crew members tried to approach them. The hangar was a bustling hub of incoming and outgoing traffic. Some ships arrived from other ends of the

Stormfell with supplies and relief crews, while others left to retrieve survivors and lost embers from the Windhammer's wreckage. Ohm and Oa paid little attention to these events as they grieved the loss of Kai and Susan.

Oa was the first to vocalize the pain they both felt. "Is it wrong to wonder why I had to wake up at the end of everything?" He stared mournfully at seeker, remembering his time with Kai and Susan. "The good things still in this world feel like a haunting echo, and friends can be lost so quickly in the havoc … I wish I could've known them longer."

Ohm slowly looked up from a rivet in the metal floor he had been intensely studying. "I woke you up because I need you, Oa. I lied when I said I don't hope anymore. I still hold on to one hope: I believe you can achieve where I failed."

"I understand that now. I won't let my purpose waver, but I still really miss Kai and Susan," Oa replied as he stared down at the floor.

"I'm sorry we had to leave Kai," Ohm said. His voice seemed tired to Oa.

"Don't be sorry, Ohm. I know I could've saved her, fixed the ARI, and even saved all the other Sky Sentinels; but I didn't get the chance. Eol somehow knew how to ruin my focus. I heard his voice when that Legion soldier attacked me. Eol seemed to feed off of my efforts, countering the power I felt inside. If he was just gone …" Oa said, letting his final words hang in the air. He let his mind forge forward, exploring all the possibilities he could think of if Eol did not haunt his steps.

"Yes, I was afraid of that," Ohm said, looking away from Oa to stare at the numerous machines that littered the hangar. Enlightened workers and soldiers bustled around, repairing and cleaning the damage. "Fred and I have continued to study our previous data collected on Seeker. It appears your power does more than anger Eol. Your arrival correlates with the accelerated advance of the Void. Your growing skill with Seeker and exploration of this world also correlates with Eol's increased influence as well."

"Your power and Eol's law appear to be equal, opposite, and infinite. My theoretical calculations have attempted to replicate such an immeasurable conflict. So far, they have culminated in an event that neither Ohm nor I can understand. By all of our knowledge such an occurrence is an impossibility," Fred said, expanding on Ohm's explanation with his monotone voice.

"So you're saying our conflict has been inevitable," Oa sighed. "My goal remains unchanged. I have an opportunity to make things right, and somehow I will stop Eol. From there, we can rebuild in the memory of Kai, Susan and your friend, Ari. We haven't lost yet. I won't let us lose," he proclaimed resolutely, as he stood, facing Ohm. "I understand why you journeyed so far to find me and to show me so much. I promise to do whatever it takes to break Eol's Law."

Ohm's head spun toward the Hangar opening. "You're going to need some of that resolve to keep your balance!" he said with happy shock.

Oa didn't have time to look as the lightning varl collided into him, tackling him to the floor. Susan nuzzled her head against Oa's face, sparking with happiness.

"Susan!" Oa laughed with joy as he embraced the creature.

The sight filled Ohm with awe and disbelief. "Impossible!"

"Improbable is the term that best defines the situation," Fred corrected smugly. Susan's bushy tail swung around, bowling Ohm over.

"Never doubt Susan," Oa said, laughing at Ohm and Fred. He ruffled Susan's head as he sat back up. "So is Kai …?" he paused, unable to finish his question as he looked into the varl's deep eyes.

Susan floated between Oa and Ohm. She lowered her head and opened her jaw slightly, letting a small gleaming stone rest gently on the ground.

"She is then," Oa said softly. His emotions were torn between joy and sadness as he saw the soul ember of his friend, resting on the floor.

"Ohm, Oa, you are alive! The lighting varl has brought victory to us all," Abur's booming voice carried over the noise of the hangar as he walked through the chaos of flight crews and machinery toward the reunion. Trae and Kendry followed silently behind him. One of the warriors walked with a slight limp.

Oa and Ohm both rose to their feet, standing beside Susan. Kai's soul ember rested between the varl's paws as she hovered lightly off the floor. Susan's head was level with Ohm's hip as she looked up at Abur with a solemn gaze.

Abur stopped in front of the trio, he looked down and noticed the soul ember. "I see," he said, sympathy in his voice. "We lost many brave Awoken on this expedition, but Kai's sacrifice was not in vain. The advance of the Void has slowed immensely. Once we deliver the refugees, we can reinforce our comrades on the second front and crush the remaining Legion. We are in debt to you, Ohm and Oa."

"Susan was the one who saved all of us," Oa said as he reached down to pick up Kai's ember. Susan's snout followed his hand as she kept her gaze on the ember. "I would like to return with you to the city on the mountain so I can learn how to listen to this ember."

"A noble endeavor, Oa," Abur complimented as his concealed face continued to stare at Susan. "Is it common for such a creature to follow an Awoken?" he asked bluntly. "Would she fight for us one more time? We would honor her forever in the temple of souls."

"She has been our companion, but I'm not sure what she will do now. Susan goes where she wants to," Oa replied diplomatically.

Ohm laughed at Oa's and Abur's ignorance. "A varl can be the most loyal friend in this world, and it is clear who Susan desires to befriend now," he turned to the creature. "Susan, whom do you protect?"

Susan flipped her head around, nudging Oa's side. She rolled over in the air, knocking him down with her playful affections. The tumble caused Oa's tunic to flip up revealing his empty chest socket. His hand instinctively brushed the tunic back down, but not before Abur's sharp gaze noticed.

"What is this abomination?" Abur snapped, stepping forward. Ohm darted in front of him. The warrior halted, hesitating at Ohm's speed and the sudden cold he felt as the air around him chilled. "My apologies, Traveler. You must understand that despite being a courageous Awoken, your friend's ominous existence was predicted by the esteemed Seven. Oa must be brought before her now that he has been discovered."

Ohm maintained a calm demeanor. "Oa will see her, but I will be with him. At no time will he be under your authority." Oa got up, gripping Kai's soul ember in his hand. He was perturbed by the sudden tension in the air.

Abur faced off against Ohm for a moment before conceding. "Very well, Traveler. We will be arriving at the mountain presently. You both will wait in accommodations we provide until the esteemed Seven requests your presence."

Hearing that they neared the city, Oa turned around to look out of the hangar. He watched as the Stormfell wheeled about. The thrusters fired in reverse, backing them toward the mountain. Oa could tell they were very high up by how close the sky was and how most of the mountain spread out below the ship. He caught a glimpse of a beautiful structure, resting on a great rock slab just beneath the peak. A fissure zigzagged down the face of the stone.

Below the rock face, the Enlightened City sat in a sheltered valley in the side of the mountain. Oa was impressed by the size. The structure was similar to Bolleworth but far grander.

An opaque white shell covered all but a few towering spires in the center of the metropolis. His view was blocked as the Stormfell cruised backwards through an opening of the shell into an enormous harbor, big enough to fit four of the sickle-shaped warships. The vessel's engines shuddered then quieted, bringing the Stormfell to a halt. The heavy structure reverberated slightly as it rested into its mooring supports.

Oa turned his attention back to Ohm and Abur. He saw Abur signal to an open-topped transport barge. Oa inspected the vehicle as it glided over to them, noting the bland design.

"We will take you to your room. Please wait there for our return," Abur instructed. His tone was removed and distant.

"Why am I so important, Abur?" Oa asked as they walked up a short ramp on the side of the craft to stand in the center of the barge.

Abur replied evenly. "You are the anomaly, Oa. I apologize, but your existence was never meant to be. Wether you acknowledge it or not, your very life aids our enemies. All will be explained by the esteemed Seven."

Oa glanced at Ohm who just shook his head subtly. The young Awoken kept silent as he stood behind the three Enlightened warriors. Inside an enclosed cockpit at the front of the barge, the pilot engaged the accelerator. The transport sped out of the docking bay and into the city below. Numerous buildings reminiscent of the ones Oa had seen in Istaar sped by. He noted that some of the architecture appeared to be exact replicas of what had been lost to the dark mists of the dead city. The shell covering the city was translucent from the inside, showing a beautiful view of the sky above. Oa gazed up toward the peak. He could make out the bottom of what he assumed was the Temple of Souls, a half-circle structure protruding from the mountainside. It had a bright profile from the light that flowed out of the peak just above the temple.

As they sailed further into the metro, Oa's keen eyes picked out Awoken milling about. A plethora of transports zipped to and fro, carrying passengers on unknown errands. There were bright signs and interesting sounds. The city was bustling with more life than Oa had ever seen. The last remaining Awoken lived life in the refuge, a diverse mixture of skills and trades. He longed to explore the streets below. He was sure he would find enough adventure there to entertain him for a very long time.

The transport barge flew to the center of one of the downtown areas. Several exceptionally tall towers rose up out of the shell that covered the rest of Enlightened City. The transport reached the edge of the highest spire and slowed to a stop before rising rapidly through the air. The wind whistled around them as they passed through one of the open gaps in the protective shell that covered the metropolis. The vessel continued up toward the top of the tower. Oa widened his stance, taking care to maintain his balance.

The barge halted at the edge of an open balcony that led into the uppermost chamber of the tower. Ohm stepped off first, stumbling slightly as the wind buffeted the vehicle. Susan and Oa followed. Behind them, Abur raised his arm and the transport dropped back down out of sight.

The chamber the friends stepped into was roomy and sparsely furnished. Several seats and reclining couches were sprawled across the spacious floor. Pieces of drab-colored art hung from the walls. Oa was more interested in the view, so he walked back out to the edge of the balcony and looked over the vast world. Far off in the distance, the Great Planes met in the black line of the Void. Down below him, the bustling life of the city was hidden beneath its opaque shell. Wind whipped around the tower, sounding a lonely wail.

Oa watched the empty stillness for some time, while Ohm paced around the chamber, deep in thought. Eventually, Oa turned and went inside. He sat on a couch and pulled Seeker from his satchel. He rolled the silver ball around in his hand. With a thought, he set Seeker floating in the air. Susan pounced from a shadowy corner of the room, sweeping the sphere up in her jaws. Oa laughed, trying to pull Seeker back. Susan growled and glowed brighter as she fought the orb's pull. She was dragged back slowly through the air. Oa gave in and let go of Seeker, allowing Susan to amuse herself with the shiny ball. Ohm flopped down in a backless chair across from Oa. A woven green rug with numerous intricate patterns lay on the floor between them.

"This place seems nice," Oa said cheerfully. His mood lightened by the knowledge of the life teeming below.

"I guess, if you enjoy the whites and grays of a holding cell. Notice there is no way out of this room other than the balcony. They do not want us to leave," Ohm replied, looking at the drab colored metal that made up the room.

"They have to know we can leave whenever we want," Oa said in amusement, pointing to Susan. "I think we should stay though. Their suspicions about me must be eased. I'm opposing Eol, not helping him."

"Their knowledge is curious. We need to find out what they know. Once we have dealt with this nonsense, we will head into town and begin hunting for more information on the ember-fission labs," Ohm replied, thinking intently. He stood up and started pacing across the floor again.

"How long do you think we have to wait?" Oa asked.

"I'm not sure, but they will contact Lida as soon as they can. Abur is in a hurry to reinforce the rest of their army," Ohm replied.

"Who is Lida?" Oa asked.

"The so-called Esteemed Seven. It appears that a creation number is still worshipped and rewarded here. I remember her. She was an arrogant and self-important leader back when I was younger. I didn't know she was still around," Ohm explained. He walked over to Oa who had taken out Kai's soul ember from his satchel. He was holding the ember intently in front of his face. Susan spotted the stone and left Seeker on the floor. She returned to Oa's side to look at Kai's ember.

"What are you trying to do?" Ohm asked quietly in an understanding tone.

"I am trying to connect with Kai's ember the way that the Enlightened do," Oa replied as he concentrated.

"That form of meditation takes time, Oa. You have no ember with which to connect to Kai's. I'm afraid such a focus may never be attained by you," Ohm said heavily as he sat down cross-legged on the couch next to his pupil. He placed the ember in his palm, focusing as he had countless times before. "I used to do this with Ari's ember," he explained softly. After some time he handed the ember back to Oa. "This is full of memories—good and bad, though the brightest by far were the weebles she shared with us, a beautiful painting of happiness and friendship. Kai died at peace."

Oa held the stone, focusing intently. "I wish I could feel that too." Frustration filled the young Awoken.

"Here, let me keep watch over her for you," Ohm said, standing up. He took the ember and placed it into the pocket on his hip. "Do not become obsessed with the embers as I did, Oa. You are a creature of more than the past or future. Unlike the Awoken around us, your gaze can pierce through what has been and what could be. You perceive how things truly should be in the p-present ..." he stumbled backwards slightly.

"Ohm, what's wrong?" Oa asked concerned.

"I am not sure ... I am losing my sight, I-I can't focus," Ohm stuttered. His hand reached up to the side of his head.

"You are falling asleep again," Fred informed.

"No, this is different. I can feel it. The timing is too coincidental. Oa, this is a trap. Do not trust her," Ohm sputtered frantically before he collapsed limply back into the chair.

"Ohm slept too recently. This timing implies sabotage of some sort. Expect them to return before Ohm wakes," Fred cautioned.

No sooner had Fred spoken the ominous prediction than the whine of an engine sounded from outside the balcony. Oa took up a defensive stance in front of Ohm as Abur and his warriors stepped into the room. Abur nodded toward Ohm's reclining figure concealed behind Oa.

"Your friend isn't well. It's to be expected from a Sleeper," Abur said. His voice held deception.

"You didn't know Ohm was a sleeper," Oa accused.

"Do not fight us, Oa. We seek only the betterment of all Awoken. Is that not your goal, too?" Abur asked, his voice slightly pleading.

Oa considered the question for a moment, then he relaxed and called Seeker back. The orb dropped lightly into his satchel. Susan hovered protectively beside him, the violet light of her eyes flashed at Abur. Oa rested his hand calmly on her head. "I'll do whatever it takes to protect these Awoken. I don't fully understand what I am, but I'm not your enemy. I'll come with you."

Abur nodded and strode from the room. Oa looked back at Ohm the Sleeper, infected and motionless. He did not know what to do. His mentor had left him at a crucial moment. He hoped Ohm's suspicions were wrong, but he felt a growing dread, as if his fate was sealed. Oa did not know what awaited him, but he held on to his desire to aid the Awoken. *I must not compromise on that conviction.* He faced forward and walked out onto the balcony with Susan. Together they boarded the transport. Susan huddled close to Oa, shielding him from the fierce wind as they returned to the city.

Back in the room, Ohm lay still. His left hand shifted suddenly, as the old Awoken fought to free himself of the infection
that had chained him for so long.

Oa and Susan were taken to the edge of the city, straight
toward the rock face that led up to the peak. As they neared the
stone, Oa could see that the fissure in the rock was actually a
trail. A long series of switchbacks had been hewn out of the
granite. The transport barge coasted out from under the city
shell, halting at the beginning of the trail. The passengers
climbed off the ship and its engines revved up, quickly returning the vessel to the city.

"We will make the remainder of the journey on foot. This
path is sacred," Abur informed Oa.

The three Enlightened warriors started up the trail. Oa and
Susan looked back at the city and the tower where Ohm was
sleeping. After a moment, they turned and followed Abur.
There were no special adornments to mark the beginning of
the path. It was simple and barren, cut deep into the rock. The
walls, floor, and ceiling were smooth. Oa wondered what had
created the path. It led in an upward slope. When it reached a
corner, the trail looped around through a brief tunnel in the
mineral to head the other way. The path switched directions
numerous times as it climbed up the peak. Oa spent most of
his time looking down as they hiked above of the city. At one
point, he noticed a glowing pale-green fuzz that poked through
cracks in the stone.

"What is this?" Oa asked, reaching to touch the soft organic
material.

Abur and his soldiers halted briefly. "The remaining life that still chooses to come from the ground. All other rock is barren but this one," he replied reverently over his shoulder.

They continued on in the fading twilight of the cycle, always moving upwards toward the peak—the pinnacle of Oa's journey. Ever since he had spotted the mountain on the horizon, he had somehow known he would end up at the point where sky met land.

The hike dragged on, as if it would never end. Oa had time to think about what potential decisions awaited him. He wished the trek to be eternal, but eventually all paths reach a destination. Oa rounded another bend in the trail and saw the route conclude before him on a ledge atop the stone they had been hiking through. Overhead, the grand structure of the Temple of Souls fanned out in a broad arc. A crystal-clear stairway climbed from the clearing high over their heads and into open air. The stairs led out to an opening in the far edge of the temple floor.

Oa hesitantly stepped onto the first step behind the confident strides of Abur, Trae, and Kendry. The lack of any railing made Oa uneasy as he tried to walk with confidence. Susan hovered close. She rested her paws on either side of him, steadying his balance as he climbed. He took comfort in the varl's company. Emerging up through the temple floor, Oa found himself standing on the edge of the platform that the Temple of Souls rested on. He was finally able to fully appreciate the view. He looked out across the mountain that extended far below. The black line on the horizon had thickened. The

Void had moved, Oa was sure of it. The abyss was closer than it had been before. *I hope this meeting is quick. The other Enlightened forces need our help dealing with the Legion*, he thought to himself.

Oa turned back and strode around the entrance in the floor. He followed Abur to the gates of the temple. The structure was an elegantly arching half-shell, opaque like the city below. Ascending up from the temple's center was a tower composed of six metal pillars. The thick columns sat in a semicircle against the flat face of the rock, stretching up to the peak. Energy coursed up the pillars, becoming a beacon in the sky. The peak lay in the brightest spot. The Awoken walked toward a set of stately white gates. A guard stood to the left of the entrance, still as stone. Abur raised his arms, and the gates swung open for him.

They entered the Temple of Souls, passing underneath the huge archway. Oa looked up at the roof overhead. The interior of the ceiling was transparent. Like the city below, it revealed the beauty of the sky above. Shards of translucent crystal hung from the ceiling of the immense chamber. Oa likened the hanging crystals to the stalactites from the Marauder's cave. He was reminded of his first adventure with Ohm. The stalactites gleamed as reflections of sky-light lit them. The rays twinkled through the facets of countless soul embers that were stored within the stalactites. Oa looked closer and realized each ember seemed to rest in a special slot that had been custom-cut for it.

At the rear of the chamber, a round flight of stairs rose up to a platform. From this platform, the six pillars rose up to the peak. In between the two center masts, another archway led to an antechamber enclosed by the colonnades. In front of the arch stood a figure clothed in white. One hundred of the finest Enlightened Warriors were stationed around the stairs, guarding the chamber. They stood in an intricate formation, unmoving and serene.

Oa followed Abur through the display, stopping at the base of the stairs. The figure above gazed down on him.

"I have brought him before you. He is a loyal comrade and was an integral part of our victory. I request your haste and fairness with these proceedings. We must depart soon if we are to aid Iron Flower and Cycle's Light," Abur said stiffly.

"There will be no need for that, Abur. I thank you for your valiant service. The end of the conflict will be decided here and now," the figure above said sweetly.

Abur and his two warriors stood to the side of Oa becoming motionless.

"Now?" Oa asked in bewilderment, but Abur did not respond. Oa looked back up toward the figure at the top of the stairs. *This must be Lida or the Esteemed Seven*, he thought to himself. She wore a long flowing white gown and her face was soft with one singular face plate, smooth and round. It glowed softly. She was the image of grace and elegance.

"Why did you bring me here?" Oa asked impatiently, his voice projecting through the temple.

"I am the Esteemed Seven. You are here because you contain the power to end this war," Lida said. Her voice was soft and soothing.

Oa stood straight. "I am prepared to do that."

"Are you?" Lida asked.

"Of course I am," Oa insisted in confusion. "I'll do anything to help the Awoken. I already proved my willingness to defend them."

"Oa, your existence conflicts with Eol's. It is a conflict that has now consumed most all of this world. I ask not for your resolve to fight Eol but for your willingness to give yourself to him," Lida said. Her soft words crashed down on Oa. From the chamber behind her a familiar figure strode out to stand next to her. Oa instantly recognized the shrouded effigy of evil.

"Eol!" Oa could not help but cry out the name in shock.

"Eol is an entity that exists to counter the mathematical impossibility you pose, Oa. An Awoken of such pure creative power cannot exist without an equally opposite creature of chaos. If you fight, the conflict will consume this world; but if you concede, Eol's lust for death will be sated, and he will leave us. In this pure glimmer of life, at the focal point of the Great Planes, we who remain shall protect our past, haunted not by the ravages of creation or destruction. It is what is best," Lida explained softly.

"Yes, Oa. Do you not want your friend Kai to be kept safe? All of her memories? The joy and happiness you shared—don't let that fade away," Eol whispered. His chilling voice rippled through the air causing Oa to shudder slightly. Susan growled next to him.

"You're lying, Eol! You will devour this city all the same," he called back.

"He is not lying, Oa. You know that it was your coming which gave Eol strength. The Void's movement accelerated when you launched from the sacred circle atop this mountain," Lida countered, her voice calm.

"Your perfect nature empowers me. It enrages me with an unending hunger, driving me to consume this world. If we oppose each other, all things will end; but if you let go and cease to be, I can preserve this existence forever," Eol said, his voice thick with a mixture of hatred, bitterness, and despair.

Oa spun around looking everywhere, seeking answers; but nothing could be gleaned from the stagnant atmosphere of the hall. He wanted to question Lida and every Awoken in the room to reason further, but his path had led him into a corner. He could no longer run. His choice was either to fight for himself or let go. No one else around would join him. *Susan would stand by me*, Oa thought happily to himself, but such loyalty should be rewarded not abused. He knew struggle would only lead to greater loss. His shoulders slumped slightly in defeat. Lida made sense. Ohm had confirmed the connection between Eol and Seeker. This was not how Oa wanted his journey and purpose to end, but he also felt doubt. Perhaps he had been wrong all along. *My dream must be flawed. If I want to stop Eol I must let go of my vision*, he thought sadly.

"Susan, please stay here. Protect Ohm now. Even if Eol goes back on his word, he should be too weak to bring the Void any further once I'm gone. You will be able to defeat him," Oa said embracing Susan. She growled in frustration but remained in her spot. She nudged Oa comfortingly as he stepped forward to slowly walk up the stairs toward his end.

"Do not be afraid, Oa. My law is truth. Your sacrifice will preserve this world and all its memories, the beauty of its entirety," Eol said with honest conviction.

Oa did not respond as he walked up the stairs in silence. He reached into his satchel and held Seeker again. His heart tugged at him, reminding him of all the potential he had, all the things he wanted to do. Oa wanted to mend others, to turn the tide of decay into a rushing wave of growth. Finally, he understood his mentor. *We feel the same. Like our existence is just a cruel trick. The only good it seems I can do for this world is to leave it.* He had failed: Buri, Ibra, Jad, and Kai had all died. Like Ohm, Oa had saved no one. Now he had a chance to act in accordance with his bold words; to protect what remained of the Great Planes. He could save the world he was responsible in part for destroying.

Oa began to walk with purpose. His beginning was inevitable, as was his end. Even in the face of destruction, he would never stop believing in the Awoken; in the good he had seen. The Marauders and Kai had given themselves to protect others. Oa had inherited the same task. The remaining Awoken would thrive in the cradle of the mountain. They would grow and create. They would find a way to give the embers life again. Somehow they would push back the Void. All would be well, and Oa's end would make sure of it.

Oa neared the top of the stairs, looking up at the last few steps. Eol stood, staff held at his side. The softly glowing face of

Lida looked down on him, her arms held out in acceptance and gratitude.

Suddenly, the peak above burst forth in the dawning of a final cycle, radiant and piercing. The sky was filled with a deep, cold blue light. From behind Oa, a thunderous crack boomed through the temple. He wheeled around and saw the gates of the temple crashing to the ground, broken in pieces. Standing tall in the entrance was Ohm, tattered clothes whipping about in the wind. The Traveler looked like a statue that had stood for all of time. Though broken and battered, the old one's will held strong; his ocular plate burned blue to match the sky above.

"Enough!" Ohm roared. His voice cut through the air strong and resilient. The voice that had woken the world had returned to protect it.

EPISODE 11

OHM'S PURPOSE

"The Destroyer! Eol, you said you stopped him," Lida cried out, her soft voice growing shrill with fright.

"Destroyer?" Oa questioned, confused. Below him the same puzzled question was being echoed through the ranks of the Enlightened warriors. He turned back to look at Lida, thinking he had misheard her. Eol moved suddenly. He leaped from the top of the stairs toward Oa, staff held high overhead.

Oa had no intention of evading the strike. He bowed his head in acceptance, averting his gaze from the impending doom. He dimly heard Ohm's shout, "Susan!"

Just as Eol's staff was about to split Oa in half, a sparking snout latched onto the weapon, halting Eol's blitz. Susan quickly let go of the staff and, with blinding speed, she head-butted the villain. Eol tumbled backwards up the steps, landing nimbly on his feet next to Lida. Oa had been knocked off balance by Susan's hasty rescue, and he slipped backwards. Ohm saw his friend tumble. Instinctively, he sprinted toward the steps. The instant Ohm's attention diverted from Eol, the demon sprung his trap. Eol whipped out a nihilistol from within his shrouds and fired. The Void bullet silenced the room for a moment. Sound returned in time for the clang of Ohm's knees hitting the floor to ring through the chamber. The bolt had pierced through his side. He did not immediately dissolve away. Instead, the wound slowly grew as the Void gnawed away at his body.

Susan had reacted immediately to Oa's fall, spinning around to catch him. As Oa fell, he saw the nihilistol being fired, watching as Ohm crumpled. Oa's scream was drowned out in the silence of the shot; and he looked away, not wanting to see his friend disappear. The lightning varl flew him down to the bottom of the stairs. Oa looked up at Eol, resting his hand on Susan for comfort. He knew there was only one way to end the monster. No one else would die. He took a step up.

"The Destroyer was never a threat," Eol snarled smugly. He never even looked at Ohm as he tossed the nihilistol away in disgust. The weapon flickered out of existence as it left his hand.

Oa halted abruptly. "What do you mean by *Destroyer?*" he asked angrily. His heart began to fear the answer.

Eol kept silent as Lida responded. "I don't know what he told you, but Ohm has another name: Destroyer, whose right hand held the power of annihilation—"

"But he rejected his purpose, and thus was powerless to save himself. Now come to me, Oa, before anyone else dies," Eol commanded, cutting Lida off. He beckoned to Oa.

The pieces tumbled into place in Oa's mind. Traveler, Destroyer, Peacekeeper: each title a different alias of the same Awoken. Could it be his friend? Could it be Ohm? Oa knew the answer. Purpose drove through his grief and he took another step. Soon he would be reunited with his comrades.

***

Ohm sat on his knees, hunched over in pain. He knew he had to act fast. "Fred, why haven't I dissolved away yet?" he asked as he reached back and pulled a microbur canister from the pack.

"I am unsure, but we are not going to last very long," Fred replied grimly.

"I was never going to live forever," Ohm growled as he crushed the canister in his hand. The metal cracked and the microburs began to leak out slowly. Ohm jammed the canister into his wound, stiffening in pain. The microburs leaked out into the gash, filling it with alloy and slowing the advance of the Void.

Ohm grunted in pain as he rose to his feet. He glimpsed Oa starting up the steps again. "Oa, get over here! Susan, grab that idiot!" he yelled across the room.

***

Oa was surprised to hear Ohm's voice. He turned and was snatched off the steps again by Susan. She whisked him over the heads of the Enlightened warriors to Ohm.

Eol's head snapped around; his crimson eyes blazed. "Impossible! You cannot resist my will!" he said furiously.

"Clearly, I can," Ohm mumbled to himself. He stood tall, straining against the heavy ache in his side.

Susan dumped Oa next to Ohm and spun around to face toward Eol, her fangs bared. Oa picked himself up and was swatted on the head by his mentor.

"What were you doing?" Ohm demanded.

"I was going to save everyone," Oa replied stiffly.

Ohm laughed, then stopped as pain quelled his amusement. "By dying? That's not how we are going to stop Eol," he stated determinedly.

"Ohm, there is no other way. If I fight Eol, you'll all die," Oa insisted.

"So stand aside, Oa. You are the opposite of me; you will heal where I have wounded. This is my duty. It always has been. I am the Destroyer. Not a researcher or wise teacher but an ender of conflicts. I cannot redeem my reputation, but I will use it to finish Eol once and for all. I am sorry I concealed the truth from you, but I had my reasons," Ohm said, stepping in front of Oa.

Oa patted his friend on the back. "I understand. You will never be just the Destroyer to me." He was not bothered by Ohm's actions. Time and disfigurement had blinded the ancient Awoken to his own nature, but Oa knew who Ohm truly was. The Traveler turned and put his remaining hand on Oa's shoulder in gratitude.

At the top of the stairs Lida's faceplate pulsed rapidly in fear. "Destroyer, why are you getting in the way?"

Ohm bowed his head for a moment, then whirled around angrily. "I have been measuring this world's worth since its birth, and it pales in comparison to Oa's potential. You would selfishly sacrifice him to try and hold onto the belief that you were meant for great things. We both remember what you did. You and I are responsible for what happened to the Great Planes."

"It was your power that desolated this world, and you'll only fail it again," Lida accused.

"Only because you sought to control it, or do they not know?" Ohm roared furiously, scanning the soldiers motionless before him.

"You all follow a coward and a fraud. The head of the regime that brought this world to its current state stands before you, and yet you follow blindly," Ohm shouted out for all the Enlightened to hear.

Several of the warriors turned and stared at Ohm "Why should we trust you? If you're the fabled Destroyer, then you have more ember dust on your hands then anyone alive," a random voice in the crowd spoke up.

"The Awoken would choose now of all times to reject my help," Ohm grumbled in frustration. His time was short. Water was leaking from his side. "None of you are old enough to truly know what the world used to be. Lida has led you to worship the past. Her vision will only leave you with longing and regret for what you can never recover. Here stands Oa, an impossible Awoken with no ember. With nothing to leave behind—he only moves forward. He can forge life where none exists. His mind is meant to see the path ahead that we cannot.

"You ask him to die for you? Well, I say we fight for him. If we stand together, we can defeat Eol. Even if it costs all our lives, it would be better to fight for someone who can make this world beautiful again than to submit and continue our stagnant existence. If you let me, I will lead you this final time," Ohm said stiffly. Resolve sounded clearly through his pain.

Oa looked at his friend. He was thankful for Ohm's faith in him. Every Awoken in the chamber had turned to listen to Ohm. Oa felt their gaze on him as well. He stood to the side of Ohm, not knowing what to say. One by one, the Enlightened soldiers stepped forward to show their allegiance. Only Abur, Trae, and Kendry did not move; hampered by their loyalty to Lida.

"Very well. I shall kill that abomination atop a pile of your corpses," Eol hissed down at the warriors. He casually spun around and drove his Void staff through Lida. "You proved less than inspiring," he taunted as she faded away into Void.

With a yell, Abur, Trae, and Kendry raced up the steps at Eol. Their hands swirled with ember energy. Eol spun the Void staff casually in his hand as Abur sprinted up the last few steps. Eol halted the staff's spin to hold the weapon behind his back. The noble Abur swung his fists, but the monster deftly dodged between the blows. Eol took a slight step back then moved with unnatural speed as he whipped his staff forward, driving it through Abur's chest.

"Now!" Abur cried out, as he gripped the staff and dropped to his knees. His whole body surged with ember energy holding off the consuming power of the Void. Trae and Kendry bounded over their fallen leader, simultaneously striking down on their enemy.

Eol was caught off guard by the ferocity of the attack. He stumbled back onto one knee, letting go of his weapon. He did not shatter from the ember-energy attack, but instead began to flicker in and out of existence. On the ground, Abur pulled the staff from his chest and melted away, unable to fight the Void any longer. Trae and Kendry were unable to grieve as they stood ready and wary of their foe. Eol flickered more erratically, emitting a screech of rage. He lifted his hand and the Void staff leaped from the ground toward him. It caught Trae and Kendry in the back of the knees cutting them down. As soon as the deadly weapon hit his hand, Eol vanished. His screech remained, echoing eerily throughout the temple.

One of the Enlightened warriors cheered awkwardly. "Too soon, stupid! It can't be that easy," his comrade whispered harshly, nudging the applauding fool.

Sirens sounded from the city below. The wailing echoed through the hall. Everyone spun to face the doors as the sound rang ominously through the chamber. Suddenly, the guard from outside the gates came rushing in screaming. "It's the city. We're under attack by the Le—" His words were cut off as a nihilistol blast silenced him forever.

Eol strode through the temple archway; the Legion following behind him. Far below, the Void ravenously feasted on the final city of the Awoken. Oa and Ohm looked at each other in shock. There was no time to register the sudden tragic turn of events.

The ice sword and shield formed on Ohm's arms. He raised the shield up, shouting for all the Enlightened to hear. "Warriors of the fallen, you know better than I how to draw strength from the memories of those you loved. Remember your past, hope in our future, now defend the moment!"

Together, the final hundred Awoken rushed to meet the Legion. Ohm tapped Oa on the chest with the ice shield. "You stay safe while we take care of these guys. When it's over, you'll be free to make that vision of yours a reality. Just promise me you won't forget why I woke you," Ohm said. His voice was hopeful and courageous, drowning out the weariness his wound was causing.

"Thank you, Ohm. I won't doubt my purpose again," Oa promised. He climbed onto Susan's back and wrapped his arms around her neck. Together, they flew to the top of the stairs.

Ohm waved to his friend one last time before he turned and sprinted to join the battle. He pushed the pain and fatigue from his mind as he lunged into the fray alongside the other Awoken. Ohm became a blur as he blocked Legion attacks, spinning rapidly as he sliced through his foes. Around him the Enlightened soldiers fought valiantly, their hand-to-hand combat unmatched. Countless cycles of training and discipline had rewarded the Awoken with the strength to hold back the tide of doom at the entrance to the temple. The close quarters kept the Legion from using their weapons to full effect. They began to burn through the protective shell around the arch. The walls melted away under the onslaught of the Void. The Legion opened a gash in the Temple of Souls through which they pushed forward, stronger in numbers and unrelenting in will. Ohm watched noble warriors fall around him as they fatigued under the unending flood.

"Fred, we have to reach Eol and end this," Ohm shouted through the fury of the battle.

"I would not advise it. We will be vulnerable from nearly every angle," Fred warned his master.

"We have to try. For those that are giving their lives right now," Ohm insisted, accepting the risk.

"Reckless as ever," Fred responded.

"This time, it's necessary, my friend," Ohm said grimly. He lifted his shield and plowed through the Legion soldier in front of him. He dove under a nihilistol shot then rolled to his feet, slicing the legs out from under several Legion. Ohm gave a mighty leap and the aqua jet activated, aiding his jump toward Eol. He held his shield in front of him with sword drawn high for a final blow. Fred's concern proved valid. Ohm's speed was not great enough to evade a stray bolt that grazed the pack's side panel. The aqua jet shut off, and Ohm tumbled to the ground short of his target. He felt the blow as if it were to his own body. "Fred, are you alright?" he called out in pain.

"My wound is consuming me at a rate much faster than yours. I am afraid my functions will be fully impeded shortly," Fred replied, his voice cutting in and out.

Ohm cried out in frustration. He lashed out at the nearest Legion soldier, slicing it in two. He spun around trying to find his way out of the chaos. All at once, the Legion backed away. Ohm realized he was alone. The remainder of the brave Enlightened warriors had fallen. Eol stood at the center of the gateway, his minions surrounding Ohm completely.

From the top of the stairs Oa started to rush down. "Stay there, Oa!" Ohm yelled, turning slightly. The young Awoken obeyed, watching in horror.

Eol's chilling voice spoke. "A worthy effor—"

"Shut up!" Ohm snapped cutting him off. "Fred, can you still activate a full fusion?" he asked softly.

"Aff-ir-mati-ve" Fred replied, faltering as his circuitry broke down.

"One last time then!" Ohm yelled. Fred lit up bright blue as he poured water forth. The liquid gushed out of the pack, spreading rapidly across the floor of the chamber. The light within Fred became dazzling until it sparked, flickered, then faded altogether. The water stopped, and the pack dropped lifeless from Ohm's back. Fred's final act had been to detach from Ohm to keep the second Void wound from spreading to his master.

Ohm hunched over as the injury in his side crippled him with pain. The microbur canister was empty and the Void was now eating away at his body. He did not let himself collapse. He knew he had one final gambit.

"This one's for you, Fred," Ohm said quietly as the pack disappeared behind him. He concentrated and droplets of water rose into the air. The drops closest to the old Awoken began to wheel around him slowly.

"End this!" Eol commanded. The Legion rushed forward raising their Nihilistols.

The Traveler drew upon his power one last time, draining the energy from the water. Harmless drops of liquid became unbreakable projectiles. He sent the ice whipping through the air in a tight vortex around him. The vortex spread as Ohm lifted more water from the floor into his maelstrom. The Void bullets were deflected harmlessly as the Legion tried to carry out their leader's order. In the center of the storm, Ohm rose to his feet. He readied himself for one last duel. He took a step forward and then another, feeling his weakened legs steady. Ohm started to trot towards Eol, intent on killing the demon. He accelerated to a sprint, hurtling through the Legion.

Eol's army was torn apart by the fury of the ice. Eol stood motionless as the edge of the storm rapidly approached him. His shrouds fluttered in the wind, and suddenly he was standing in the tempest. Countless Legion soldiers were shredded, but the ice never hit Eol. He stood calmly waiting.

In the midst of the gale, the Traveler appeared. Charging forth, he sliced his sword with deadly speed and accuracy at Eol's head.

Eol parried the blow with his staff, taunting Ohm, "Your words to Oa where truly words of a friend. I'm sorry you will turn on him," he taunted cryptically as the two fiercely struck at each other, evenly matched in a dance of death.

"Silence!" Ohm yelled, driving Eol back.

"You can't keep this up. You are broken," Eol continued, enraging Ohm even further.

"I have to! I will not fail Oa," Ohm gasped, fighting within himself to become faster and stronger even as his senses dulled and his energy drained out of the wound in his side.

"You are a creature to be pitied, but the Destroyer will be whole again. I will make sure of it," Eol said, dodging to the side of Ohm's attack. He slipped his hand through Ohm's defense grabbing him by the side of the head. "It is time for you to remember, Ohm. It is time for you to accept your purpose," he snarled.

***

Oa stood atop the stairs, holding Susan tightly in suspense as he watched the ice storm rage below him. The ceiling above had been torn apart, and the ember stalactites had crumbled under the force of Ohm's fury. Suddenly, Oa saw a blue flash from the center of the vortex, and then the maelstrom ceased. As the white storm cleared, Oa saw Eol at its center. In his hand he held Ohm's mask. Oa spotted his friend a short distance away, lying on the floor. Fred was gone and so were Ohm's weapons. The hole in his side had grown to a gaping wound, and water was now only dripping from it. Ohm feebly tried to crawl away from Eol but the shrouded monster strode forward and gripped him by the tunic. Eol dragged Ohm up the steps toward Oa. Oa was frozen in horror when he saw what Ohm's mask had been hiding. Half of his head was gone, eaten away long ago by the Void. Eol tossed Ohm to the ground and stood facing Oa.

"I'm sorry, Oa. I failed," Ohm said wearily.

"You were never meant to serve him!" Eol snapped. He knelt down next to Ohm, resting his hand on Ohm's damaged head. "You strayed from your path, but you can never escape your fate. I am you. The part of your programming you tried to rid yourself of in that cave so long ago. Your negligence killed Ari. So you threw your gift into the abyss. I was too weak to stop you then, but I am stronger now. You will submit to me. You will submit to our purpose. Now remember!"

"No, you can't be. The researchers at Istaar must have triggered my power when they detonated the ember fission bomb. You, I mean it, killed Ari ..." Ohm recalled in shock, refusing to accept the truth even as the gap in his mind was mended. "But I drove my right arm into the Void core, I-I got rid of you."

Eol shook his head slowly. "I am you, Ohm. Now turn on this enemy of ours. Accept the responsibility you forsook—Me! The will of the Void! Our purpose is good—it's what the Creator intended." Eol lifted Ohm off the ground and drew him into the shrouds of Void. The rags wrapped around Ohm, slowly enveloping him until he had disappeared into them. One of Eol's eyes turned blue as Ohm remerged with his lost programing. The Destroyer stood anew in front of Oa.

Finally the infection and disfigurements made sense. In an attempt to cleanse himself from the title of Destroyer, Ohm had unwittingly created Eol.

"Ohm?" Oa asked hesitantly, hoping his friend was still alive somewhere in the darkness. There was a long pause as he waited in suspense.

"Oa, they're here. Everyone is here. Ari and Kai, all of them," Ohm replied slowly. There was another long pause. Oa could not fathom what his friend meant. He put his hand on Susan for comfort. The varl growled reassuringly, adopting a defensive stance.

"Their souls now rest in me. I-I wasn't a Destroyer ... I preserved them," Ohm stammered in realization. His voice began to mix with Eol's. The demons voice was an ominous whisper, it waited patiently as the old wanderer gradually lost control of his will.

"But Ohm, I don't understand," Oa said, growing increasingly worried as he tried to grasp Ohm's words. Next to him, Susan bared her fangs at the shrouded figure before them.

The menacing shadow paid no attention to the varl's threat. "I see it now, the reason I devoured the soul embers. The Creator knew all things must end, so he built me to protect this world, to preserve it. Every memory, every joy, every pain, every success, and every mistake of this world—it's all here, frozen in my ember. I can see Ari and you and Kai, everything all at once. It's chaos, but it's how things should be. It's how they've always been," Ohm said in bittersweet acceptance. He took a step toward Oa.

"You said I needed to trust my cause and not follow the past," Oa said, nervously taking a step back.

"I am sorry, Oa; my purpose has always been to protect what the Creator made. I have not failed yet. My greatest challenge was always meant to be you. The Void is closing in, Oa. Only one of us will be left. You must yield," Ohm said with an eerie calm. Eol's voice softly echoed each syllable he spoke. Oa backed up through the archway between the pillars onto a round platform. There was no roof or walls aside from the pillars. A hole the size of a birth cell sat in the center.

"You made me promise never to let go of my vision," Oa pleaded. "You awoke me!" Susan growled a warning as the Destroyer stepped through the arch and onto the platform.

"I was wrong, Oa. I know what it is like to feel betrayed by the Creator. I know you must despise yourself as I did, but it is not your fault. Without you, I would not exist. Our conflict is inevitable, but I will preserve your memory for all of eternity here," Ohm said, tapping his chest. His voice had grown cold.

Oa felt alone, more alone then he ever had before. He wondered why he had to be pitted against his friend. He tried to think of a way around the situation, but the Void had already eaten halfway through the temple. The oily black tide erased everything in its path. Oa never wanted to fight for just himself; he had hoped others would join his convictions. Now his friend, who had encouraged him the most, was telling him he was wrong. Oa looked next to him. Susan was still by his side; she turned and opened her jaws in a smile, her tongue rolling out to lick his face with an explosion of sparks. Oa knew he had to trust in himself and in the comrades who had gone before him. *I must trust in their faith. In Susan's faith in me now,* he decided.

"Ohm, I don't care what you know now. I see a better existence than this. I see a future, and I will fight for it. I will not die and leave you trapped in this incomplete creation," Oa said. His words were steely.

Susan roared. She lit up, preparing for a final fight. The remainder of the sky above still shone bright as the energy from the pillars coursed up into it.

"So be it. I cannot protect you any longer," Ohm said. His voice splintered, then shattered. The pieces drifted away as madness took him. The blue eye beneath Eol's shroud changed back to red.

"Do you know how a lightning varl is born?" Eol's voice oozed out like poison to fill the air. Oa could no longer hear any trace of his old friend. He did not respond as Eol stalked around him on the platform.

"Two varls must meet—a male and a female. They must spend a lifetime together for their energies to merge. When they are completely attuned to one another they die together. Out of their ashes, a newborn varl rises—a complete combination of the parents. The species progressively dwindles down, leading up to an ultimate varl, the culmination of the entire species. Wouldn't that be special? The beginning of something new.

"There were two penultimate varls. I hunted down and slew the one atop my head, but the other stands beside you now. Susan, you call her? Kai thought she was the ultimate varl; but alas, she is merely the failed remnant of a species I broke," Eol said, his voice even and deadly. Despite the danger, Oa was still sadly reminded of one of Ohm's lectures. The memory drove him to fight for the Awoken's legacy all the more.

"Take a lesson from the varls, Oa. You, like Susan, are merely a creature meant to carry potential but never to fulfill it. Such a feat is impossible, and I exist to uphold that law. Perfection cannot exist!" Eol snarled, lunging forward.

Susan roared, rearing up to meet Eol. She caught his swinging staff with her paws. The energy inside her began to pour into the Void weapon. Susan snapped at Eol's head, but he ducked underneath the attack; twirling his weapon around to catch Susan behind the head. The blow struck hard, draining more energy from the lightning varl. She retaliated quickly with a swipe of her paw.

Oa snatched Seeker from his satchel, ready to truly fight for the first time in his life. Seeker blazed to life in his hand and suddenly the platform began to float upwards. Oa rushed forward, sending Seeker flying toward Eol. The orb of light struck Eol's staff, preventing it from dealing another blow to Susan. She darted forward, lightning spewing from her mouth. Eol brought his staff back around to block the energy. The Void consumed the purple fire, further draining Susan's life force. She faltered slightly, shaking her head in confusion as she tried to recover. Eol took advantage of the pause to knock Susan out of the way and sprint toward Oa.

Oa called Seeker back to his hand as Eol's staff sliced down toward him with blinding speed. Oa's arms were too slow, but his mind was fast enough to move Seeker into a parry position. His arm was a blur as he mentally positioned Seeker to counter each of Eol's attacks. Susan charged in, causing Eol to split his attention. The demon was still too fast. His ferocity increased as he battered down harder on Oa, causing the young Awoken to stumble back.

"You are alone, Oa! Stop fighting!" Eol thundered.

"Never! My friends are always with me. Their hopes and dreams will live on in me. I will carry those hopes and never let them fall to the likes of you!" Oa shot back as he locked Seeker with the Void staff. The opposing forces pushed against each other as the platform rose up through the pillars of light, higher and higher. Oa strained with all his physical and mental might. The Void closed in around them, eating at the pillars and the sky above. Susan tried to tear Eol apart, but with each attack her essence only drained into the monster instead of harming him.

The platform reached its destination and halted. The only light came from Seeker and Susan. The darkness had closed in, hovering around the edge of the platform. The sky was gone along with the rest of the world. All that was left was Eol, Oa, and the final lightning varl, locked in a duel of fate. Oa lost his footing and Eol flung him backwards across the platform. Oa landed on his back, hard. He looked up to see Eol charging toward him, but Susan intercepted the assault. She moved as fast as Eol did. The varl's size fluctuated rapidly as she outmaneuvered her foe. She darted around Eol's attacks, delivering blow after blow, but the shadow could not be moved.

Susan poured out the strength of her ancestors, the life of the Great Planes. She fought out of loyalty and love for Kai, Oa, Ohm, and her lost mate. The whirlwind of violet burned brightly even as it drained away into the Void. In the end, Susan grew tired. Her spirit was far from infinite. Oa got up and ran toward the varl to protect her, but he was too late. The final lightning varl faltered, and Eol laughed victoriously. He battered her down, driving his staff through her body and pinning her to the ground. Susan let out a yelp as she was mortally wounded. Eol drew the staff out and backed away, pleased with himself.

Oa skidded to a halt beside Susan. Her aura flickered and dimmed, as the churning energy in her chest slowed. The varl looked up and spotted danger behind Oa. Susan spent the last of her strength as she curled around the young Awoken and blocked a swipe of Eol's staff. She whipped her tail around and threw Eol across the platform. She uncurled from Oa and he held her head as she gave a final howl. Susan's light faded completely and the creature of sky lay dead.

Oa remained knelt next to Susan. Eol stalked toward him, but still the Awoken did not move.

"Have you finally given up?" Eol asked.

Oa did not respond at first; but when he did, he spoke as if to a friend. "No, I haven't. I have this strange ability to believe that things can end for the better. I won't fight anymore, but I will never stop believing in my dream and in my friends—or in you Ohm."

"Fool!" Eol shouted as he swung his Void staff. It sliced through Oa's torso and sent him skidding back across the platform. Seeker glowed dimly at Oa's side as Eol's red eyes stalked toward him. Oa let his mind wander, remembering the times he had spent with Kai and Ohm and Susan. A vision of all of them, together once more, played in his mind. Eol halted next to Oa. He raised the staff high to deal the finishing blow that would end the story forever.

Suddenly out of the shrouds that covered Eol's chest, a figure burst forth. With a yell, Ohm pulled himself halfway out of the Demon of Void. He froze Eol's final blow with sheer will.

Ohm reached out his hand toward Oa. His blue ocular plate flickered faintly.

"Oa, I will not let you die, but I am the Destroyer. I-I must fulfill my purpose," Ohm said with the last of his sanity, fighting to get every word out. He drew his left hand back, reaching up to his chest. He grunted in effort as he unclasped his cloak. The cloth parted revealing Ohm's soul ember. He clasped the stone in his remaining hand; the hand of life. The First One pulled with all his strength, yelling in effort. Eol began to regain control, his staff continuing its swing down towards Oa. With a mighty crack and flash of light, Ohm's soul ember pulled free. The light in his ocular plate died. Instantly, the oily black of the Void stopped churning. It froze, hardening into a solid black wall. Eol froze in place as well, becoming a mere husk. Ohm's body slowly relaxed, slumping forward. His arm swung down and his left hand gently opened. The soul ember resting in his palm tumbled out onto the ground with a clink.

Oa lay on the cold metal floor in pain. He was tired; and even though he considered healing himself, he did not have the strength. His laceration did not expand, but life slowly drained away through it. Oa thought about all he had been through and about everything he had seen. He thought about his vision and how he had wanted to make something better out of the world. He pondered all this as he lay at the end of all things.

Two Ones—what an odd idea. Ohm and I awoke so far apart, and yet, we grew so close. Why were we so different in the end? Oa thought to himself. *Myself, made with no ember, and Ohm made to consume everything. What was the Creator thinking …?* he let his thoughts drift off.

Suddenly, he realized what he had to do. With every last bit of energy Oa had, he rolled over and crawled toward Ohm's soul ember. He reached forward and, straining to his limit each time, he pulled himself a little closer. Every fiber of his being was focused on reaching that ember. Oa stretched out his hand again to pull himself closer, and he felt the crystal. He gripped the ember feebly and rolled onto his side. With grim resolve, he set the stone in the empty cavity in his chest. He was too tired to even try to align the connections. Oa collapsed onto his back, finished. Seeker flickered and went out.

Inside Oa's chest, the soul ember rose up and rotated around. It oriented itself correctly then dropped back down into his chest socket with a single flare of warmth. Seeker began to glow brilliantly. Tendrils of energy flowed out of Seeker and into Oa's body. Countless rays of light shot out of the orb until the sphere had melted away completely. Oa's body could no longer be seen. Only a being of pure light remained.

***

Oa awoke. He sensed his body sit up slowly. A sliver of his mind registered that he was encased in a small, dark room, trapped in the remnants of a dead world. This did not bother him. He finally felt unhindered, as if a great weight had been lifted from his shoulders. The strange symbols no longer bombarded his inner sight. Oa looked down, only one symbol remained at his core. He looked closer. The strange glyph seemed to beckon him, calling out. Oa plunged into the singularity. He could see nothing other than the symbol. He was mesmerized by the depths of the aura within his chest. The sounds of life teamed around him. He could hear it; he could feel it.

"Hey, Oa!" Kai's voice called out to him. Oa felt her slug him in the arm. "Took you long enough, but you did it. We're are all here. There's that guy and what's her name—pretty much everybody. Cale and Jess want to meet you later," she said unable to contain all of her excitement. "Whoa, look out! Susan wants to say hi." Oa felt the familiar tickle of static across his face. He heard Susan's happy bark.

A friendly voice laughed, "That can wait Kai. I'm sure Oa would like a moment to get his bearings." Oa felt Ohm's hands on his shoulders.

Oa heard himself speak. "I did it," he said happily.

"Of course, you did," Kai's voice echoed back warmly.

"So what now, Oa? You ready to show us that vision of yours, or is this it?" Ohm asked, teasing.

"Yeah," Oa said. He paused for a moment as he fell deeper into the light, following his friends. He laughed or smiled; he could not tell which. "Of course, I'm ready. First, we have to grow. Things are too small here. I'm thinking bigger, much bigger." He reached toward his dream; his potential.

"Not so flat this time, though. They're gonna want more room to soar in," Kai said. Her voice sounded far away. The sound of cheerful laughter and music filled Oa.

"Just show us where to go," Ohm whispered. His words carried softly through the sounds of joy around Oa. "*Your will shall be.*"

"Yes, it's time to go," Oa said. He sprinted faster and faster toward the symbol of light. He stretched out his hand and took hold.

***

In the center of the chamber, a shining figure sat floating in the air; legs crossed, hands resting calmly on its knees. The radiant being began to grow, filling the room. Illumination surged around the husk of death, a broken law. The empty, shrouded carcass melted away as the aura of life pushed against its confined existence. The noise of countless voices filled the space, laughing and cheering together in a song of hope. The song echoed throughout the universe as light pushed against its boundaries. All at once, the walls shattered. Rays of creation burst forth, forging ahead in pursuit of what lay concealed in the deep.

—The End.

Connect with the Author

Well, you made it to the end. Congratulations!

Thank you for going on this journey with me. I hope you enjoyed reading the story as much as I enjoyed crafting it. If at any point in the future you feel the urge to contact me with questions or comments, you may reach me at my Author Page:

https://www.amazon.com/author/asouth